NEVER
CONSPIRE
With A SINFUL
BARON

D0380496

Also by Renee Ann Miller

Never Kiss a Notorious Marquess

Never Deceive a Viscount

Never Dare a Wicked Earl

Novella
The Taming of Lord Scrooge

Published by Kensington Publishing Corporation

NEVER CONSPIRE With A SINFUL BARON

RENEE ANN MILLER

ZEBRA BOOKS
KENSINGTON PUBLISHING CORP.
www.kensingtonbooks.com

ZEBRA BOOKS are published by

Kensington Publishing Corp.
119 West 40th Street
New York, NY 10018

All Kensington titles, imprints, and distributed lines are available at special quantity discounts for bulk purchases for sales promotion, premiums, fund-raising, educational, or institutional use.

Special book excerpts or customized printings can also be created to fit specific needs. For details, write or phone the office of the Kensington Sales Manager: Attn.: Sales Department. Kensington Publishing Corp., 119 West 40th Street, New York, NY 10018. Phone: 1-800-221-2647.

Zebra and the Z logo Reg. U.S. Pat. & TM Off.

First Printing: June 2020
ISBN-13: 978-1-4201-5003-2
ISBN-10: 1-4201-5003-0

ISBN-13: 978-1-4201-5004-9 (eBook)
ISBN-10: 1-4201-5004-9 (eBook)

10 9 8 7 6 5 4 3 2 1

Printed in the United States of America

It is universally understood that a gentleman with an excessive amount of debts must marry a wife with a sizable dowry.

Chapter One

London, England
May 1881

"How about Lady Sara Elsmere?" Lord Adam Talbot asked, looking up from his copy of Debrett's Peerage, a guide to the nobility.

Elliot Havenford, Baron Ralston, leaned back in his chair and propped his booted feet onto the corner of his desk. Obviously, Talbot was a half pint short of a full cup. Though Lady Sara possessed a handsome enough face, the woman suffered from a nervous hyena-like laugh whenever a gentleman stepped within two feet of her. Elliot couldn't imagine what bedding her would be like. Well, actually he could, and there stood the crux of the problem.

He shook his head. "I'd rather wed old Lady Winton."

Talbot snorted and flipped to another page in the thick book. The smile on his friend's face dissolved, and his gaze shot back to Elliot. "Good God, man. You're joking, right? Surely, you aren't seriously considering marrying that battle-ax."

Of course, he wasn't. Lady Winton was in her dotage and as mean as a dog fighting over a bone. He motioned to the glass of liquor in Talbot's hand. "Old chum, you've had too much of my brandy if you can't tell when I'm jesting."

"Elliot, this liquor is so inferior, I bet I couldn't get tipsy even if I downed the whole decanter."

Elliot lifted his own glass and swallowed a mouthful. Talbot was right. Bloody awful. His current circumstances had reduced him to buying rotgut. A year ago, he'd been a content fellow. Not a rich man, but a comfortable man. Oxford educated, he'd made several rather clever investments. Now, he was heading toward destitution, having sunk nearly every farthing he possessed into his entailed properties. The only thing he still owned of value was Swan Cottage, in the Lake District, which he wished to give to his sister.

The storm raging outside Elliot's town house intensified, and a bolt of lightning lit up the evening sky. The rain pounding against the windows sent sheets of water over the mullioned glass, causing rivulets to run down the inside of the panes and settle in a puddle on the interior's wide sill.

Damnation. The property still needed more repairs. His estate in Hampshire stood in worse condition than the London residence. Elliot feared the next storm might send the country home toppling to the ground. His uncle, the last Baron Ralston, a bachelor, had spent more money on his tailor, traveling, and his string of mistresses than on any of his properties.

"Ah." Talbot tapped a firm finger on a page in Debrett's. "How about Lady Nina Trent?"

Nina Trent? Elliot rubbed his shaven jaw, already coarse with bristle this late in the evening, and pictured the raven-haired beauty, a close friend of his cousin Victoria. He could easily envision taking Nina to bed *and* enjoying the expedition.

"She's quite pretty," Talbot said, breaking into Elliot's lurid thoughts. "Though a bit too thin for my taste. If you know what I mean." His friend winked.

He knew exactly what Talbot meant. The man liked breasts as big as melons.

"And her eldest brother, the Marquess of Huntington, is rolling in money." The grin on Talbot's face widened.

Indeed. Lady Nina Trent would be perfect. He liked the woman, and he'd bet his last coin Huntington would offer a sizable dowry. The funds would help solve his financial woes and allow him not only to make repairs to his derelict properties but also to give his sister, Meg, the come-out she deserved next year. Yes, Lady Nina might be the answer to all his problems.

"Aren't her brother and sister-in-law hosting a ball next week?" Talbot asked, taking a pen and writing something in the thick tome before tossing it on a table.

Elliot laced his hands behind his head and leaned back in his chair. "Yes, and I'm attending. So, Lady Nina it is."

"I don't know, Elliot. Even if you win her over, her brother might object to the match. Some say Lord Avalon proposed last year, and Huntington didn't allow her to accept the offer."

Not precisely true. Elliot's cousin Victoria had sworn him to secrecy. Nina had accepted the earl's proposal, but before the family announced it, she'd found out the man had a pretty French mistress in Paris. "Everyone knows Avalon is a cad."

Talbot's bark of laughter sounded like a small explosion. "And you aren't? You better convince the chit that you love her, or her brother will never let you wed the girl. Huntington dotes on his wife and feels only a love match will do for his sister."

A love match? What rubbish. There was no such thing. His own parents had resided in separate homes. It was a miracle he and Meg had ever been conceived. His grandparents' marriage had been worse. They'd needed to reside in separate countries.

Another roll of thunder shook the walls of the town house. A piece of the ceiling's plaster landed on the floor with a *thump*.

"Bloody hell!" Talbot stood and brushed the flecks of plaster off his clothes.

Elliot released a slow breath. Before this blasted town house came crashing down around him, he'd convince Lady Nina to wed him.

Sitting in the drawing room of her family's Park Lane residence, Lady Nina Trent tried not to say a word as Grandmother lectured her. Arguing with the woman would only cause the matriarch to repeat everything she'd said in an elevated voice. The best way to contend with this situation was to remain as quiet as a church mouse until the sermon concluded.

"Are you listening to me, child?" The old woman thumped her cane.

"Of course, Grandmother." Nina forced a sugar-infused smile.

Nina's eldest brother, James, had always said Grandmother lived by three rules: God, country, but most of all, honor to the Trent family name. In Grandmother's eyes, her grandchildren had botched the latter. Though James, once known as the "Murdering Marquess," had redeemed himself, her brother Anthony had not. He gambled too much, drank too much, and fornicated too much. And

Nina's broken betrothal to that bounder Lord Avalon had only added to the old woman's displeasure.

"I heard a new whisper of scandal regarding you."

Nina's gaze narrowed on the woman like a hawk spotting a field mouse. A cold chill moved down her spine. "What is being said?"

"That Avalon decided not to propose to you because of some character flaw you possess." Grandmother's hand tightened around the gold knob of her cane as if she wished to thrash something with it.

"That is balderdash. He did propose." Though it had not been publicly announced. "I ended the engagement, and I am not the one with a character flaw. That cad is. Hopefully, such an *untruth* will die in the wind."

"Or it might pick up speed and sweep through the ton with the intensity of a gale force. If that happens, then your chances of making a good match will wither away. I wish you'd overlooked Avalon's shortcomings and married the earl."

Shortcomings? Is that what Grandmother called them? The man had professed his undying love to Nina until she'd found out he had a mistress—a very pregnant mistress.

"I refuse to marry a man who intends to keep a paramour." Nina squeezed her hand so tight, her nails bit into her palm.

"Some married men keep a mistress."

"Then I pity their wives." Nina was sure Grandmother knew why she hated adulterous men. Her father had been unfaithful, and her mother had spent her life collecting more heartache than any woman should have to endure while dealing with her philandering husband.

Grandmother thumped her cane again. "It is your duty to stem the flow of gossip. You have a responsibility not only to the Trent family name but to your brother James."

A stab of guilt poked at Nina. James had recently crawled out of his own pit of gossip and reestablished himself as a prominent member of the nobility.

"You don't want to hurt his renewed standing in society, do you?"

She didn't. She loved James. He'd not only been a brother, but a father to her and she wanted to please him more than anyone else in this world.

Grandmother leaned forward, and her light gray eyes pinned Nina. "The Duke of Fernbridge has recently arrived in London and is looking for a wife. He'll be attending your brother's ball. If you were to marry a man of such high standing, it would disavow any whispers that taint your name. You need to set things right. You owe that much to your brother."

Chapter Two

From where Nina stood behind a potted fern, she surveyed the Duke of Fernbridge. The man possessed the blondest hair she'd ever seen—like a halo, it almost glowed under the string of lanterns and moonlight on her brother's terrace. She parted two leaves to get a better look.

Though he was not classically handsome, his features were striking.

Since her conversation with Grandmother, she'd found out more about the gentleman. He was twenty-seven, didn't run with a fast crowd, rarely gambled, and didn't keep a mistress.

"What are you looking at, poppet?" a deep, masculine voice asked.

Like a mouse cornered by a cat, Nina squeaked and spun around.

Lord Elliot Ralston favored her with a lackadaisical smile.

The man was a scoundrel of the highest order, perhaps even more wicked than Nina's shameful sibling Anthony— a hard feat indeed. He was the type of man a sagacious woman should never choose for her husband—even if his dark wavy hair and deep blue eyes made him more visually appealing than any other man of her acquaintance.

She opened her mouth to chastise him for startling her. "Lord Ralston—"

"Eyeing the Duke of Fernbridge?"

"I wasn't eyeing him." She crossed her arms over her chest.

His smile broadened. "Do you realize when you lie your cheeks turn a lovely shade of pink?"

Nina fought the urge to deny it, but she could feel the warmth flooding her face. "What concern is it of yours?" Her words came out a bit sharper than she wished. Ralston possessed an odd ability to turn her normally serene mood tempestuous.

"I've known you since you and my cousin Victoria became friends. How long has that been, five years?" He arched a brow.

Nearly six. And she could still remember the way her fifteen-year-old heart had leaped the first time she'd met Ralston. He'd stepped into the room where she and Victoria had been playing a duet on the piano. His bespoke clothing had accentuated his impressive physique. He'd leaned close to her to turn the page of the music sheet, and she'd gotten a whiff of his scent—a mixture of soap and vetiver. The same pleasant scent that presently filled her nose.

"Nina?" His silky, deep voice pulled her from her thoughts.

She blinked. What had he asked her? Ah, if they'd known each other for about five years. "Yes, about that amount of time," she agreed, though she knew it longer.

He placed his index finger under her chin and tipped her head back, bringing her gaze to his. "In that time, we've become friends, so I want to make sure you get what you want."

"And what do you believe I want?" she asked.

He jerked his chin in the direction of the Duke of Fernbridge. "I presume, like so many other women this season, you want an introduction to that milksop, hoping he'll choose you for his duchess."

Milksop? Perhaps the duke didn't possess Ralston's urban manners or breath-stopping looks, which caused women to risk society's wrath and make complete cakes of themselves, but Fernbridge *was* the type of man she wished to marry. Trustworthy and—

"Safe?" Ralston said.

The man really possessed the uncanny ability to know what she was thinking. It was unsettling, to say the least. Ralston was a warlock. "Better to marry a man like Fernbridge who is steadfast than a scoundrel like you."

He theatrically set his hand over his heart. "You wound me."

Doubtful. Ralston possessed a conscience as impenetrable as a suit of armor being prodded by a feather. He flirted with women to several degrees beyond what propriety dictated; then, after they fell like toppling lawn pins, the black-hearted devil moved on to his next conquest.

"I went to university with the man, and I know exactly what he wants in a wife, and you are too free-spirited for him. He'd do better to marry someone like my cousin Victoria."

Victoria? No, that wouldn't do. Victoria was as sweet as a petit four and just as cute, but Grandmother was right. Fernbridge would be perfect for Nina. Marrying him would stifle any vicious gossip and please James. "I disagree."

"Sweeting, do you really wish to be with a man who still prefers country dances to the waltz? Whose idea of excitement is hunting with his hounds?" He spoke in a low voice. "Who's in bed by nine o'clock? And once married most likely without his wife."

The heat already flooding her face traveled to her ears. Beyond the pale for Ralston to mention such things.

"You don't want to marry a man as dull as unpolished silver, do you?" Ralston's blue eyes held her gaze as he stepped even closer. So close, his breath touched her lips.

If she didn't know better, she'd think he was trying some of his womanizing sorcery on her. But he didn't dally with those looking for a husband. Widows were more to his liking.

She glanced over her shoulder and peered through the fronds to where Fernbridge still conversed with Lord Pendleton. Most likely, Ralston was trying to discourage her, so his cousin could become a duchess. It would explain the reason he was paying her so much attention. He probably hoped to distract her, so Victoria could swoop in. Didn't he know his cousin was sick and wouldn't be attending tonight?

"It sounds like a *very* comfortable existence," she replied.

"Comfortable existence? Don't you mean dreadfully dreary?"

In truth, life with Fernbridge did sound rather dull, but wasn't that what she wanted? A reserved man who would be faithful. And though her brother James would not want her to marry a man she didn't love, she knew he would be pleased if she chose someone sensible like Fernbridge, and Grandmother would be ecstatic.

"The gentleman spends all his time rusticating in the country," Ralston said.

"What is wrong with that? I enjoy reading and horseback riding. I'd have more time to do so."

"Darling, there can be more to do once one is married than either of those activities." The curve of his lips left no doubt as to what he meant.

Scandalous man. She huffed and peeked at Fernbridge again.

"Very well, I see there is no dissuading you. Do you wish for an introduction?"

"Yes, would you present me?"

"Of course, anything for you, poppet."

When younger, she'd enjoyed him calling her by that endearment. Now, it grated on her nerves. "Must you call me that? I'm nearly twenty-one."

"Practically on the shelf." He grinned and offered her his arm.

The man irritated her to no end. Yet, after she set her hand on his sleeve and they moved across the flagstone terrace, an unsettling sensation crept over her. Ralston probably had such an effect on all women. It was the way he smiled with his sensual lips, along with the way his blue eyes held a woman's gaze as if she were the only woman in the room. Nina gave herself a mental slap. Victoria had revealed one too many stories about her cousin's womanizing exploits. The rogue had probably perfected his seductive smile at a young age while peering at his reflection in a mirror.

As they crossed the terrace, Lord Pendleton, who'd been conversing with the duke, strolled away.

"Fernbridge, old chum, how are you?" Ralston asked, shaking the other gentleman's hand.

The two men looked like night and day. Fernbridge was blond with a fair complexion, while Ralston's brown hair verged near black and his skin was a warmer, sun-kissed shade, as if he'd recently spent time outdoors.

As Ralston made the introductions, the Duke of Fernbridge took her gloved hand in his. "A pleasure to meet you, Lady Nina."

"I hope you are enjoying London, Your Grace." Nina offered her most congenial smile.

He wrinkled his nose. "I must admit I'm anxious to return to the country. These late London hours take some getting used to."

From the corner of her eye, she noticed the I-told-you-so curve of Ralston's mouth.

"It's only ten o'clock, Fernbridge. The merriment is just getting under way," Ralston said.

His Grace released a slow breath as if the thought of staying up a minute longer weighed heavily on his shoulders, and in truth, they were nice shoulders. Not as broad as Ralston's but impressive, and he stood close to six feet, a couple of inches shorter than the scoundrel standing next to her.

Fernbridge possessed a round, pleasant face. His eyes were a pale shade of gray as if watered down, and his blond hair tended to curl at the ends. He looked like an angel in comparison to Ralston.

Yet, her stomach didn't flutter when she looked at him. But Nina realized compatibility and genuine regard could grow between two people once married. One's heart didn't need to ache for one's spouse for a marriage to be successful. Loving someone left one vulnerable to heartache. Hadn't she witnessed that firsthand watching her mother? Though, like her mother, Nina seemed to have a propensity to gravitate toward scoundrels. She'd proven that last season when she'd fallen for Avalon. Now, she wanted a man who would be steadfast.

Nina pitched her distracting thoughts away. "Your Grace, since arriving in Town, have you taken in any plays?"

"No. Not yet." He turned to Ralston. "How went the hunting season in Hampshire?"

"I wouldn't know. I haven't gone hunting in some time."

"If I recall correctly, when we were boys, you were a dashed good trap shooter." Fernbridge frowned.

Ralston gave a weak smile, but something in his expression seemed odd. "Yes, but I've not engaged in the sport lately."

The musicians struck up the first song of the evening, and Nina glanced through the French doors to the orchestra.

"Ah, a waltz," Ralston said. "Might I have this dance, Lady Nina?"

She wanted to kick him in the shin. She'd hoped Fernbridge would ask her. She tried not to grit her teeth as she forced a smile. "Of course, my lord."

"If you'll excuse us, Fernbridge." Ralston offered his arm.

As they strode inside, she narrowed her eyes at him.

"I told you he doesn't waltz," he said, once again reading her thoughts. He leaned close. "You know, the best way to snag a man is to make him realize you are a prize catch. Especially a man like Fernbridge who enjoys the hunt. You are going about this the wrong way, darling. If you seem too readily available, he's less apt to be interested."

She frowned. What was he saying? That she could win Fernbridge's eye if he thought someone else was also vying for her hand? Surely, Ralston didn't mean he was willing to play the role of a gallant suitor to make Fernbridge more interested. "Are you offering to play the faux competition?"

Ralston cringed as if the idea were distasteful; then a slow smile lifted one corner of his mouth. "Why not? It might be entertaining. Yes, I'll sacrifice myself for the good of the cause."

"*Sacrifice?* I always thought you a smooth talker. Now

I'm wondering what draws women to you like bees to a single flower in a field of dried grass."

As they reached the dance floor, he set his warm hand to her back and pulled her close. As he spun her into the flow of those moving in tandem to the music, he whispered, "It's not the way I talk to a woman, darling. It's something much more wicked."

Chapter Three

As Elliot twirled Nina around the dance floor, he gazed at her. She was lovely with her large, honey-colored eyes, dusted with long lashes, and lips the same shade as her cheeks when she blushed. If he won her over, he would enjoy tasting her sweet mouth and every other inch of her body.

"Lord Ralston," Nina whispered, drawing him from his lustful thoughts. "You're holding me too close."

"Yes, darling, but notice the way everyone's attention is centered on us." He glanced around. Fernbridge had entered the ballroom, and though standing with a group of other gentlemen, he watched them as well. "Even your duke is looking at us. We will be gossiped about in every drawing room tomorrow. Many will think me asking you to dance means that I've set my sights on you."

"Why would they think you've set your sights on me? Everyone knows you have no interest in marriage."

"Then why would I ask an eligible lady, such as yourself, for the first dance?"

"True, and I'm nothing like most of the women you dance with." Her bow-shaped lips turned up. "Your dance partners usually are blinded by your handsome face and believe they might reform you. Whereas, I am aware you are a cad who will never be tamed."

Getting Nina to marry him might be a bit harder than he thought. "How you like to wound me."

She laughed. "A hard feat indeed. You wear a shield around your heart."

True, but I will have you believing otherwise, poppet. A stab of guilt prodded him over his planned deception. He squashed it as his sister's face flashed in his mind, along with the memory of her lying on the ground, crimson blood spreading over the skirt of her green cotton dress. He shoved his guilt and the disturbing image aside. Next year, he wanted to give Meg a spectacular first season, with the finest silk gowns from Madame LeFleur's—the most fashionable modiste in Town. He owed his sister that much and more.

It won't ease your guilt over what happened to her, a voice in his head whispered.

Attempting to chase away his demons, Elliot concentrated on Nina, twirling her fast as they took the turn at the end of the dance floor.

Pleasure lit up her eyes.

Her countenance made it crystal clear that Fernbridge wasn't a good match for her vivacious personality. Elliot was doing her a favor steering her away from such a wet nappy. Nina might think she'd enjoy a staid existence, but she would be bored senseless. At least life with him wouldn't be boring.

"You look miles away," she said. "What are you thinking?"

"Thinking? Why, how becoming lavender looks on you." It wasn't a lie. The color with her dark hair was striking.

Her cheeks flushed.

Smiling, he took her into another fast turn. She slipped her hand from his upper arm to his shoulder and tightened her grip. Though he knew several members of the ton who were sticklers for propriety would frown at them, the smile on Nina's lips broadened.

Fernbridge wasn't the right gentleman for her. Not with her free-spirited nature.

He shifted his gaze away from her attractive face and glanced around the massive ballroom. Everything about the space confirmed Huntington was well off. The arched ceiling possessed a mural that rivaled the masters. The walls were freshly painted. The flower arrangements, set in Sèvres vases, were larger than most and sported costly, exotic florals.

In the crush of people, Elliot noticed Nina's brother James Trent, the Marquess of Huntington, staring daggers at him. He didn't need to worry only about winning Nina's heart; he needed to worry about her brother accepting the match. Unless he could get Nina into a compromising position that would dictate she marry him.

Elliot pinched his lips together. When had he become so manipulative?

When his uncle had left him a barony two farthings away from insolvency. When he'd had to put nearly every bit of savings he possessed into repairing his dilapidated London town house. Money that should have helped Meg. At least he still had enough for her to continue at Mrs. Gibbs's School for Girls.

He scanned the ballroom again. Penny Granger was dancing with Lord Pendleton. The American heiress's father was a wealthy banker. Perhaps, he should try to woo her instead of Nina. Dollar princesses knew what their parents wanted. They were to marry into nobility in exchange for their sizable dowries.

Elliot looked at Nina's shimmering dark hair, intricately styled with pearls weaved in her upswept locks. As if sensing his regard, she tipped her face toward his and smiled. Her cheeks were slightly elevated in color.

No, he'd not change course now. He'd already set this ship in motion and would do his best to convince Nina to marry him.

The last cords of the Venetian waltz whispered in the air, and Elliot offered Nina his arm as they strode to where her brother Huntington stood with his wife.

The marquess hurled a disapproving scowl at Elliot, so disapproving it might have shriveled a lesser man's bollocks. Next to Huntington, his wife smiled congenially. Lady Caroline Huntington looked like a harmless sprite, but everyone knew the truth. She was not easily intimidated. She was the editor of the *London Reformer*, a progressive newspaper, and had proven she was no toady. She also cared for her husband's family and would defend them relentlessly, even Huntington's cantankerous grandmother.

Elliot glanced around. Come to think of it, he hadn't spotted the Dowager of Huntington, better known as the Dragoness of Huntington. "You grandmother is not attending tonight's festivities?"

"No, she has a megrim."

As they stepped up to Huntington and his wife, Elliot greeted them, then turned to Nina. "Thank you, Lady Nina, for a most enjoyable waltz."

He thought he heard Huntington growl. But just as the marquess opened his mouth, his wife set a hand on her husband's sleeve, drawing the man's feral gaze to her.

Huntington's granite-hard face softened.

"Darling," Lady Huntington said, as if she knew how to soothe the beast with her generous smile, "I believe our gathering is a success."

The marquess patted his wife's hand. "Yes, dear, a real crush, though we invited several people who should have been cut from the guest list."

Easy to hear the agitation in Huntington's voice. Also, easy to decipher who he referred to, and if any uncertainty lingered in Elliot's mind, the direct gaze the marquess kept on him dispelled any residual doubt.

Lady Huntington sucked in a startled breath. She knew it the height of impropriety for her husband to utter such a statement where he might be overheard.

Next to Elliot, Nina appeared a hairsbreadth away from strangling her brother. "James," she hissed.

The way she chastised the marquess pleased Elliot. He liked women who didn't wither under a man's gaze. Women who knew how to stand their ground. They tended to act more adventurous in life and in bed.

Trying to soothe the situation, Lady Huntington said, "Lord Ralston, how are you?"

"I'm well, my lady. Your gathering *is* a success, and I thank you for the invitation." He faced the marquess. "As I do you, Huntington."

The man's eyes narrowed a fraction. "Surprised you're not in the card room, Ralston."

He didn't have the funds to piss away, but he couldn't let members of the ton know that, so he'd have to play conservatively. "On my way right now, but your sister's beauty forestalled me. So much so, I couldn't resist asking her to waltz." He took Nina's hand in his and kissed her gloved fingers. "Thank you for the honor of a dance. It was most enjoyable."

Nina held his gaze, then briefly glanced at Fernbridge.

The man had paused in his conversation with Lord Templeton to watch them.

Elliot noticed the pleasure the duke's regard brought

Nina. He cocked an eyebrow, clearly stating he was right about men and competition.

Fernbridge ran his hand over his jaw, said something to the men in his group, then strode toward them.

As the duke approached, Nina tensed with obvious anticipation. She would be sorely disappointed if she hoped the man intended to ask her to waltz. Elliot hadn't lied. Fernbridge didn't waltz.

Smiling broadly, Huntington shook Fernbridge's hand. The welcoming expression on the marquess's face declared Fernbridge a fit suitor for his sister. Did he really wish Nina to marry such a stodgy chap?

"Weren't you going to the card room, Ralston?" Huntington asked, obviously trying to get rid of him.

"I wonder if Sir Walter is in there," the duke said. "I wished to ask him how the fishing is in Kent. I'll join you."

Elliot saw the disappointment on Nina's face. Why the hell was she interested in Fernbridge anyway? A quick glance at Huntington and Elliot realized the answer. Not only did Nina want someone safe, she also wanted to please her brother.

As Ralston and Fernbridge walked toward the card room, Nina tried not to frown. When she'd noticed the Duke of Fernbridge watching her waltzing, she'd hoped he would ask her to dance. Instead, he'd gone off in search of Sir Walter. Perhaps Ralston had told her the truth and His Grace did not favor waltzing. Nina hadn't missed the I-told-you-so expression on Ralston's face when the man had confirmed he didn't care for staying up late. Perhaps Fernbridge was too bland.

Lord Avalon's face appeared in her mind's eye. He'd

made her believe he loved her, only to trample on her heart. No, Fernbridge was a steady fellow. He would be perfect.

Standing next to her, James cleared his throat, drawing her from her thoughts. She knew what her brother was thinking—Lord Elliot Ralston was a cad like Avalon, and she should stay as far away from him as possible. What she couldn't tell him was that Ralston's attention toward her was nothing more than a ruse. A game of sorts for Ralston, who wished to prove his point about the way the male mind worked.

"Nina, I hope you are not setting your sights on Ralston," her brother said.

She held his direct gaze. "James, it was only a dance. I might have been naive last year, but I've learned my lesson."

As the night went on, Nina kept an eye on the card room, hoping to spot the Duke of Fernbridge exiting it. It appeared Ralston was correct. The duke had no interest in waltzing, which was a shame since she dearly enjoyed it.

Her mind recalled how smoothly Ralston had led her across the dance floor. She shoved the memory from her head. Falling for a confirmed bachelor was more foolish than falling head over shoulders for that snake Avalon. At least Avalon had wished to marry her.

Ralston stepped out of the card room.

Speak of the devil.

"Excuse me," she said to the group of women she stood with.

He appeared to be heading to the French doors, left open to cool the warmth caused by the crush.

"Lord Ralston," she said, catching up to him.

He turned around. "Yes, darling?"

She frowned. She didn't like him calling her darling any more than she liked him calling her poppet. The endearment sent an odd tingling through her body when he said it. "Is the Duke of Fernbridge still in the card room?"

"No. He left over an hour ago."

Drat. She must have been dancing when he exited the room. She glanced around, looking for his tall form and blond hair.

"I doubt he is still here. He's probably safely tucked into his bed." He grinned. "Have you thought about my offer?"

"Do you truly believe if you pretend you are pursuing me it will capture His Grace's attention?"

"I do."

She was tempted. Extremely tempted. "Thank you, but no."

"If you change your mind, let me know. I'll even include lessons."

Lessons? Her heart picked up tempo. "For?"

He leaned nearly as close as he had on the terrace. Once again, his breath touched her lips. "Instructions on how to win a man's heart."

She set a hand on her hip, then lowered it, knowing such a stance might draw attention. "I don't need any lessons."

He flashed one of his devilishly handsome smiles that probably turned most women's brains to mush. "Are you sure?"

"I am." She strode away before temptation caused her to agree to the scoundrel's plan and his wicked lessons.

Chapter Four

A moist breath fanned against the back of Elliot's neck. He cocked open one eye and glanced at the morning light seeping through a slim gap between the curtains in his bed-chamber. Another heavy breath puffed against his nape, and he opened the other eye and stilled.

He didn't recall inviting anyone to his bed after Lord and Lady Huntington's ball, which meant only one thing. He slowly rolled over.

Two large, bloodshot eyes stared at him from under droopy lids. Without warning, a long, wet tongue lapped against his cheek.

Good God! He jerked back.

This was not the first time over the last year that he'd awoken to find Zeb in his bed. Besides inheriting the barony, Elliot had also inherited his uncle's godforsaken bloodhound.

This scenario with the animal had played out more times than he wished to recall. Each time it happened, he woke up with an even smaller sliver of the mattress, along with the dog snuggled up closer to him, but never this close.

"Damnation, Zeb. I'm practically clinging to the edge of the mattress."

The dog stared at him with his solemn brown eyes.

He sat up and pointed to the velvet-covered pallet on the floor. "That. Is. Your. Bed."

The bloodhound shifted closer.

Disgusted, Elliot flopped onto his back and let out a frustrated sigh. Perhaps the animal was suffering from some sort of melancholy over Uncle Phillip's passing. Yes, that must be it. "Sorry, boy, but as much as we both wish it, the old fellow isn't coming back."

The dog whimpered.

Elliot folded an arm behind his head and reached out with the other to pat the dog's head. "Maybe you need a companion. How about a sexy poodle?"

As if thinking the offer over, one of the dog's drooping brows lifted.

A rather disturbing vision of Zeb getting cozy with a lady friend while in Elliot's bed flashed in his mind. On second thought, getting the dog a companion might not be a wise decision.

"Would it cheer you up if I took you for a walk in the park today?"

While gasping at his last breaths, Uncle Phillip had also asked Elliot to take Zeb for walks regularly. A monotonous undertaking, since the animal tended to fall asleep during them.

Zeb placed his paw on Elliot's chest and excitedly thumped his tail.

"How odd you understand that, but nothing else I say. Let us make a deal. You crawl onto your bed and let me sleep a few more hours, and I'll take you."

The bloodhound tipped his head sideways as if Elliot were speaking some foreign tongue.

Hadn't he learned this conversation never worked?

Apparently not, since he continued to try to bargain with the animal to no avail.

A few hours later, unable to fall back asleep with Zeb breathing down his neck and nudging him, as if impatient to go for a walk, Elliot stepped out of his town house with the hound.

When he was young, Elliot had owned a black retriever. The dog had moved at a frantic speed, dragging Elliot around as if their roles were reversed. That was not the case with Zeb. The animal, like the servants his uncle had employed at his town house, moved at a turtle's pace.

Zeb's steps slowed and he plopped down and rested his massive head on the flagstones as if intending to fall asleep.

"Don't even think about it," Elliot warned.

The hound peered at him from under his drooping brows.

Good Lord, the animal was a pain in his arse. "Come on, boy. Get up."

The dog closed his eyes.

A girl with two blond braids and a lad with a mop of brown hair stopped and stared.

"Hey, guv'ner, what's wrong with your dog?" the boy asked.

Too many things to list. "Nothing."

The girl peered at Zeb with her large hazel eyes. "Mister, I think he's dead."

The word *dead* caused several other strollers to slow their steps and stare.

Elliot drew in an agitated breath. "No, he's not dead. He's resting. You should move along before he awakes. He can be vicious."

Instead of shrieking and dashing off with fear, the two imps glanced at each other and laughed.

"He looks so old, I bet he don't have any teeth." The girl folded her arms over her chest and flashed a challenging expression.

"He does, and they are quite sizable, and he's particularly fond of eating children, especially cheeky, blond-haired girls." He gave the child a hard stare.

Uttering a disbelieving snort, she flipped one of her braids over her shoulder.

Elliot released a long-agitated sigh. "Don't the two of you have parents who are wondering where you are?"

"Nah," the boy said. "Mama told us to go outside and play and stop traipsing under her feet."

"So she sent you out into the world to spread your cheer to others?"

In unison, they both smiled, oblivious to his sarcasm.

The temptation to pick up the eighty-five-pound dog and walk away with as much dignity as he could muster nearly overwhelmed Elliot.

Thankfully, Zeb stirred and lifted his head.

"See. He's waking up. Now you both better run and hide because he eats legs first."

The girl rolled her eyes.

As if a heavy leaden weight were strapped to the dog's back, Zeb slowly got up on all fours, took two steps, then sat down again as if exhausted.

With a burst of laughter, the lad slapped his thigh.

Chuckling, the two children strolled away.

Elliot pulled out his pocket watch. In a few hours, he had an appointment with a plasterer about repairing the ceiling in his drawing room. At this rate, he'd be late.

"Lord Ralston," a woman called out.

He glanced over his shoulder. Lady Amelia Hampton and her cousin Priscilla Grisham approached.

Hell and fire. He stifled a moan. The woman who'd recently wed old Lord Hampton was clearly looking to start up an affair. She'd practically flashed one of her breasts at him during the last house party they'd both attended. He couldn't escape talking with her unless he picked up Zeb and ran—which would surely prompt people to conclude he verged on madness.

He forced a smile. "Ladies."

She gave Zeb a quick glance and wrinkled her nose. "My lord, how nice to see you again. I've been wondering if you'll be attending Lady Randall's house party?"

Lady Randall's house parties were full of revelry and dissipation. Doubtful Nina would attend. "No, I don't believe so."

"No?" She pouted. "It would be *so much* more enjoyable if you did."

Good Lord, the woman was bold.

Next to her, her timid cousin's eyes grew round.

Elliot glanced at Zeb, who slowly shifted onto his feet. "If you'll forgive me, ladies. I must be rushing off. I have an appointment shortly."

"Of course. I hope to see you soon," she purred.

Elliot forced another smile and strode away.

That afternoon, Mr. Crumb combed his fingers through his long gray beard as he surveyed the damaged ceiling in Elliot's drawing room. The plasterer set up his ladder, climbed it, and poked and prodded at the area near where the plaster had fallen off the ceiling.

"Hmmm," he mumbled and pulled on his beard.

Elliot feared that, every time the fellow did that, the amount he intended to charge grew by astronomical proportions.

"Well, m'lord. I fear it isn't good news." The plasterer climbed down from the ladder.

It never was when it came to this property. So far, Elliot

had hired a mason, several carpenters, a window glazer, a plumber, a roofer, and a chimney sweep.

"Do you have an estimate?"

"Yes, m'lord, let me figure it out, and I'll give you the cost before I leave."

The man said *m'lord* as if Elliot pissed gold and had a money tree growing in his garden.

"Sad situation. Sad situation, indeed." Mr. Crumb withdrew a small notepad from the inside of his coat pocket and removed the pencil tucked above his ear. As he wrote, the man would sigh every few seconds, as if this quote were as painful for him as it would be for Elliot.

Mr. Crumb tore the paper out of the notepad and handed it to him.

Elliot stared at the inflated figure and bit back the urge to grab the man by the scruff of his coat and toss him out the door. He forced a smile. "Thank you, Mr. Crumb. I have several other contractors who will be giving me an estimate. I have your card and will be in touch if I intend to hire you."

"Several other estimates?" the plasterer echoed, suddenly looking nervous. "Perhaps I can do the job for less, m'lord." Obviously, the man had thought Elliot so plump in the pockets, he wouldn't squabble over the price. Mr. Crumb took the paper from Elliot and jotted a new figure on it and handed it back.

Even with the price drastically reduced, Elliot still couldn't afford the repair. "If I wish to hire you, Mr. Crumb, I'll be in touch," Elliot repeated.

With a dejected expression, the fellow nodded, picked up his ladder, and exited the room.

Elliot's gaze veered to the ceiling. "I wonder if I could fix it myself?"

Zeb, sprawled on the hearth rug, lifted his head and gave him a doubtful look.

"Don't look so dubiously at me. I think I could do it."

The dog uttered a huff, which clearly conveyed the animal's misgivings.

"Well, I need to at least try." His life was worse than he thought if he was trying to gain the bloodhound's approval.

Mrs. Lamb, the housekeeper, stepped into the room, wiping her hands on her yellowed apron. Beside inheriting his uncle's run-down London town house, crumbling country estate, and depressed bloodhound, Elliot had also promised his uncle on his deathbed that he would continue to retain his uncle's ancient valet, Wilson, and the housekeeper, Mrs. Lamb, who was losing her hearing.

Elliot crumpled the paper in his hands and tossed it onto the cold grate.

"Tried to swindle you, did he, my lord?" the housekeeper asked.

"Yes, but afterward he gave me a decent price," Elliot replied in an elevated voice.

"So you intend to hire him?"

"No. I'm going to try to do the repair myself."

As if she hadn't heard him correctly, the housekeeper removed the hearing trumpet she kept in her pocket and set it to her ear. "What was that, my lord?"

"I said, *I'm* going to attempt to repair the ceiling myself," he repeated.

Mrs. Lamb laughed as if Elliot were joking.

"I'm serious."

"Really?" The woman pursed her lips. "I don't mean to sound impertinent, my lord, but do you think that a wise move?"

No. Not particularly. But in his financial situation, it remained the only option currently feasible to him.

* * *

The inside of Madame LeFleur's shop with its colorful bolts of fabric was like the Yorkshire moors on a spring day—a rainbow of hues. Nina plucked off her gloves and ran her fingers over a bolt of green silk that shimmered under the chandeliers.

"Oh, that shade of green would look fetching on you," Caroline said.

Nina lifted the end of the material and placed it next to her sister-in-law's cheek. "I was thinking, with your green eyes, you should have a gown made from it."

"Goodness, I have enough dresses and . . ." Caroline's cheeks flushed with color. She glanced around as if checking to make sure the modiste assistant who'd greeted them remained out of the room. "I believe I'm with child."

Uttering a squeal of pleasure, Nina embraced Caroline. "I'm to be an aunt again?"

"I believe so. And if I am, I shall be reduced to wearing a tent in a few months." She gave a low laugh.

"You look lovely when enceinte."

"Ha! I look as if I'm going to tip over."

"Does my brother know?"

"I think James suspects. I've been craving chocolates like I did when pregnant with Michael. But please don't say anything to him. I want to be sure, and I've not seen the doctor."

"I won't say a word."

Caroline touched a bolt of amethyst silk. "How about this shade? It's close in color to one of your other evening gowns, but lavender suits you."

"That's what Lord Ralston said."

Caroline tugged slightly on her earlobe. "Might I ask what is going on with you and Lord Ralston?"

"Going on? Nothing. We are friends." She avoided Caroline's direct gaze and drew her finger over a bolt of blue velvet. Both Caroline and James would think her mad if she told them she'd almost agreed to Ralston's plan to capture the Duke of Fernbridge's attention.

Caroline touched Nina's arm, concern evident in her sister-in-law's eyes. "You're not smitten by him, are you?"

"No. Anyway, Lord Ralston is not interested in marrying, and even if he was, I learned my lesson when Avalon broke my heart last year. I will not make the same mistake. I wish to marry a steady fellow who does not run with a fast crowd. Both you and James need not fret."

"Darling, there is no need to rush into marriage."

Obviously, Caroline hadn't heard the latest rumor about Nina possessing some unknown character flaw. She didn't wish to tell either her brother or sister-in-law what Grandmother had said. It would only upset them. "I know, but several of my friends have already made matches."

"Nina, it is not a race. You have years to find a husband. You do not need to rush and set up your own household. James and I love having you with us. As does your nephew."

"Grandmother says it's my duty to marry well."

"Pish. It's not a duty. It is a choice. I wish you to marry for love."

"Caroline, what you have with James is a rare commodity."

The bell over the shop door jingled, and the sound of two women chatting caused Nina to glance over her shoulder.

Lady Amelia Hampton and her cousin Priscilla Grisham stepped into the modiste's shop. The three of them had made their bow to the Queen together. Last month, Amelia had married the Earl of Hampton, a man

nearly three times her age. Nina didn't like the woman for
three reasons. One, she thought herself everyone's better.
Two, she was a notorious gossip who didn't give a tinker's
curse whom her cruel words hurt. And three, she was the
first cousin of Lord Avalon, Nina's former betrothed.
Though the engagement had not been made public, their
families had known about it.

Amelia lifted her gloved hand, whispered something to
Priscilla, and tittered.

She could imagine what Amelia had said. The whole
family probably knew she'd almost made a fool of herself
over a man who'd not truly returned her affection. She'd
been nothing more than a means to an end. Once she'd given
him an heir, he'd probably have spent all his time in his
mistress's bed.

That Lord Avalon would not marry the woman he truly
loved said more about him. An actress was not worthy. She
would taint Avalon's precious bloodlines. What poppy-
cock. In her opinion, Avalon did not deserve the woman.
Not the other way around.

"Pay no mind to Amelia," Caroline said, breaking into
Nina's thoughts. "She should not be gossiping. I have half
a mind to . . ."

"To what?" Nina arched a brow.

"Tell people what I recently learned about that harpy,
but then I would be no better than her."

"What is it?"

Caroline's expression turned sly. "An employee at Harrods caught her walking out of the store with a scarf she'd
not purchased. When the manager realized who she was, it
was all kept hush-hush, but one of my reporters got wind
of the incident."

Somehow, it didn't surprise Nina. Amelia acted as if
everyone owed her.

Amelia headed their way. As always, Priscilla followed her cousin as if the other woman had her tethered to a leash.

"Hello," Amelia said, smiling like a cat about to pounce on a bird with an injured wing. "Nina, I haven't seen you since my cousin and you . . ." She made a little O shape with her mouth as if catching herself before saying something indelicate. "I mean, how are you?"

Nina forced her chin up. "Splendid." She deliberately let her gaze settle on the paisley scarf Amelia wore. "What an eye-catching scarf. Might I ask where you *bought* it?"

The other woman's cheeks turned pink. "At Harvey Nichols."

"Really?" Caroline said. "I would have sworn I'd seen one identical to it at Harrods."

The feline grin on Amelia's face vanished.

The modiste's assistant rushed through the green velvet curtain that separated the fitting rooms from the front of the shop.

Amelia flicked the girl a look of disdain. "What took you so long? I have an appointment to be fitted! No one greeted me when I walked through the door. Customers would never be treated this way at the House of Worth in Paris."

"Forgive me, Lady Hampton." The assistant motioned to the curtain. "Please come this way. Madame LeFleur is eager to help you."

"About time." Amelia stormed toward the fitting room. "Come along, Priscilla."

After the other women stepped into the back, Caroline wrinkled her nose. "Isn't she charming?"

"Yes," Nina replied, "if one has an odd disposition toward viragos."

Caroline chuckled.

After they'd chosen a bolt of fabric, another of the modiste's assistants led Nina and Caroline into one of the three fitting rooms in the back of the shop. Each room was named after a flower. They were led to the Orchid Room, which boasted cheval mirrors, a skirted dressing table, a divan, and upholstered chairs with button-topped ottomans, all in cream velvet. A pot with a white orchid sat on the round marquetry table.

"Madame LeFleur will be with you shortly." The assistant placed the bolt of lavender silk Nina had chosen on the round table and stepped out of the room.

Nina opened the design book placed next to the potted orchid. It featured sketches specifically designed for her. The first page had a beautiful ball gown with sleeves as sheer as a butterfly net, a low, rounded collar, and flowing silk skirt with a sheer overlay in the palest pink.

"It would look *magnifique* on you," Madame LeFleur said in her thick French accent as she entered the fitting room and stepped beside them. The modiste pointed at the bolt of lavender silk fabric. "I could do it in this material. I have the perfect shade of violet organza to complement the fabric."

Caroline gave Nina a hopeful look. "What do you say, dearest?"

"It *is* lovely." Nina ran her finger over the edge of the page.

"It will draw a man's regard but do nothing more than tease his eyes. It is what one wishes to do, *oui*?" Madame LeFleur grinned as she pulled out her measuring tape. "Please, if you will . . ." She motioned to a small dais. "I will recheck your measurements, my lady."

"Nina, while you are being measured, I'm going to visit the bookshop next door. I will be back in a few minutes."

Nina nodded, and Caroline exited the fitting room.

A few minutes later, Amelia's shrill voice filtered in from across the hall. "You stupid cow. Get me Madame LeFleur this instant!"

The modiste's assistant stepped into the fitting room. "*Excusez-moi*, Madame LeFleur." The woman strode over to where they were and whispered, "That *mégère* is insistent I change the figure I wrote for her waist. She says it should be two inches less. I have measured it three times."

Nina tried not to smile at the French woman calling Amelia a shrew. She could add a few less charitable words.

Amelia's grumbling could still be heard. "Madame should be attending me. Not Nina Trent. Doesn't she know she was jilted by my cousin? There must be something terribly wrong with the girl because my cousin is the sweetest man. No man will want her now."

Nina balled her fingers into a fist and fought the urge to confront the other woman. She was sure the gossip-monger knew Nina had ended the relationship. Most likely it was Amelia spreading the lies about her.

Thank goodness Caroline hadn't heard. Her sister-in-law would have marched over to the other fitting room and said something. Words that would only cause someone like Amelia to behave more viciously. Nina would take care of this in her own way.

She would show both Amelia Hampton and her cousin Avalon that she could snag the most sought-after man of rank. She was now more determined than ever to get to know the Duke of Fernbridge and see if they would be a good match. And she knew just the scoundrel to help her.

Lord Elliot Ralston.

Chapter Five

Like the morning before, and the one before that, etcetera, etcetera, Elliot woke up with Zeb's warm breath puffing against his nape. Without opening his eyes, he shifted away and landed on the floor with a loud *thump*.

Damnation! He rubbed the back of his head. He should have realized the dog had once again taken over nearly the whole mattress, leaving him a small fraction. This was like a bloody nightmare that kept repeating itself. Naked except for his drawers, Elliot stared at the ceiling and the cracks that spread across the surface like the branches of a deciduous tree.

Yesterday, he'd bought the ingredients to make the plaster compound to attempt to fix the drawing room ceiling. If successful, he'd work on this ceiling next.

Zeb made a noise and peered over the edge of the mattress. The bloodhound cocked one of his drooping brows as if to say, *What an odd human you are, lying on the floor.*

How had his life come to this? "Must you stare at me during this moment of disgrace?"

Zeb made a grunting noise, and his massive head disappeared from Elliot's view.

Hell and fire. The hound was probably drooling on the pillows.

The door opened, and his valet slowly shuffled into the bedchamber. Wilson wore the thickest eyeglasses Elliot had ever seen. He also looked older than the Parthenon and moved at a pace comparable to Zeb's.

"Good morning, my lord. A missive has arrived." The valet offered the note to the dog lying in the bed.

Elliot sat up. "I'm here, Wilson. That is Zeb you are handing the note to."

"Really?" The man's eyes blinked behind his thick lenses.

Releasing an exhausted breath, Elliot stood and took the note. The flowery script indicated a woman had written it. He opened the envelope.

Dear Lord Ralston,
    I've changed my mind about your offer. I'll be attending Lady Clifton's musical this afternoon at two o'clock. I would be so very grateful if you could meet me there.
Yours sincerely,
Nina Trent

Elliot grinned. Under normal circumstances, he'd rather swallow a flame thrower's sword than attend a musical and listen to an endless list of debutantes perform.

"Should a reply be sent, my lord? The messenger who dropped off the note didn't wait for one."

Understandable. Nina wouldn't want him to send a note to her brother's house. Elliot stood and tossed the parchment into the cooling embers in the grate. The paper smoldered and curled at the edges before it burst into flames. "No, but I need to send a note to Lord Talbot."

Three hours later, Talbot knocked on Elliot's bed-chamber door. "What the bloody hell is taking you so long?"

Elliot jerked the door open. "I'm nearly ready."

Talbot stepped into the room and frowned at the dog sprawled out on the bed. "Blimey. How often does that beast sleep there?"

"Lately? More often than he should."

Zeb cracked open one eye, gave Talbot a disinterested look, then rolled over.

"You should give him away. What do you need a blood-hound for? You don't even like hunting."

If the animal had ever been a good hunting dog, those days were gone. "I told you, I promised my uncle on his deathbed I would keep the dog."

"Well, he won't know if you don't keep your promise." One side of Talbot's mouth lifted in a sly, crooked grin.

"I gave my word. I'll not go back on it."

Talbot narrowed his eyes at Elliot's valet as the ancient servant stepped out of the dressing room. Wilson's feet shuffled slowly over the faded Aubusson carpet. The man held up two silk neckcloths, which were identical, and studied them through his thick glasses as if deciding the future of the English crown.

Talbot, obviously comprehending what was taking Elliot so long, let out an impatient gust of breath and flopped onto the upholstered chair in the corner of the room.

"I'll wear this one," Elliot said, pointing to the one closest to him, attempting to move the process along.

"You should wear this one, my lord," Wilson said, draping the opposite one around Elliot's collar. "The color is better suited to your waistcoat."

Talbot opened his mouth as if intent on informing the valet the ties were the same.

Elliot shot him a scathing look, and his friend clapped his mouth closed.

After it took Wilson an ungodly amount of time to tie the neckcloth and assist him with his coat, Talbot and Elliot climbed into his friend's carriage.

Talbot shot him a hard stare. "Why do you keep that fossil about? The man is as blind as a bat, and he's atrocious at his job."

"You know why."

"A blind and slow-as-molasses manservant, a hard-of-hearing housekeeper, and an old bloodhound, along with two neglected residences. I'm starting to think your uncle didn't like you much."

His uncle had cared for him more than his own father had. He'd spent time with him, whereas Father had acted as if Elliot were an imposition thrust upon him. Father had shipped him off to boarding school as quickly as he could. It was his uncle who'd invited him to spend holidays with him on the Continent. They'd traveled to France and Italy and stayed at lavish hotels.

He'd never realized that Uncle Phillip had lived well beyond his means until his uncle's solicitors had shown Elliot the debts the man had accrued. His uncle had preserved grand impressions while traveling on the Continent, but nothing else. Uncle Phillip had possessed a penchant for his mistresses, along with a kind heart to those who were loyal to him. Too bad he hadn't possessed any sense of how to invest wisely.

As the carriage weaved through the busy London streets, Talbot released a long-suffering sigh. "Why do you wish to attend one of Lady Clifton's tedious musicals?"

"Lady Nina will be there."

A grin spread across his friend's face. "So, you are already attempting to woo her. You old dog."

"I am, but she's set her sights on the Duke of Fernbridge."

"What? You mean she hasn't fallen into your arms like a lovesick puppy?"

"No."

"Which means she has good sense." Talbot laughed.

"With friends like you, I'm not sure why I'd need any naysayers about."

"Oh, I don't doubt by the end of the season you will have charmed your way into the girl's heart. Anyway, in school, Fernbridge was rather tedious, and he hasn't changed much, but the man is a duke and as rich as the queen."

That fact caused a tightness to wrap itself around Elliot's chest. If Nina's power-hungry, cantankerous grandmother wished for a marriage that would band two powerful families together, then marrying Fernbridge would be like grabbing the brass ring.

Talbot glanced out the window of the carriage, then at Elliot again. "I've noticed the way that American, Penny Granger, all but drools when you walk by. Perhaps you should try to win her instead. They say her father's Second Avenue mansion in New York City has so much gilded furniture it blinds a man. Leave it to a *nouveau riche* American to live so ostentatiously."

He'd noticed the woman's glances as well, and she seemed pleasant, but for some stubborn reason, he wanted

Nina. Perhaps it was nothing more than what he'd said—men enjoyed the chase along with the competition.

"You know I despise Lady Clifton's musicals," Talbot grumbled, breaking into Elliot's thoughts. "I cannot believe I agreed to go with you."

"I don't care for them either."

"Lady Clifton is a complete bore. She wishes to marry off her eldest daughter, Georgiana, this season, and I fear she hopes I'll be the one snagged. Every time that mama sees me, I feel like I'm a rat being cornered by a Jack Russell."

"Not the most favorable analogy for either you or her ladyship."

Talbot grinned. "It isn't, is it? Sometimes I regret I'm to inherit my father's title and properties."

Elliot blinked. Talbot's father was a wealthy duke who, unlike Elliot's uncle, had invested wisely. He hadn't cared a whit that some members of the peerage still looked down on those in trade. The man had realized that living off one's ancestors' wealth was a thing of the past. And that the income at their country homes in this age of industry could not save them. Their grand homes were now weighty anchors about their necks. They needed to invest wisely or be dragged down like a ship with a hole in its hull.

He ran his hand over the damask curtains in the carriage and gave Talbot a sardonic look. "Quite terrible being wealthy."

"I freely admit, I enjoy my family's wealth, but one wants to eclipse the achievements of one's father. I fear I shall never do so."

Talbot's father was a hard man to please. His overbearing personality was what had made him such a good businessman. He made all the decisions and had not allowed his son virtually any control. Perhaps it explained why Talbot, who'd been such a good student in school and admired by fellow students, now acted so frivolous.

"Talbot, have you ever thought about starting your own business?"

"Doing what?"

"Have you heard of Langford Teas?"

"I've seen their horse-drawn wagons with the name painted on the sides."

"I overheard Samuel Langford, the proprietor, at the Reform Club saying he wishes to retire. If you purchase it, I'll run the business for a share of the profits."

"What do you know about tea?"

Two weeks ago, he'd known nothing, but since overhearing Langford talking to another man about the possibility of selling the business, Elliot had done extensive research. "I've looked into the man's business. I visited the London Tea Auction and found out that Langford is set in his ways. He still purchases Chinese tea. But a new batch of growers is taking root in Ceylon. Their product is cheaper."

The old exuberance that used to light up Talbot's eyes returned. "What is the quality like?"

"Good. Also, Langford has never branched out past the lower counties. At one time, tea was the drink of the wealthy, but times have changed. Like pubs are for men to gather and talk, now tea houses are being built to cater to women. I forecast the number of tea houses popping up across Great Britain will increase. Langford hasn't expanded his brand to them. He seems content with his small sliver of the pie."

Talbot laughed.

"What's so funny?"

"My father just purchased Old Towne Teas. How I'd

love to be his competition. To grow this business and surpass him in sales."

A small flash of hope exploded in Elliot's gut. "Then what do you say? Are you interested in purchasing it and letting me manage it for a cut in the profits?"

His friend held his gaze. "No."

All the excitement in Elliot's chest released on a heavy breath.

"I have a better idea. We can be partners."

"You know I don't have the funds. I've sunk nearly every dollar I own into my wretched properties, and I cannot spend what little I have left. I need it, and more than what I have, for my sister's season and dowry."

Talbot scratched at his chin. "Then I'll help us secure a loan by providing the initial capital. The contract will stipulate that we both own the business equally, but you will take a smaller cut of the profits and manage the business until you have matched my investment."

Elliot stared at his friend. He bloody well looked serious. "Do you have enough capital?"

"People might think me a useless popinjay, but I've been speculating. And I'm damn good at it. I've been waiting for an investment, but we need to form a company. If we purchase the business, I don't want my father to find out that I'm one of the owners." Talbot rubbed his hands together. "If this works out, I'm going to best my sire and prove to him I'm his equal."

"You're sure you want to do this?" Elliot's heart was beating fast.

"Definitely!" Talbot thrust out his hand for Elliot to shake.

For the first time in weeks, a sense of hope settled in Elliot's chest. But unless he grew Langford Teas profits quickly, most of his share would initially go to paying off

Talbot. Which meant he still needed to try to win Nina's hand to give his sister a proper season and repair his neglected properties.

The rumbling of the carriage's wheels slowed as the vehicle pulled before Lady Clifton's town house.

Talbot moaned.

Elliot smiled. Inside, Nina waited for him.

Chapter Six

After handing their hats and gloves to the servant in the entry hall, Elliot and Talbot stepped into Lady Clifton's music room.

Their hostess rushed toward them.

"Here comes the Jack Russell," Talbot mumbled.

"Lord Talbot, Lord Ralston," Lady Clifton said. "How utterly pleased I am you both could attend."

As Talbot could do when he wished to, he turned on the charm and greeted the woman. "We wouldn't miss it for the world. Even highwaymen could not have waylaid us."

She tittered and glanced around the room. "Where is my eldest daughter, Georgiana?"

Elliot could almost hear Talbot's teeth gritting. As his friend chatted with the woman, Elliot searched the room for Nina. She sat in the front row of chairs, facing the Bösendorfer grand piano. Her yellow dress set off the dark color of her hair, which was loosely pinned up and accented with a glistening silver hair comb. Nina turned slightly to talk to the gray-haired matron sitting beside her. *Good Lord*. The Dowager of Huntington, Nina's grandmother, sat next to her. Elliot released a silent sigh. He had hoped Nina's sister-in-law would accompany her. It would be beyond beneficial if he could win the woman's approval if he was to get anywhere with Lord Huntington.

After making small talk with Lady Clifton, Elliot said, "If you will excuse me."

Talbot looked like he wanted to strangle Elliot for abandoning him.

"Lady Huntington, Lady Nina," Elliot said, stepping up to them. "How wonderful to see you here."

The Dowager of Huntington lifted her lorgnette and scrutinized him with her steely gray eyes. "Goodness, Lord Ralston, what is a rascal like you doing here?"

Nina smiled. "I'm sure he is here for the same reason everyone else is in attendance. To enjoy the music."

"Pish. I doubt that."

He brought the old woman's gloved hand to his lips and kissed it. "I take great pleasure in listening to music."

"Humph. You take great pleasure in widows," the Trent family matriarch said. "Which must mean your newest *friend* is attending." She pointed at the young widow Eliza Finston. "She's most likely the reason."

"Actually, my lady I was hoping to claim the seat next to your lovely granddaughter."

The dragoness's hand tensed around the knob of her cane as if she was contemplating lifting it to smash it over his head.

"That would be nice." Nina placed her hand over her grandmother's white-knuckled grip, apparently fearing the matriarch might cause him bodily harm.

"Thank you." He bowed his head and sat.

"Will you be performing?" Elliot asked Nina, realizing he couldn't ask her about her missive, since her grandmother was listing toward them like the Leaning Tower of Pisa and might overhear every word spoken between them.

Nina's pink cheeks deepened. "No. I'm not accomplished at the piano."

"But I remember you and my cousin playing a duet."

"You remember?" Her stunning brown eyes with their specks of gold widened.

"Of course, I thought you played quite well."

"I fear your memory is faulty. Victoria is the pianist. My playing is average at best."

"Will you be singing instead?"

"No one would wish that. My singing is worse than my piano playing. My brother Georgie's dog at our home in Essex howls when I sing. Then he retreats to under the nearest table and places his paws over his ears."

Perhaps he should invite her over to get Zeb off his bed. An image of Nina lying in his bed appeared in his mind. He cleared his throat and attempted to clear the wicked thought. "Surely, your singing cannot be so terrible."

"Sadly, it is. James even hired a vocalist to try to improve my singing. She quit after a month and claimed me hopeless."

Elliot grinned. Her honesty was refreshing. How many times had he heard mothers and debutantes praise their talents, only to learn it was false bravado?

"Are you laughing at me, sir?"

"Of course not."

She grinned. "Yes, you are."

"Well, I'm envisioning your brother's dog taking refuge under a table." That wasn't true. He was still envisioning her lying in his bed.

"My lack of being able to carry a tune does have its advantages."

"Does it?"

"Yes, when I wish to be alone, I start singing. I can clear a room as rapidly as a fire."

Elliot laughed. He was enjoying himself, even with the knowledge that at any moment a pixie-faced debutante would command the attention of those seated and most likely sing or play the piano off key.

Lady Clifton strode over to Nina's grandmother. "Lady Huntington, how wonderful to see you here."

Thwarted in her eavesdropping, the Dowager of Huntington straightened and gave a clearly forced smile. "Yes, Caroline was supposed to accompany Nina, but is feeling under the weather, so I had no choice."

As if used to the old woman's bluntness, Lady Clifton smiled and sat next to the dowager, forcing her to turn to the woman.

"You received my note?" Nina whispered.

"I did."

"If you truly think pretending you are pursuing me will spark Fernbridge's attention, I'd like to take you up on your offer."

This day was getting better every minute.

"You understand it won't only be me acting as if I am considering courting you, but also giving you lessons?"

She glanced at him, then quickly glanced at her hands, folded in her lap.

Curiosity sparked in her eyes. Nina might act the proper miss, but underneath her façade was a woman who wished to experience life to its fullest. Fernbridge was so wrong for her.

"No lessons," she said.

"We will see." He grinned.

She looked like she wanted to kick him.

Good God, something about her excited him far more than was necessary for the task at hand.

"And since we have known each other so long, I think when alone, you should call me Elliot."

Her lips pinched into a tight line, but she nodded.

Lady Clifton stood and walked away.

The Dowager of Huntington leaned forward, peered past her grandchild, and pinned him a withering glare. "What are you two whispering about?"

"Just the weather," Nina replied.

"Switch seats with me, Nina," the old woman said, as if he carried smallpox or some other contagious disease.

Nina was saved from replying by Lady Clifton standing before the rows of chairs and ringing a small brass bell. "Everyone, please be seated. We are about to start." As the woman spoke, her daughter Georgiana sat at the piano.

Talbot lowered himself into the chair next to Elliot. "Have you heard her play?"

"No," Elliot said.

"If you think you are in for a treat, you are mistaken. I think the chit and her mama are tone deaf," Talbot said sotto voce. "You will be forever indebted to me for dragging me here."

Two hours later, Talbot looked ready to doze off if he had to endure another piano performance. Elliot hoped the woman playing an exceedingly slow rendition of Beethoven's *Moonlight Sonata* was the final performer.

The young debutante hit the last key, and everyone applauded.

Lady Clifton strode back to the front of the room. "Ladies," she said, then turned and looked at Talbot and Elliot. "Gentlemen, refreshments will be served in the drawing room."

A nerve ticked in Talbot's jaw. "Elliot, please do *not* tell me you want to stay for tea. I'm anxious for something a bit stronger to relieve the megrim I've gotten while sitting here."

Elliot smiled at him, then stood and offered Nina his arm. "Might I escort you to the drawing room?"

"No, you may escort me," Nina's grandmother said, leaning her weight on her cane and standing up.

"Of course, Lady Huntington."

As the matriarch placed her hand on his sleeve, she gave him a death stare. "What are you about, Lord Ralston?"

"I'm not sure what you mean, madam."

"Oh, don't act guileless with me. I know you're up to something. And it better not be you've set your sights on my granddaughter. I was not feeling well, so I did not attend my grandson's ball, but I have my way of finding out things. I heard you danced the first waltz with Nina."

He didn't doubt the woman had her spies. Most likely servants who feared her and quaked when she glared at them with her icy gray eyes.

"My granddaughter has set her sights on the Duke of Fernbridge. It would be an auspicious union, which I look favorably upon."

"The man is as dull as a tarnished quid. She'd be bored married to him."

"That is of no concern. She has a duty to her family to marry well."

He was so tired of hearing about one's duty. He was in dire financial straits because of the duty placed on him. Surely, there was more to life.

"Go sniff at someone else's skirt. Or else . . ."

Elliot might have set out to marry Nina for her dowry, but now he just wanted to save her from this old woman's machinations.

"Madam, if you think you will scare me away with your threats, think again," he said in a low voice. As they stepped into the drawing room, he forced himself to smile at the old bat as he led her to a chair. After she sat, he turned to Nina and Talbot, who walked several yards behind them.

Nina smiled at something Talbot said to her, but her gaze kept veering to him and her grandmother as if she realized the woman had been warning him off.

"Madam." He nodded at the dowager and strode toward Nina before the old woman could continue flailing him with her sharp tongue.

"I feel rather left out of whatever conversation you two were having," Nina said.

"We were conversing about how fetching you look in your yellow gown." Elliot smiled.

The way she pursed her lips clearly betrayed she didn't believe him, but a slight blush colored her cheeks as if she still took pleasure in the compliment.

He enjoyed seeing her blush, and contrary to what her grandmother wanted, he was now more determined to win Nina's hand and thwart her grandmother's ill-advised matchmaking.

Three days later, Elliot toured Langford Teas on Mincing Lane with the proprietor. Talbot, concerned his father would find out he was a partner in this venture to purchase the company and try to outbid them, had suggested they keep his involvement secret. While Elliot attended to the legal stuff, Talbot would remain anonymous, but provide the initial capital.

Inside the business, the scent of tea infused the air. Elliot had always preferred coffee to tea, but suddenly this scent was nearly as sweet as a woman climaxing beneath him. If he could make this business more profitable, he could become a full partner, not an indebted one.

They stepped into a long, narrow room. Men wearing

dark aprons stood at tables packaging tins of tea from large vats. Stacks of crates stamped TEA filled an adjacent storage area. This morning, Elliot had also toured Langford's dockside warehouse in Wapping, where the tea was stored after arriving from China.

Elliot noticed another room with glass windows, making the occupants inside visible. Several men were placing tea leaves on a scale, then mixing them with other ingredients.

"That is the blending room," Langford said, motioning Elliot to precede him.

Inside, the air was thick with the scent of spices. Two gentlemen sipping tea engaged in a robust conversation on which blend they preferred.

As Langford explained the workings of the blending room, Elliot found it odd that not a single taster was a woman since they did most of the shopping and enjoyed tea houses. If Langford agreed to his terms for purchasing the business, Elliot would hire a couple of female tasters. Perhaps create brands just for them. This idea of marketing specialty teas for women, along with using a direct supplier from Ceylon instead of purchasing higher-priced Chinese tea from the auction house, would hopefully increase revenue.

They exited the blending room and entered Langford's office.

After two hours of robust negotiations, Elliot stood and reached across the proprietor's desk to shake the tea merchant's hand. "So at the end of next month, we will sign the purchase agreement for the amount we discussed." Elliot still wanted to examine the ledgers more thoroughly and have an inventory done at the warehouse.

Standing, Langford grasped his hand and pumped it enthusiastically. "Yes. I'll contact my solicitor today and have him begin drafting the sales agreement."

Elliot knew the amount he'd offered for the business was a bit steep, but he was sure he could increase the company's profits and wanted to convince Langford to agree to the sale before another potential buyer made a bid.

The door behind him opened, and a man who looked in his early twenties stepped into the room. "Sorry, Uncle Samuel, I didn't realize anyone was with you."

Langford walked around his desk. "Lord Ralston, might I introduce you to my nephew, Harry Connors. Harry, his lordship is to be the new owner of Langford Teas."

Elliot offered his hand to the other man.

Ignoring it, Connors stared blankly at his uncle. The man opened his mouth, then closed it, betraying his shock. "You're selling the business?"

"I told you I wish to retire."

Connors clenched his jaw, causing a nerve to visibly pulse. "Yes, but I thought the business would be kept in the family."

Looking uncomfortable, the older man's gaze slipped to Elliot before returning to his nephew. "We will discuss this in private, Harry. This is not the proper time."

"Is Aunt Tilly aware of this?" An unpleasant sneer twisted the man's lips.

"Yes, and as I've said, we will discuss this later." Langford's cheeks turned red.

Connors gave one last look of unabashed disgust before he exited the office, slamming the door in his wake with such force the walls rattled. A painting of a clipper ship at sea slipped off its hook to fall askew onto the floor with a *thud*.

"I'm sorry you had to witness that, my lord." The man released a deep, audible sigh. "My wife has seen fit to spoil her sister's boy, being he is our only living relation. He lives a flamboyant lifestyle on my generosity. However,

I cannot see to giving him the business my father started. I fear it would come crashing down under my nephew's tutelage. I hate to speak ill of the man, but he is a spendthrift with a penchant for gambling at the horse races."

The smell on young Harry Connors's breath had also revealed he indulged in blue ruin.

"Then you aren't questioning your decision to sell me the business?"

"No, I will not change my mind, my lord. I have shaken your hand, and that is as good as a legal contract."

Elliot nodded. He felt sorry for Langford. This decision to sell the business had obviously not come easy to the man, but he understood his desire to see Langford Teas flourish. Elliot aimed for it to do so once he and Talbot purchased it.

But now, he needed to center his mind on trying to woo the lovely, raven-haired Nina, who would be at Lord and Lady Pendleton's ball tonight.

Chapter Seven

Lord and Lady Pendleton's ballroom glittered under the crystal chandeliers. As Nina and her grandmother entered the massive space, Nina searched the crush for the Duke of Fernbridge. Her stomach gave a nervous jump when she spotted him in a crowd of men that included Lord Elliot Ralston.

The duke looked bored, whereas Elliot said something and the men gathered gave a hearty laugh. Elliot was not only a lady's man but also a man's man, admired for his easy, carefree way. As if sensing someone watched him, he turned and flashed a rakish smile at her.

Her heart picked up speed. Maybe that nervous jump in her stomach had nothing to do with Fernbridge and everything to do with the rake standing next to him.

Nina gave herself a mental shake. The man was a rogue. She needed to remember this was nothing more than a game for Elliot. His blatant flirtatious looks meant nothing. He just wished to prove he could help her bring Fernbridge up to snuff with some competition.

Next to her, Grandmother grumbled. "I forgot how dashed crowded these things get. The smell of so many perfumed bodies crushed together like plums in a pie is nauseating."

Nina released a silent sigh. An hour before James, Caroline, and she were to leave for Lord and Lady Pendleton's ball, James had knocked on her bedchamber door and informed her Grandmother would be accompanying her. That could only mean one thing. Caroline was not feeling well. Queasiness had plagued her sister-in-law at the beginning of her last pregnancy.

"I need to sit," Grandmother snapped, giving an imperious thump of her cane, pulling Nina from her thoughts.

Around the perimeter of the ballroom, gilded chairs had been placed for those who wished to sit. On one wall sat several of Grandmother's old cronies.

"Grandmother, look who is here." Nina motioned to the gray-haired women, hoping the sight of them would elevate the matriarch's sour mood.

"Good God. I do not want to sit next to Lady Filbert. She complains incessantly about her bunions." She glanced around the ballroom. "Ah, there is the Dowager Lady Campden. I wish to sit next to her. She's originally from America. When she talks with her Bostonian accent, I pretend I cannot understand her, and she finally stops chatting. She's perfect."

Nina led the dowager to the chair next to Lady Campden. "Grandmother, I see my dear friend Lady Sara Elsmere. I shall be over there conversing with her."

Like a periscope, Grandmother tracked the girl down with her steely gray eyes and frowned. "Isn't she the girl who possesses that atrocious nervous laugh?"

"Not always," Nina said defensively.

"Go now before she comes over here. I fear her wretched laughter might bring on another megrim."

As Nina pivoted to walk away, Grandmother's gnarled fingers wrapped about her wrist, stopping her departure. "I see the Duke of Fernbridge is here. Remember, child, you have a duty to your family. If you marry the duke, it will snip any unfavorable gossip in the bud and please your brother."

Nina nodded, then strode toward Sara. Her friend, dressed in a simple cream-colored gown with little ornamentation, seemed to be attempting to blend into the wall. Gatherings like this made Sara as panicky as a cat getting bathed. As always, the sour-faced duenna Sara's father hired to attend these functions with her stood by her side.

As Nina joined her, Sara straightened her drooping shoulders and turned to her chaperone. "Mrs. Appleton, you may find a seat. I shall be fine with my friend Lady Nina."

The old woman strode away.

"Nina, I'm beyond happy to see you here. I'm like an octopus out of water at these events, but Papa still insists I attend."

Nina tried not to smile at her friend's description. Sara tended to replace words in idioms, making them unique, as she had now done using *octopus* instead of *fish*. She clasped Sara's hands and lifted her arms outward. "You look quite attractive, and I assure you, you have only two arms."

"I wish I did have eight. Then Papa would stop forcing me to attend these gatherings and sell me to a carnival instead."

"Sara, no one shall ask you to dance if you hide in the corner of the ballroom."

"That is precisely why I am here. You know what happens when a man so much as glances at me."

"Perhaps when dancing with a gentleman, you can imagine they are your dance instructor, Mr. Arneau."

Red crept up Sara's neck to settle on her cheeks. "Mr. Arneau quit yesterday. I giggled even when he danced with me."

"I'm sorry."

"I'm not. The man acted like a general in the army. He had no patience. I feared he might strike me. Honestly, Nina, I wish Papa would let me stay home and hide away in the library, but he has threatened to bolt the door closed if I do not attend this season. If he would attend with me, he'd witness firsthand how I am a leper."

Nina squeezed Sara's hand. "You are no such thing."

"No gentleman wishes to dance with me, and I cannot blame them." Sara's eyes grew large. A nervous-sounding laugh bubbled up her friend's throat. "Oh dear, Lord Ralston and the Duke of Fernbridge are cutting a path through the crowd and heading this way."

Nina turned and watched as both men strode toward them.

A moment later, Elliot inclined his head. "Lady Nina, how are you?"

"I'm well."

"May I introduce you both to Lady Sara . . ." Nina's voice trailed off as she noticed Sara had disappeared. "I'm sorry, Lady Sara was here a minute ago." She searched for her friend, then turned back to Fernbridge. "How are you, Your Grace?"

He released a bored-sounding sigh. "Well enough." He glanced about. "Ah, if you'll excuse me, I see Lord Alstead. He's got a stocked lake on his property. One of the best fishing places in all of England."

The man strode off.

Nina stared at Fernbridge's back as he walked away. "Maybe if I stripped naked, he would notice me."

Elliot's bark of laughter caused her to peer at him.

Goodness, had she spoken out loud, or was he once again reading her thoughts?

"I'm sure he would." Humor gleamed in his eyes.

Heat warmed her cheeks. "Tell me you have telepathic powers, and I didn't say that out loud."

"No such powers, but I wish I did." He bent his head closer to hers and spoke in a conspiratorially low voice. "I'd truly enjoy knowing what you're thinking, especially if it involves getting naked. Tell me what other wicked thoughts you have?"

Wicked? At this moment, they were abundant. When Elliot leaned close, she wondered what it would be like to have his sinful mouth on her skin. She stepped back. "My thoughts are quite pure."

"What a shame." The corners of his mouth turned upward into that devilishly handsome smile he'd perfected. "Though I'm sure you walking about sans clothing would have caused your grandmother to swoon."

The mention of her grandmother caused Nina to glance at the old woman. Thankfully, she was engaged in conversation with Lord Pendleton and hadn't noticed Nina and Elliot.

"The lessons I have planned for you are much subtler." Elliot's low and sensual voice sent an unwelcome shiver down her spine.

"I told you I don't require lessons. And I don't think this plan of yours will work. Fernbridge hardly notices me. He probably wouldn't even if I was naked. Perhaps if I wore a feathered grouse costume and squawked like a bird."

"Nina, tell me why you are interested in Fernbridge?"

"I have my reasons."

"Because he is a duke?"

If she married Fernbridge, she would finally win her grandmother's approval. But more important than that, it would please James, and her brother had sacrificed so much for them. Fernbridge might not be the most attentive person, but she believed he would be a steady husband. Not a man like her father or Avalon.

She held Elliot's intense gaze. "Will you help me or not?"

For a long minute, he didn't say anything. "I will, but there *will be* lessons, and the first one is, don't practically drool when you look at the man."

Without thinking, she touched her chin. "I do not drool."

"No, not literally. But you hang on his every word, and you try too hard to engage him in conversation."

"I'm being polite."

"You are, and you're exceptional at it, but it adds to his sense of self-importance."

"What do you want me to do? Ignore him?"

"No, but don't try so hard. Remember a man like Fernbridge wants to feel you are a challenge."

Nina opened her mouth and clapped it closed when Lord Talbot walked up to them.

"How are you, Lady Nina?" the man asked, looking as if he was attempting to hide behind them.

"I'm well."

"What are you about, Talbot?" Elliot narrowed his eyes at the other man.

"Lady Clifton spotted me as soon as I stepped into the ballroom. I'm trying to avoid that matchmaking mama."

"Lord Talbot!" Lady Clifton waved at the viscount as she marched toward them with her daughter Georgiana in tow.

Talbot mumbled something under his breath and glanced about as if searching for a quick escape. "Damnation. No avoiding her now. If you'll excuse me."

"I take it Lady Clifton is hoping for a match." Nina smiled at Elliot.

"Talbot will be a duke one day, and it appears dukes are in high demand."

Nina felt her cheeks warm. Somehow his comment had made her sound mercenary, or as if she'd somehow disappointed him. Well, she would not allow a rascal like Lord Elliot Ralston to make her feel guilty for contemplating wedding a man who didn't run with a fast crowd.

"The musicians are warming up their instruments." Elliot offered his arm. "Might I have this dance?"

"I don't wish to dance with you," she answered, still feeling the sting from his unspoken censure. He did not understand how much she owed James. How he'd raised them after Mama's and Papa's deaths. She wanted to please him, especially since her brother Anthony was causing James so much distress.

"You enjoyed it last time."

"I didn't. I just pretended I did."

"Liar," he whispered.

She tried to ignore the way her stomach fluttered. "Your conceit is overwhelming."

"Oh, darling, how you enjoy wounding me." He flashed his white teeth in a devil-may-care smile. "How are we to pull off this ruse if you won't dance with me?"

Elliot was right. If they were to pretend he was interested in courting her, she needed to dance with the scoundrel. She placed her hand on his sleeve. "I'm only dancing with you because I want Fernbridge to see us. No other reason."

As they joined the flow of others waltzing, she tried not to smile. He was correct. She did enjoy dancing. Moving in tandem with a man as the strains of a waltz filled a ballroom could be thrilling. However, dancing with Elliot verged on provocative.

Perhaps it was the way he looked at her. Truly held her

gaze for long moments of time while twirling her around the room. Many of the men she'd danced with were peacocks who watched the crowd to see who observed them, but Elliot's attention centered on her.

It made her feel as if they were the only two dancers in the room. It also made her feel hot—not only where his gloved hand touched her back, but everywhere. And occasionally, little sparks flickered in her stomach. Agitated by her reaction, she forced her gaze away from his blue eyes.

"No one will believe you are enchanted with me if you continue to frown."

"You're holding me too close," she said snappishly, more irritated with herself than him.

He pulled her incrementally closer. "I didn't think I was holding you close enough. Tell me why you're so prickly?"

"It's exceedingly hot in here."

The next thing she knew, he guided her through one of the open French doors.

"Elliot, we cannot be out here alone."

With a slight lifting of his chin, he gestured to several other couples who danced on the terrace. "We're not alone."

"But my grandmother—"

"Was still engaged in conversation with Lord Pendleton. Probably advising the man on how they could achieve world domination."

She laughed. "You might be right. But I thought your whole reason for dancing with me was to impress upon Fernbridge your interest in me."

"Glance to your left."

She turned her head slightly. The duke was standing with three other gentlemen at the far corner of the terrace. She hadn't noticed him leave the ballroom. Probably because she'd been too entranced by Elliot.

"Us dancing under the stars will get his attention."

Stars? She glanced up. Indeed, there were stars scattered above as if someone had tossed them haphazardly into the heavens. Though only a short distance from Town, Lord and Lady Pendleton's Richmond residence felt more like a country home since it was absent the fog that clung over London like low clouds.

The strains of the waltz stopped, and Elliot pointed at the sky. "There's Ursa Major."

"You know the constellations, my lord?"

He gave a short laugh. "Does that surprise you?"

It shouldn't, but she didn't want to think of him as anything else but a rogue. Placing him firmly in that category made him less appealing, and he already appealed to her more than she thought wise, especially since all his attention was a ruse.

He held her gaze, waiting for her response.

She shouldn't answer. If she said yes, it would be insulting. If she said no, it would inflate his opinion of himself. Yet, she didn't want him to think she thought him too perfect. "A little."

As if used to others underestimating his intelligence, he said nothing. That bothered her. As a woman, she contended with men who questioned her intellect. Not her brothers, but others. Her sister-in-law, Caroline, had grown up with a father who had not thought her worthy of conversation. Nina was sure it was the reason Caroline had wanted to become a journalist. Elliot had given her a glimpse of himself—something she didn't think he often did because of his carefree reputation. She liked him more than she wished to admit.

Guilt prompted her to ask, "How do you know about the constellations?"

"When younger, my family holidayed in the Lake

District. Like here, the stars shine brightly. Since my sister enjoys astronomy, I bought her a book on the constellations, and at night, we'd search them out." The tone of his voice clearly betrayed his affection for his sister. Victoria had mentioned the girl but knew little about her. From the story Victoria told, when Elliot was younger, his parents had taken to living in separate homes. The sister had gone to live with her mother in the country, then to a private school after her mama's death.

"Victoria mentioned you have a younger sister."

"Yes. Margaret, but I've always called her Meg." His smile cemented Nina's opinion that he cared deeply for the girl.

"Do you and she still stargaze?"

"Occasionally, though we haven't been to Swan Cottage in many years."

"Swan Cottage?"

"That's the name of the property I own in the Lake District. It will be part of Meg's dowry."

Nina wondered if Elliot was as protective of his sister as James had become of her since Nina's botched betrothal to Lord Avalon. Thoughts of her eldest brother reminded her he wouldn't be pleased she stargazed with Elliot. Neither would her grandmother. "We should return. Grandmother is probably wondering where I've gone off to."

He smiled. "She might already be plotting my demise."

She grinned. "What, my sweet Grandmother?"

He laughed. "Earlier, Fernbridge mentioned he will be attending Lord and Lady Hathaway's house party. Will you be going?"

"Yes. You?"

"I will, now that you are."

They moved to reenter the ballroom.

Near the French doors, Fernbridge still chatted with

several other men. Odd, she'd completely forgotten about the man. That sentiment seemed mutual. Fernbridge also seemed oblivious to her presence. "I don't think your plan is working one whit."

As if on cue, Fernbridge turned and glanced over his shoulder at her.

Elliot offered her his arm. "I wouldn't be so sure of that."

As they walked toward the French doors, the duke strode toward them. He offered a warm smile. "Lady Nina, Lord Ralston."

She opened her mouth to ask him if he was enjoying the unseasonably warm night. Remembering what Elliot had said about acting indifferent, she clapped her mouth closed. Such advice seemed odd, but Elliot did have the ability to make women swoon, and most likely the more the rascal ignored a woman, the harder she would vie for his attention.

Nina forced her expression to remain bland. "Your Grace."

The smile on his lips slipped a notch.

She glanced into the ballroom as if it held more appeal than the duke's company.

"Pleasant weather this evening," Fernbridge said.

Goodness, Elliot clearly knew what he was talking about. The more indifferent she acted, the harder Fernbridge tried to engage her in conversation.

"Yes, very nice weather. If you'll excuse us, Your Grace, I've promised the next dance to Sir Thomas. I should return to the ballroom." With that said, she and Elliot walked back into the ballroom, but she could feel the duke's gaze on her.

When they were out of earshot, Elliot laughed. "Well done, darling."

* * *

Back inside the ballroom, Elliot watched Nina and Sir Thomas as they moved across the dance floor to a Venetian waltz. His regard shifted to Fernbridge, who stepped into the ballroom. The man's gaze, like his own, followed Nina and her partner. The duke's interest was piqued. Elliot wondered why he was helping Nina get Fernbridge's attention. It was as if he was sabotaging his own plan, but it had been the only way he could figure to compel Nina to spend time with him.

From the corner of his eye, he saw Fernbridge heading toward him. Elliot took a glass of champagne off a passing footman's tray.

His Grace cupped his chin as if in deep thought. "Ralston, tell me about her."

"Who?" Elliot knew damn well Fernbridge referred to Nina. The man's gaze followed her like a bear's tracking salmon moving upstream.

"Lady Nina Trent."

The idea of listing several disagreeable habits Nina possessed flashed in Elliot's mind, yet he couldn't think of anything. He could make something up, such as she had a terrible habit of picking her nose or suffered from excessive flatulence, but he couldn't lie. He'd sunk low, but not that low.

Instead, he offered the truth. "She's lovely."

"Yes, she's quite handsome."

Of course, the man thought he solely referred to her beauty, but Elliot had meant it as so much more.

Fernbridge cleared his throat. "So, tell me why Avalon stopped courting her? I've heard gossip."

It wasn't his place to say that Avalon had a very pregnant mistress. A woman he was presently entertaining in France. That, contrary to his family's desires, Avalon had not been willing to give up his lover. "He didn't stop courting her. *She* was not interested in furthering an alliance."

"I'd heard differently."

Yes, some vicious gossipmonger has been spreading that lie. He wished he knew who. He wanted to grab them by the shoulders and shake them senseless. He blinked, startled by his vehemence. "A misinformed tattler."

"Ah, I'm learning London is full of them. I've heard some colorful things about you."

"Have you?" Not surprising.

The man smiled. "Lady Nina is not a widow. Does that mean you wish to court her?"

"She interests me." Elliot tipped the champagne flute to his mouth.

"Then that makes two of us," Fernbridge said and walked away.

He'd suspected his interest in Nina would draw the man's attention. In school, Fernbridge had always tried to compete with him.

Well, hopefully the lessons Elliot had planned for Nina at the Hathaways' house party would remove all thoughts of Fernbridge from her mind.

Chapter Eight

Elliot sat in his club in St. James with several chums, which included Talbot, Roger Monroe, and Lord Joshua Winters.

"You look like you haven't slept in a fortnight, Elliot." Winters grinned. "Who's been warming your bed?" The man leaned forward and placed his elbows on the table as if awaiting a titillating story.

Talbot burst out laughing. "Wait until you hear. Go on, tell them, Elliot."

Elliot shot Talbot a scathing look.

"Good Lord, who is it?" Roger leaned back in his chair and tipped his mug of coffee to his mouth.

"Veer your minds away from any salacious thoughts. Only that massive bloodhound he inherited." With a hearty laugh, Talbot pounded his palm on the table.

Roger half-laughed, half-coughed, sending a spray of dark brew into the air. "Zeb?"

Of course, Zeb. He didn't own any other eighty-five-pound bloodhounds who insisted on sleeping with him.

Winters wrinkled his nose and sat back. Though Elliot wasn't sure if it was disappointment over not hearing some lurid tale or disgust over the coffee specks Roger had spat all over the sleeve of Winter's coat.

"I'm glad you gentlemen find humor in this." Elliot scrubbed a hand over his face. "I haven't had a decent night's sleep in—"

"A dog's age?" Talbot's grin broadened.

"You should send him to your country home, so he might roam about." Winters picked up a napkin and dabbed at the coffee flecks on his sleeve.

Elliot had contemplated that idea. Most bloodhounds would enjoy the country, but Zeb wasn't like most dogs. He was old and melancholy, and he didn't roam, he slugged. Besides that, who would take care of him at Ralston House? He'd let everyone go except the housekeeper and a groundsman. If they ignored the animal, his ennui might worsen.

"Or give him to someone else," Winters continued. "You don't hunt."

"That's what I suggested," Talbot said.

Who would want a bloodhound who didn't hunt? One who laid about all day? He ignored the suggestion. "Are any of you going to the Hathaways' house party this weekend?"

They all answered in the negative. Lord and Lady Hathaway's house parties were usually subdued affairs.

"Why are you going there?" Roger asked, looking rather put off by the idea of attending such a tame gathering.

"Lady Nina Trent will be at the house party." Talbot winked at the other men.

"Don't tell me you're seriously considering settling down?" Winters looked at Elliot as if he'd decided to cut off a leg.

"Lady Nina's quite pretty." Roger twisted the end of his moustache and gave a salacious grin.

Elliot wasn't sure why, but the look on Roger's face made him want to invite the other man to Clapton's Boxing Club and trounce him. Without answering the question,

Elliot pushed back his chair and stood. He needed to leave before he did something foolish, plus he'd promised to take Zeb for a walk. A rather depressing adventure.

Outside of his club, Elliot pulled on his leather gloves. The warmth that had cloaked London yesterday had given way to the return of Old Man Winter. He settled inside his carriage. Normally the interior of one's vehicle on a bitter day would be a blessing, but Uncle Phillip's equipage lacked benevolence. An odor one could only call unpleasant clung to the faded brown upholstery like a forlorn lover.

"Walk," his coachman, Rigby, instructed the horses.

The two bays moved, sending the rattling of their harnesses and clopping hooves to add to the composition of sounds that filled the busy London street. They'd no sooner turned off Pall Mall when the carriage hit a rut. Elliot bounced so high on the seat his head almost rammed against the roof. Besides needing new upholstery, the carriage needed new springs.

As he stretched his neck to relieve the tension in it, an image of Swan Cottage burrowed to the forefront of his mind. If he sold the property, he would be able to place his feet more firmly on solid ground, perhaps even crawl out of the financial pit he was sinking into like quicksand. Yet, he couldn't bring himself to do it. Meg loved the cottage. Plus, he'd already promised it would be part of her dowry. He would not go back on his word. He owed her that much, and so much more, after what he'd done.

He glanced out the window as they turned onto Charles Street. The equipage slowed as it neared the front of his town house. It gave a violent shudder before the left rear corner of the vehicle's compartment slammed against the pavement, causing an explosive noise like a clap of thunder.

Elliot, tossed sideways, slid across the seat. His shoulder rammed against the side of the thin squabs.

Christ. They'd lost the left back wheel.

The sound of the metal axel scraping against the street filled the interior of the compartment, along with his coachman's frantic calls to the horses, attempting to keep them calm.

The smell of sparks, as if one took metal to a grinding wheel, filled the air.

"Whoa. Whoa, boys!" Rigby called out to the neighing horses.

Frantic voices rushed toward the carriage as the vehicle finally came to a stop.

"Are you hurt, my lord?" Rigby called out, jumping down from the perch.

"No," he said, making his way to the opposite side of the vehicle to force the door open. Bracing his hands on the sides, he lifted himself out and jumped down to the pavement.

A crowd of startled faces, eyes wide, mouths gaping, stared at the lopsided vehicle. Several men rushed over to help his coachman unharness the horses so they wouldn't drag the carriage farther up the street and cause more damage.

Elliot walked around to the other side. Crouching, he examined the axel. Thankfully, it wasn't bent.

"Forgive me, my lord." The coachman stepped beside him and shifted nervously from one foot to the other as if he feared Elliot would sack him.

It wasn't the coachman's fault the vehicle was old and in need of repairs.

"Saints preserve!" Wilson said, dashing out of the house. The manservant stared at the carriage through his thick glasses. "You could have been killed, my lord." His gaze volleyed to the coachman. "And you as well, Mr. Rigby."

True. Years ago, Elliot had witnessed two spooked

horses pulling a carriage. The frightened animals had turned so fast, the vehicle had teetered and fallen on its side. The noise had caused the anxious horses to continue their mad dash until the carriage had been little more than kindling wood, and the occupant inside dead. Yes, both he and the coachman were lucky the man had controlled the horses.

He helped the men lift the rear of the carriage so the wheel could be placed back on.

"The cotter pin is missing," Rigby said. "We must have lost it when the vehicle hit that rut. I'll go to the wheelwright and get a replacement and have him put the bill on your account."

Damnation, more money he needed to spend. Brushing off his hands, he thanked the men and strode into the house with Wilson.

Mrs. Lamb approached with Zeb on his leash. "He's raring to go for a walk, my lord."

Elliot rubbed at his sore shoulder and realized the housekeeper hadn't heard the commotion outside.

"Are you daft, old woman?" Wilson asked. "His lordship's been in an accident."

The housekeeper cocked her head to the side and pulled out her hearing trumpet. "What?"

The valet just shook his head at the housekeeper before turning to Elliot. "I will take him, sir."

"No, I will." He couldn't let the half-blind manservant take the bloodhound out. The man would probably step in front of a carriage, and one accident for the day was enough. He took the dog's leash and headed toward Hyde Park.

Conversations during luncheons at the Trent family table were rarely dull. Caroline and James discussed politics.

Grandmother scoffed at everything they said and called them radicals while arguing a counterpoint. Georgie, who was ten, mostly talked about his favorite subject, which this week was steam locomotives, but next week would be something different. The only one besides Nina who sat quietly was Anthony, and that was only because her scandalous brother usually spent his nights gadding about Town and looked close to catatonic at this hour of the day.

Yesterday, Nina had overheard James in his office railing at Anthony for his dissipated lifestyle, which included spending his nights playing cards and sharing his mistress's bed.

"Though I enjoy sparring with you, Grandmother," Caroline said, "I have an editorial to write. I need to go to my office at the *London Reformer*."

Grandmother's steely gray eyes hardened, and the lines in her face deepened. "What radical agenda will this editorial be about?"

"Ah, you will have to read next week's edition to find out." Smiling, Caroline stood.

The matriarch made a derisive noise. "James, I wish you'd learn to control your wife."

James's response was to kiss Caroline's cheek and offer to walk her to her carriage. "I'll be in my office looking over my land steward's report if anyone needs me."

"And what are you going to do?" Grandmother turned her angry glower on poor Georgie.

He stood and swiped a napkin over the crumbs on his chin. "I have to finish a math assignment my tutor gave me."

"Good gracious, boy, shouldn't they be shipping you off to boarding school soon?" A week didn't go by in which Grandmother didn't ask that question.

"James and Caroline said I don't have to go yet." Georgie dashed out of the room, obviously thinking the math assignment awaiting him was better than staying with their irritable grandmother.

Grandmother snapped her finger in front of Anthony, who appeared to have fallen asleep. "Wake up, Anthony, before you land face-first in your soup."

When he appeared not to hear her, she slammed her open palm on the table, rattling the dishes.

Anthony bolted upright and peered around as if trying to reorient himself to his surroundings. He set a hand to the side of his head and got up from his chair. "I need to find James's valet, so he can fix me one of his tonics, then I'm going back to bed. I've got a splitting headache."

"Humph." Grandmother picked up her cane, which leaned against the table, and stood. "If you didn't engage in debauchery at all hours of the night you wouldn't look like a corpse in the afternoon."

Anthony gave her one of his devil-may-care smiles, then bent to give the woman's cheek a kiss. "Admit it. You adore me." He exited the room.

"Yes, like one adores a toothache," Grandmother said.

"I heard that!" Anthony called out from the corridor.

The dowager pinned Nina with her piercing gray eyes. "Are you still interested in the Duke of Fernbridge?"

She took a sip of her tea. "I am."

"Wise choice, girl. At least one member of this family realizes their duty to the Trent name." The matriarch quit the room, leaving Nina alone.

Blessed quiet. She ate a spoonful of rice pudding and looked at the copy of the *London Reformer* that Caroline had left on the table.

SUFFRAGIST BEATRICE WALKER
TO HOLD RALLY AT
SPEAKERS' CORNER IN HYDE PARK

Caroline had mentioned the rally. *It might be interesting*, Nina thought as she plopped a piece of tomato into her mouth. Yes, she'd attend.

A few minutes later, Nina slipped her small sketchbook into her reticule and made her way down the steps. She'd reached the entry hall when Grandmother stepped into the room.

"Where are you off to?"

"I'm going to Hyde Park to draw." Telling Grandmother the truth would only start a row.

"Alone?"

"Grandmother, the park is no more than a stone's throw from here."

"You still need a chaperone."

Nina released an audible sigh. "Maybe when you were a young woman, but nowadays women have more freedom to move about."

"It's obvious you've been listening to that progressive sister-in-law of yours. What has this family come to? Caroline runs a radical paper. Your brother all but encourages her, and Anthony is out all night doing God knows what. Most likely whoring, and you believe walking about unchaperoned is proper."

Georgie stuck his head out of the morning room. "What's whoring?"

Nina gave her grandmother a reproachful look, then patted her young brother's head. "I'll let Grandmother explain that."

And without looking back, Nina slipped out of the house.

A sizable crowd had gathered at Speakers' Corner in Hyde Park. Nina lifted her hand to her forehead to shield the sun from her eyes and surveyed the throng of mostly women. Standing to the rear of those gathered, she withdrew her sketchbook and unwrapped her piece of charcoal from the paper she'd placed it in.

A tall, slender woman dressed in a white blouse, navy skirt, and matching woolen jacket stepped onto a crate.

Hisses and boos mixed with applause.

Ignoring the naysayers, Beatrice Walker welcomed the crowd. She talked about the strength and intelligence of women and their growing place in the world.

As Nina listened to the suffragist's impassioned speech, the charcoal in her hand stilled. The woman's rallying cry sparked something inside of her. It made her understand Caroline's dedication—her desire to be a journalist and help further the cause of the women's movement.

"We should have as much say in our lives as a man." Beatrice Walker's voice shook with emotion. "We—"

The suffragist's words were cut off by a tomato landing mere inches from where the woman stood. Red pulp splattered in the air and onto her skirt.

Nina sucked in a shocked breath. Caroline had told her how poorly some members of the crowds treated the suffragist when she spoke, but she'd found it difficult to believe.

As if nothing had transpired, the woman continued talking over several people who jeered.

Spotting a policeman, Nina slipped the sketchbook and charcoal into her reticule and marched over to him. "Aren't you going to do anything?"

"About what?" With the nail of his index finger, he picked at the space between his two front teeth.

She almost growled in frustration. Was the man blind? She jabbed her finger toward the suffragist at the exact moment a head of cabbage sailed past Beatrice Walker's head.

The suffragist ducked and continued speaking.

"I presume you didn't see that either?"

"Nope." The policeman folded his arms over his chest, peered over her head, and stood as silent as one of the Queen's Guard at Buckingham Palace.

Nina kicked at the ground, sending dirt onto the policeman's shiny black shoes. "I bet you didn't see that either."

That got his attention. He grabbed her wrist and pulled her toward the paddy wagon.

Her heartbeat picked up tempo. "Where are you taking me?"

"To the magistrate."

"So the men tossing food at Miss Walker are to be ignored, yet I am to be arrested?"

Several women in the back of the crowd turned to the commotion and started yelling at the bobby.

From the corner of her eye, Nina noticed a slender young lad peering at her. The boy cranked his arm back.

Knowing what was about to happen, Nina ducked.

The tomato whipped through the air and struck the constable in the shoulder.

Startled, the officer momentarily released her and searched the crowd.

She cocked an eyebrow. "Bet you saw that."

With a growl, the policeman grabbed her wrist again. "Come on, missy, get in the wagon."

"Hold on there," a familiar male voice called out.

Elliot and a large bloodhound walked toward them.

"None of your concern, sir," the constable said. "Be about your own business."

"Lord Ralston, I don't need your assistance in this matter. I look forward to going before the magistrate. I will inform him how this policeman didn't see fit to arrest several disorderly people at an otherwise peaceful rally."

The policeman appeared to not hear a word she said. He was staring at Elliot. Probably pondering what might happen if he crossed a member of the House of Lords. As if thinking better of it, he released her wrist.

"She's all yours. God help you, my lord." Swiping at the juice dripping down his face, the constable strode away.

"Nina, what was that about?" Elliot asked.

She pointed to the crowd and the suffragist who was finishing her speech. "Beatrice Walker was doing nothing more than talking about the advancement of women when a lad threw a tomato at her. One idiot in the crowd threw a head of cabbage, and that policeman did absolutely nothing. He just stood there smirking. So, I kicked dirt on his shoes."

Elliot's dark brows lifted. "You what?"

"The lummox should not have ignored the situation. My sister-in-law, Caroline, told me about what went on at these rallies, but seeing it firsthand . . ." She shook her head.

A slight smile turned up one corner of his mouth. He offered her his arm, and they walked toward the Marble Arch. "Your grandmother might have suffered apoplexy if you'd been arrested."

She'd been so agitated, she hadn't even thought about that. Or James's reaction. "I could not stand idly by."

The slight curve of his mouth broadened.

"Elliot, I see no humor in this."

He sobered. "Neither do I."

"Then why are you finding it difficult to keep a straight face?"

"Because you are full of surprises."

She wasn't sure if that was good or bad, but she didn't regret her actions. "Well, I would do it again."

"Would you now?"

"Indeed. So what do you think of that?"

"It places you in my high regard."

His words startled her. "Really?"

"Yes. Standing up for what you believe in is important."

"You are full of surprises as well, my lord." She peered at the dog. Occasionally, Elliot had to coax the animal to continue walking. "Is he yours?"

"Regrettably, yes."

The displeased look on his face made her smile. "You're not fond of dogs?"

"I like them very much. This one is just a bit unique."

"How so?"

"He's older than dirt, and stubborn."

As if offended by the comment, the dog not only slowed down but sat.

"Come on, old boy." Elliot gave a gentle tug on the leash.

The animal looked away as if disinterested.

"See." He frowned. "Zeb, get up."

The dog slowly got onto all fours.

"Were you sketching before you decided it would be entertaining to kick dirt on the constable's shoes?"

"How did you know?"

With a tip of his chin, he motioned to her hand. "The charcoal smudges on your glove. My sister gets them on her fingers when she draws."

Once again, a smile touched his lips when he mentioned his sister. It made her curious about the girl. "Do you see your sister much?"

"During holidays."

As they reached her family's Park Lane residence, he grinned, and pulled out a handkerchief from the inside breast pocket of his navy coat and offered it to her. "You've tomato pulp on your face."

It was warm from his body's heat and smelled like soap

and starch and him, an utterly wonderful scent. "I saw the lad a few seconds before he tried to hit me with the tomato, so I ducked, and the policeman was struck. You should have seen the startled expression on his face."

"I can imagine. Karma."

"Do you believe in that?" she asked, wiping her cheek.

"Yes." Conviction edged his voice, but he didn't expand on his succinct reply. "You missed a spot." He took the handkerchief from her fingers and brushed it gently over her cheek, while his intense blue eyes held her gaze.

Her heart stuttered in her chest and warmth tingled through her body.

The clopping of hooves and rattling of harnesses pulled her regard away.

Caroline disembarked from her carriage, looking a bit puzzled by Elliot's presence. She narrowed her eyes at a spot at the shoulder of Nina's green walking outfit. "Are those tomato seeds on you?"

"They are. I went to the rally you mentioned." Nina brushed them off.

"Oh, don't tell me those wretched tomato-throwers were there again."

"Yes, and a constable did absolutely nothing."

"The scoundrel. I wish I had been there." Caroline peered at Elliot. "You were attending the rally as well, Lord Ralston?"

"No, Lady Huntington. I was walking my dog."

Caroline glanced at the animal, smiled, then returned her gaze to them.

"I don't wish James to know, Caroline, but I was nearly arrested." Nina released a frustrated breath.

"Arrested?" Her sisters-in-law's green eyes turned wide.

"Yes, if Lord Ralston hadn't interceded, I would have been. I got a bit agitated with the constable."

"Ah, Nina, I'll make you a suffragist yet." Caroline grinned and faced Elliot. "Thank you, my lord. You must stay and have afternoon tea with us."

Nina blinked, startled by the invitation. Surely, her sister-in-law realized James would not be pleased to see Elliot.

Chapter Nine

"I'd be honored to take tea with you." Elliot smiled at Lady Caroline Huntington, then glanced at the dog sitting by his feet. "I'll just walk Zeb home and return shortly."

Nina glanced at the bloodhound. "No need. My younger brother, Georgie, loves dogs. He'll probably want to play catch with him in the garden."

Catch? Good luck with that, unless the boy was a miracle worker.

"Please, come inside." Caroline motioned to the front door, which was painted in a bright yellow.

Elliot gave a gentle tug on Zeb's leash, and luckily the animal followed him into the house. He remembered the grand entry hall from when he'd attended the ball. Its opulence made it difficult to forget. It sported a black and white marble floor in a diamond pattern. Arched niches displayed costly tall Grecian urns, and to the right, a wide marble staircase led to a balcony decorated with more arches and thick cornices.

Male voices could be heard down the corridor. Huntington and a stony-faced butler stepped out of a room. The smile Huntington offered his wife disappeared when he noticed Elliot.

"Darling." The marquess kissed his wife's cheek, then glared at Elliot.

"James, dearest, Nina and I happened upon Lord Ralston, and I invited him to afternoon tea." She patted her husband's hand affectionately.

Elliot surmised that Caroline would not mention Nina's attendance at the suffragist rally. Not that Elliot thought the man against the women's movement. To the contrary, his backing of his wife's newspaper, and the editorials she wrote, confirmed Huntington supported it. However, the fact that Nina had nearly been arrested would not sit well with the marquess.

"Ralston." Huntington stepped up to him and grasped his hand in a bone-crushing clasp that might have broken a less hardy man's fingers.

He'd seen the man engage in several rounds at Clapton's Boxing Club and knew him a worthy opponent, but if he thought his glower and the pressure of his grip would scare Elliot off, it wouldn't.

A snore that sounded more like a steam engine choking caused everyone's gazes to shift to Zeb. He lay sprawled out on the floor, asleep as if it were as comfortable as Elliot's mattress.

Mirth lit up Nina's eyes.

Peering at the dog, Huntington frowned, then motioned to the stairs. "Shall we go to the drawing room?"

Good Lord. Elliot glanced at the sleeping dog. He'd probably have to carry Zeb up the flight of steps.

"Since it's such a fine day, let's take our tea on the terrace," Nina suggested.

Elliot breathed a silent sigh of relief.

Nina smiled as if reading his thoughts.

"What a splendid idea." Caroline turned to the butler,

who stood patiently waiting for instructions. "Menders, we'll take our tea on the terrace."

"Yes, my lady."

Georgie came barreling down the stairs. "Oh, jolly ho," he said, spotting the sleeping bloodhound. The lad crouched next to the dog. "Who's this fine fellow?"

Elliot squatted next to him. "Master George, might I introduce you to Zeb. As you can see, he is rather old and doesn't have much bounce in his step. If you wish to pet him, he's quite tame."

As Georgie ran his hand over the animal's flank, Zeb opened his droopy-lidded eyes and wagged his tail.

"Georgie, do you want to take him outside and into the garden?" Nina asked.

"May I?" The child peered at Elliot.

If the lad could get the dog to go with him, Elliot would be grateful. "Of course."

"Come on, boy. Want to play outside?" Georgie stood and took the dog's leash.

For a moment, it looked like Zeb was going to just lie there like a stone statue, but he slowly got to his feet and followed Georgie down the corridor.

"Shall we?" With a sweep of her hand, Lady Huntington gestured toward the arch.

Outside, they sat at a cast-iron table on the terrace. Before Elliot could assist Nina with her chair, her brother was by her side. Huntington sat next to Nina, while motioning Elliot to sit in the chair opposite them.

If the marquess had his way, Elliot didn't doubt, he'd have been seated at another table or perhaps in the middle of Park Lane, so a carriage might run him over.

Zeb's bark caused him to look at the dog. Elliot almost rubbed at his eyes to make sure he wasn't hallucinating. The bloodhound was fetching a stick.

"Georgie is marvelous with dogs," Nina said, noticing the direction of his gaze.

"I see that." Elliot wondered if they'd notice the lad missing if he kidnapped him. Probably. They seemed like a close family. Unlike his own, in which children had been seen but not heard. Georgie looked to be around ten years old. By that age, Elliot had already been shipped off to boarding school. Though, in truth, he hadn't minded—better than listening to his parents' quarreling. A few years after Meg was born, his parents had all but given up on their marriage and taken to separate residences. Meg had gone off with Mother, Elliot with Father. Two children who were more of an inconvenience than anything else.

The French doors opened. The butler pushed a tea cart to the table and spread a pristine white tablecloth over the surface.

Caroline served the tea while the butler placed several tiered trays with cucumber sandwiches and biscuits on the table.

"Will you be attending the Hathaways' house party, Lord Ralston?" Caroline handed him his cup.

"I will."

"Ah, we are attending as well." Nina smiled and took a sip of her tea.

Elliot noticed the way Huntington's hand clenched at his delicate teacup. If the man didn't loosen his grip, the porcelain would shatter.

The French doors opened, and Nina's brother Anthony stepped outside. Elliot had played cards with the man several times. He was the black sheep of the family. Where Huntington was serious, Anthony acted carefree. A rascal who liked to enjoy life a little bit more than one should. His current mistress was an actress or an opera singer.

The appearance of his scapegrace brother seemed to

turn Lord Huntington's mood darker, especially when Anthony strode closer and one could see his clothes were wrinkled as if he'd slept in them. Or perhaps he'd not slept home, but in someone else's bed and just crawled out of it. The dark stubble shadowing his jaw added to his unkempt aura. Appearing oblivious to the disapproving glower with which his brother was favoring him, Anthony grinned and clapped Elliot on the shoulder. "Ralston, how are you?"

"Well. And you?"

"Capital." Anthony slumped into one of the chairs and glanced at Huntington. The smile on the younger man's face faded. "Dash it all, James, you look like a mortician with that scowl on your face."

Though Anthony was only around his mid-twenties, up close Elliot could see the signs of dissipation on the man's face.

Anthony lifted a hand to shadow his eyes from the sun and pointed to Georgie and Zeb.

"Goodness, when did we get a pony?"

Nina laughed. "Anthony, are you drunk? That's Lord Ralston's bloodhound."

Leaning forward in his chair, Anthony blinked. "Well, I'll be. . . . It is a dog. What does he weigh? Six stone?"

From having had to carry the stubborn dog about on several occasions, Elliot knew Zeb weighed close to that. "Yes."

Nodding, Anthony picked up a sandwich and took several sizable bites.

"Your garden is lovely, Lady Huntington." Elliot pointed to an area to the left of the terrace. "The bark of the birches with the rhododendrons must look stunning when the latter blooms."

Everyone's gazes swung to him as if he'd dropped his trousers and flashed his arse.

Nina blinked. "You are familiar with plants, my lord?"

"A bit." He'd been working and studying the plants in his garden at his country estate. He and his gardener, Mr. McWilliams, had torn out those that were half dead and unsalvageable and divided overgrown plants. He might not have the funds to repair the country residence, but he had the physical ability to garden and plant. He'd found masses of bluebell bulbs that he'd dug up and replanted near the meandering pathways on the property. This spring, a profusion of purple, carpet-like flowers had rewarded his labor.

"I fear I cannot take any credit for the gardens, my lord," Caroline said. "I know little about gardening except what I find visually appealing." She gave a small laugh. "I'm not even sure which plant is . . . what did you call it, a rhododendron?"

"Those." Nina pointed at the bushes. "Remember, you asked the gardener to clip some of their flowers last year?"

"Ah, yes. I recall they were purple. As you can see, Nina knows more about them than I do. She likes to sketch them."

"Do you, Lady Nina?" He smiled at her.

"I do."

"I'd love to see your sketches," Elliot said.

Her eldest brother made a noise that sounded like a growl.

"Suffering from dyspepsia, James?" Anthony asked, oblivious.

Tired of her eldest brother's boorish behavior, Nina set her teacup in her saucer. "Would you like a tour of the gardens, Lord Ralston?"

Elliot glanced at James and smiled. "Yes, I would."

She had to give Elliot credit; he wasn't the type of man to cower.

As if intending to accompany them, James pushed his chair back.

Caroline set her hand on her husband's, halting his movements. "Georgie is there."

Elliot offered Nina his arm.

They strode down the terrace steps and onto a garden path.

"Does your brother own a set of dueling pistols?" Elliot asked. His mouth turned up, forming a lopsided grin.

Nina couldn't help her laugh. "I believe he has inherited my grandfather's."

"Is he dashing from the terrace to retrieve them?"

She glanced over her shoulder. "No, but if looks could kill . . ."

"Ah, I can handle looks. Bullets are more difficult to dodge."

Another small laugh escaped her lips. "So, was that a lucky guess as to which plants are rhododendrons, or do you really have an interest in horticulture?"

"I can point out a rhododendron just as easily as a forsythia or berberis."

"I'm impressed, my lord. Constellations and a knowledge of plants. Perhaps there is more to you than your handsome face."

"You are free to examine me all you want." His voice was low, seductive.

The tone, along with the implication, made her body heat. She swallowed hard. "You know there is no need to play this game with me when the Duke of Fernbridge is not about."

"But I enjoy the way you blush. And if I'm honest, I like torturing your brother."

Nina glanced at James. He watched them like a hawk. If her brother knew about the lessons Elliot wished her to partake in, he *would* be running for Grandfather's old dueling pistols.

Georgie and Zeb strode up to them.

"He's lost interest in fetching," Georgie said, his tone reflecting his disappointment.

Elliot took the dog's leash and ruffled the lad's hair. "Master George, that's the most I've seen him move. He usually does little else besides sleep. You are a miracle worker."

Her young brother proudly puffed out his chest.

"I best be shoving off or Zeb will fall asleep halfway home, and I'll need to carry him the rest of the way."

She nodded.

Elliot thanked Caroline and James, while not seeming the least bit put off by James's glower.

Nina walked him to the door. "So, I will see you at the Hathaways'."

"Yes, and we will begin our lessons in earnest."

Last night, while in bed, she'd wondered what Elliot's lessons would involve. Lesson one—to not fawn over the Duke of Fernbridge—had been easy, but she feared some of Elliot's lessons would be more titillating.

Nina's heart picked up speed. She averted her gaze and patted the dog's head. "I do not think there is anything you could teach me that I don't already know."

He leaned close and whispered in her ear, "Oh, darling, there is so much I could teach you."

And with that said, he strode out the door, leaving her body tingling just from his words.

Chapter Ten

The following day, Elliot raked his fingers through his hair as the carriage he'd hired at the train station drove between the stone pillars flanking the entrance to his country house. He reached into his coat pocket and withdrew the unsettling letter he'd received.

What in God's name was Meg doing in Hampshire? Why wasn't she at Mrs. Gibbs's School for Girls? Since receiving the note from Mrs. Newcomb, the housekeeper at Ralston House, he'd tried to make sense of it.

The carriage slowed as it neared the residence. From the outside, the Jacobean country home looked impressive. Previous barons had added additions during the sixteenth and seventeenth centuries. At one time, it had been a showplace that held grand balls and house parties. Now, the dilapidated inside reflected only a shadow of its past.

When the vehicle stopped, Zeb, sprawled on the opposite seat, lifted his head and gave Elliot a droopy-eyed glance. Without waiting for the door to be opened, Elliot disembarked, anxious to find out what was going on.

"Lord Ralston. I hope you had a pleasant journey," the gardener, Mr. McWilliams, said, walking toward him.

No. Thoughts and concern over his sister had made the journey seem interminable, and Zeb's snoring, which at times sounded like a hand bellow with a clogged nozzle, hadn't helped.

"McWilliams, is my sister inside?"

The old man nodded.

The driver opened the boot to remove Elliot's valise.

"I'll get your bags, my lord," the gardener said.

"Thank you." Elliot entered the house.

Mrs. Newcomb rushed toward him and gave a quick curtsey. "Oh, thank goodness you are here, Lord Ralston. I didn't know what to do."

His heart rate quickened. "To do? What do you mean? Is something wrong with Meg?"

The woman gave several vigorous shakes of her head like a dog trying to dislodge a flea in its ear. "No. Not exactly."

He wanted to rail at the woman over her ambiguous reply. "Yes, go on."

"Well, my lord, she's been cleaning the place since she arrived a few days ago. I cannot get her to stop. A lady of her station shouldn't be getting calluses on her hands."

Cleaning? "Where is she?"

"Upstairs in the blue drawing room. She's taken the curtains down and is washing all the windows and sills in there."

Elliot took the steps three at a time. His sister shouldn't be cleaning. Not with her bad leg.

He flung open the double doors and stepped into the room. Meg stood over a bucket of water, wringing out a sopping rag. She wore a maid's uniform. A white mobcap covered her long dark hair, but a few tendrils clung to the dampness on her flushed face. A long smudge of dirt ran from her nose to her cheek. If he'd seen his own sister on the street, he would not have recognized her.

She glanced up and smiled. "Elliot, what are you doing here?"

"What am I doing here? What are you doing here? Why aren't you at school?"

Meg placed the rag on the edge of the bucket and wiped her damp hands on her soiled white pinafore. She peered at him with her dark blue eyes that looked so much like his own. "I didn't like it there."

"You love it there. Did someone say something to you? A new student?"

"No, I . . ."

"What?" He strode up to her and gently set his hands on her shoulders. "Tell me, Meg." He tried to keep his voice calm, but if someone had hurt her, he would make them pay.

With a sweep of her hand, she motioned to the room. "Look at this place. Pieces of plaster molding are missing, the floors are warped, the white ceiling is full of soot because the chimney in here is clogged. I know this residence and the London town house are bleeding you dry. You cannot afford to pay for Mrs. Gibbs's School."

"Oh, Meg." He pulled her close, and she rested her head against his chest. "Is that why you are here? The last thing you should be worrying about is money. Since you are away at school, and I live in London, I am making repairs to the town house first. I will repair this monstrosity in good time. I have everything under control."

"You do?" Her eyes grew wide.

"Yes." He took her hand in his and led her to a group of chairs.

Today, her limp was more exaggerated. All this physical work surely exacerbated the pain in her left leg. "Please, sit." He gestured to a chair upholstered in faded blue velvet.

Though she tried to hide it, the way the skin around her mouth tightened proved her leg plagued her.

The fact that Meg scrubbed this accursed house because of her concern for him made him want to hit something. "You shouldn't be doing this. I plan to go into trade with Adam Talbot." He wouldn't tell her how close to insolvency he was, or he'd never get her to go back to school. And he'd definitely not tell her about his other plan, regarding Nina.

"Talbot?" Meg crinkled her nose as if forced to smell spoiled fish. "Are you mad? He's a rapscallion. A ne'er-do-well. An immoral rascal. A . . ."

He held up a hand. "Yes, but he's also smart, and he has the capital to get us started."

"I hope you're not tying a noose tighter around your neck."

He hoped he wasn't either, but Elliot believed he could build Langford Teas into the most well-known tea merchant in the world. And in time, the most profitable.

"Come see what I've done." Without waiting for his response, Meg slowly stood and strode to the double doors.

Though noticeable, her limp didn't appear as exaggerated as a few minutes ago.

He followed Meg down the corridor to the library. The space usually smelled of musty books—the stagnant odor as potent as a freshly peeled onion, but today the scent of lemons filled the air. The polished wooden shelves, those not broken, reflected the light streaming through the clean windows. Even the dingy, threadbare rugs, were more vibrant.

"You did this?"

A proud smile wreathed the lower half of her face. "With Mrs. Newcomb's help. We rolled up the carpets and beat them." She laughed. "We both suffered coughing fits from all the dust."

"I'm amazed they didn't disintegrate. I thought the dust coating them most likely held them together."

"We had to toss half the books away. Even putting them in the sun would not have saved them. Book bugs had destroyed so many."

He took his sister's chafed hands in his. "You worked a miracle, and I'm grateful, but you need to return to school."

"I won't return. No matter what you say." She gave him that stubborn look he remembered from when she'd been knee-high. "You've spent hours on the gardens here, and they reflect your efforts. I can be of help as well. You see what I've done. I want to do more."

Meg was a baron's sister, not a maid, but it was futile to argue with her when she was in this mood. He'd try to talk some sense into her later.

"You are as stubborn as a mule," Elliot said, the following morning as he sat across from his sister, eating breakfast.

She spread marmalade on her toast and grinned.

"It's not funny, Meg." He reached across the table and turned her hands palm side up. "You have blisters."

"Tell me something, Elliot. When I read your letter last month, I could sense the pride you felt after you and Mr. McWilliams transplanted bushes and planted bulbs. Admit it. Admit the satisfaction you felt afterward. When I look at the library, I feel the same way. Tell me why you're dressed in rough wool trousers and a Guernsey sweater this morning?"

He opened his mouth, but she held up a hand. "I know why. You intend to go into the garden and work there because it gives you a sense of accomplishment."

True. "Have you ever thought of becoming a barrister?"

Meg frowned. "You know women are not allowed."

"I bet if you argue that injustice, you might win that point as well. You're too damned stubborn for your own good." He stood. He was getting nowhere arguing with his sister. Needing to burn off some steam, he strode from the room. As he stepped outside, he pulled his leather work gloves out of his back pocket. The scent of grass and freshly turned soil filled the early morning air.

Even in his piss-poor mood, he smiled at the sight of the garden below the terrace. Meg was right about one thing, seeing what he and Mr. McWilliams had done over the last few months did give him a sense of pride. The crushed-stone walkways were lined with flowering bulbs; while some spring bushes dropped spent flowers, others were budding. Seeing a shovel leaning against a concrete bench, he picked it up, and with the heel of his boot, Elliot jabbed the metal edge into the ground around a dead bush.

An hour later, he glanced up at the back of Ralston House. From where he stood, he could see Meg inside the blue drawing room again, washing the windows.

As a child, Meg had been stubborn, but now she acted simply unreasonable. He mumbled a curse.

Zeb, who laid a couple of yards away in a patch of grass, opened one eye.

"I thought you were stubborn," Elliot said to the animal. "But my sister has you beat by a mile. She cannot stay here." He thrust the shovel farther into the soil and tried to lift the root ball out of the ground. "Perhaps I should drag her back to school before I attend the Hathaways' house party." He peered at the dog, who now had both bloodshot eyes open. "What do you think?"

"Does the dog usually answer you, my lord?" Mr. McWilliams asked.

Elliot glanced over his shoulder at the gardener, who strode toward him, pushing a wheelbarrow. The man's weathered face donned a wide smirk. Over the last several months, Elliot and the old geezer had attained a more relaxed relationship with each other. The man knew a great deal about gardening and had taught Elliot everything from composting to transplanting.

"I don't want to hear any of your sarcasm today." He rammed the shovel deep, releasing the bush from its underground tethers.

The man laughed. "In a testy mood, are ye, laddie?"

"If you had a mule-headed sister like mine you'd be cranky as well." Elliot put his weight into prying the root ball out of the ground. The dead bush toppled over. The brittle branches snapped as it landed on its side.

"I've got seven sisters, my lord. All still living, too."

"Good God, seven? They should canonize you."

Together, they lifted the dead bush and placed it into the wheelbarrow. Elliot drew the sleeve of his shirt over his damp forehead.

"Worse, I was the only boy," McWilliams said. "You know what it's like to have seven older sisters who all think they are your mother?"

"I can imagine. Purgatory?"

"At times, but I wouldn't have traded any one of them for the world."

"I don't want to trade Meg; I only want her to return to school. Is that such a terrible request?"

"I don't see her as much different than you, my lord."

Elliot stared at the man as he brushed the dirt off his leather work gloves. "How is that?"

"Everyone wants to feel useful. I think this is her way of feeling a sense of accomplishment. She's probably been told most of her life that she cannot accomplish tasks. She wants to prove she can."

"I never told her she couldn't do things."

The old man arched a bushy gray brow. "Maybe you never said it in so many words, but perhaps the way you've treated her?"

"I haven't . . ." Or had he? Elliot glanced back at where his sister continued to scrub at the thick grime on the windows.

"Maybe all she wants is to feel useful. Or prove to you she is capable of what others can achieve."

Hadn't Meg told him the same thing? Elliot nodded, set the shovel into the wheelbarrow, and marched toward the house.

Inside, Meg turned when he entered the blue drawing room. Her gaze flicked to his before she continued running her soiled rag over the filthy panes. Rivulets of dirty water slid down the glass.

"I don't wish to argue with you anymore." She dunked the rag into the water and wrung it out.

After the accident, since Meg had learned to walk again, Elliot always rushed over to her when he entered a room, so she would not have to limp over to him. He forced his feet to stop and put out his hand. "Please, come here, Meg."

She set the rag onto the wide sill. As he watched her move toward him, Elliot fought the urge to rush to her side or tell her to be careful. Perhaps McWilliams was right. Perhaps Elliot made Meg feel incomplete. That thought wrenched at his heart. He'd never meant to do that. Perhaps he only tried to shelter her or makes things easier for her because of the guilt that held on to him like a metal clamp.

Meg set her hand in his and frowned as if she thought there would be a repeat of the argument from earlier this morning.

He cleared his throat. "I'll be leaving in a few short hours for London. I have a business appointment with Talbot, and then I'm to attend a house party."

She wrinkled her nose, most likely over his mention of Talbot, or perhaps because he smelled of the manure from the garden soil. "I will return in a month's time. You may stay here while I'm away."

"Really?" She smiled.

"Yes." He glanced around the room. "Forgive me if I haven't told you how proud I am of what you've accomplished."

Her smile broadened. "Thank you."

"But when I return, we will take up the conversation again about you returning to school."

Meg's lips pinched into a tight line, but she didn't say anything.

Chapter Eleven

The carriage had barely come to a stop in front of Lord and Lady Hathaway's country residence when two liveried footmen rushed out to assist Nina, Caroline, and James.

"Nina!" someone called out.

She turned. Her dearest friend, Victoria, who was also Lord Elliot Ralston's cousin, walked arm in arm with him. The memory of his softly spoken words only seconds before he'd exited her family's London house drifted through her mind. *Oh, darling, there is so much I could teach you.*

An odd dichotomy of apprehension and titillation coursed through her. The latter another sign that she seemed to gravitate toward scoundrels. If one possessed an inner compass regarding men, hers was broken. Once again, she reminded herself this was nothing more than a game to Elliot. A ruse.

Victoria embraced her and brushed her cheek to Nina's.

Over her shoulder, Nina heard Elliot greeting her brother and Caroline. Without seeing James's face, she could imagine the sneer her protective brother was bestowing on the baron.

"I'm so pleased you are better, Victoria." Nina stepped

back and surveyed her friend. She looked well after having been ill.

"I would have recovered quicker if my mother hadn't forced me to drink the bitter possets our cook concocted." Her friend wrinkled her nose.

"Where *is* your mother?"

"She caught my cold, but after making me drink those unpleasant concoctions, she has refused to even sniff them. I'm here with Great-aunt Gertrude." Victoria grinned.

Great-aunt Gertrude was close to ninety and napped frequently. She was an abysmal chaperone. Not that Victoria would take advantage of the situation, but it was a break from her domineering mother.

"Hello, Lord Ralston," Nina said, turning to him. He wore no hat, and his dark hair looked a bit wind tossed, adding to his rakish appeal.

"Lady Nina." He bowed his head but kept his gaze on her.

Her body tingled, and she forced her regard to return to Victoria.

Her friend glanced at the watch pinned to the bodice of her dress. "Lord Hathaway has planned an excursion to his newest folly. A miniature version of a Greek temple. The tour will start at three o'clock." Victoria slipped her arm through Nina's. "Say you will join me. You can bring your sketchbook."

"I'd love to."

"Anyone else?" Victoria asked.

James stared at Elliot as if waiting to hear if he intended to participate in the outing before he responded.

"I'll have to pass. I've promised Lord Chambers a game of chess," Elliot said.

"Do you wish to go, dear?" James asked Caroline.

"No, I'd like to rest a bit." As if queasy, Caroline set a hand over her stomach.

Nina wondered if Caroline had told James she was most likely with child.

James and Caroline strode toward the country home.

A crested carriage pulled up behind theirs, and the driver jumped down from his perch to assist the occupants.

Lady Amelia Hampton and her cousin Priscilla Grisham alighted the vehicle.

A tight coil of tension twisted at Nina's muscles. Remembering what the mean-spirited woman had said at the modiste made her hands clench. She forced them to relax.

As if Victoria and Nina were invisible, Amelia greeted Elliot. "Lord Ralston, fancy seeing you here." The words came out like a purr.

Could the woman be any more obvious? Doubtful.

"Lady Hampton." He bowed his head.

"Victoria. Nina," Amelia said, the sensual lilt of her voice absent.

Both Nina and Victoria greeted Amelia and her cousin, who seemed more timid than usual when she mumbled a low hello, while offering a tentative smile. An atrocity that Priscilla allowed her unkind and overbearing cousin to cower her.

"Will Lord Hampton be joining you?" Victoria asked.

Amelia waved a hand in the air. "My husband is busy with estate business in Wiltshire, so I am without him this weekend." She glanced coquettishly at Elliot.

The thought of Amelia and Elliot together made Nina's skin crawl. She hoped he had better taste than that. But what did she care beside the point it might spoil her plans to make Fernbridge think Elliot was his competition? Yet, her stomach fluttered as she waited for Elliot's reaction.

His mouth remained in a straight line.

From what Victoria told her about her cousin, he didn't dally with married women. Ever.

"I need to get settled," Amelia said. "I hope I have a bedchamber with a canopy bed. I love the privacy they offer when the curtains are pulled closed. Even servants cannot see you in bed if you don't wish them to." She smiled at Elliot again.

Nina realized her mouth was gaping as wide as Victoria's and snapped it closed.

"Come, Priscilla." Amelia tapped the area over her thigh as if calling a loyal lapdog to attention.

Amelia strode away, Priscilla trailing after her.

A half hour later, Caroline's lady's maid helped Nina unpack her clothes from her trunk.

"Now, miss, let's get you out of that dusty traveling dress," Maggie said. "Do you know what your host and hostess have planned for the day?"

"Lord Hathaway is taking several guests on a tour of the parklands and to visit the new folly he's had built." Nina noticed the slight wrinkling of Maggie's nose at the mention of their host's name.

"Yes, I know he's a bit pompous."

The little lady's maid's eyes widened. "Oh, no, miss, I wasn't thinking that."

"Ha! Yes, you were, and so was I. And both our thoughts shall not be mentioned outside of this room."

Grinning, the lady's maid placed her fingers before her lips as if locking them with a key. She lifted a yellow walking dress out of the trunk. "I think this would be perfect."

"Yes, I agree."

The maid pointed to the blue ironstone pitcher and bowl on one of the low mahogany dressers. "There's fresh water in there, miss. I'll take this gown belowstairs to run an iron over it and be back shortly."

The door clicked closed behind the lady's maid.

Nina unfastened the row of buttons lining the front of her traveling dress and stepped out of the garment. After wetting a flannel, she drew the cloth over her arms and face. The cool water felt good against her dusty skin.

Hearing voices outside the open window, Nina parted the sheer under-curtain slightly. Below the window, Amelia Hampton stood on the terrace talking with two other women. From this distance, she couldn't hear what the nasty gossipmonger was saying, but most likely something disparaging against another guest, perhaps her.

Maggie entered the bedchamber. The smile on the young woman's face faded. "Something wrong, miss?"

"No. Nothing."

The maid stepped next to Nina and peered out the window. As if smelling refuse floating in the Thames, Maggie wrinkled her nose. "Lady Huntington told me all about Lady Hampton. You pay her no mind, miss."

Nina forced a smile at the maid. Knowing Amelia might be spreading caustic lies made the gossipmonger difficult to ignore.

Maggie assisted Nina with her walking gown and was styling her hair when a knock sounded at the door.

"I'll get it, miss." Maggie slipped the last pin into Nina's loose chignon.

Almost bouncing on her toes with excitement, Victoria entered the bedchamber. "Nina, are you ready? Lord Hathaway is a stickler for punctuality. If we are not in the entry hall in five minutes, he will leave without us. I don't want to miss the tour. You know how I love Greek architecture."

"I do." Nina linked her arm with her friend's, and they started down the corridor to the grand, winding staircase. "I hope Amelia will not be joining us."

Victoria made a face as though she'd been forced to

drink another medicinal posset. "Did you see how she blatantly flirted with Elliot?"

"Do you think . . . Well, is it a possibility he is interested in her?" She didn't care. Really, she didn't.

"Doubtful. My cousin might be a rake, but he has better taste than that."

Nina fiddled with the edge of her sleeve. "I think Amelia is spreading lies about me."

Victoria stopped walking. "What?"

"I overheard her at Madame LeFleur's."

"Why, that witch. What did she say?"

"She mentioned something must be wrong with me for her dear cousin not to offer."

Her friend's mouth gaped. "The scoundrel did offer. Perhaps if you ignore her, she will stop her vicious prattle."

"I thought that as well, but in truth, I'd like to wring her neck."

They stepped into the entry hall. A party of around fifteen people had formed for the outing. Nina's gaze sifted through those gathered. Thankfully, Amelia was not in the group. With his blond hair, she spotted the Duke of Fernbridge, nearly immediately. Next to him stood Elliot.

What was he doing here? He'd said he'd already scheduled a chess match.

As if feeling the heat of her regard, Elliot looked at her. His gaze traveled from her face down the length of her body, then back. He flashed one of those wicked smiles he'd perfected.

She found herself smiling back.

Next to her, Victoria tightened her grip on Nina's arm. "Is something going on with you and Elliot?"

Nina shook her head.

"Then why is my cousin smiling at you like you're the last dessert on the table and he's about to snatch you up?

Please tell me you aren't foolish enough to think you could tame him."

The muscles in Nina's stomach tensed. Perhaps it would be best if she told Victoria about the plan Elliot had proposed. Otherwise, her friend would think she'd gone daft to allow such a scoundrel to give her too much attention. Victoria might think her daft either way.

Without answering, Nina motioned with a slight tip of her head to Lord Hathaway, who was giving them a reproachful glare for whispering while he addressed the group.

"Let us be off," their host said.

As they walked through the entry hall and down the wide central corridor to the French doors that led to the back terrace, Elliot shifted through the group, positioning himself next to Nina.

A line creased the smooth skin on Victoria's forehead. She eyed Elliot suspiciously. "I thought you had a chess match."

"I canceled it."

"Really?" Her large blue eyes widened. "Since when are you interested in Grecian architecture?"

"I have great admiration for anything Grecian."

Victoria gave an indelicate snort. "Since when?"

Lady Pendleton stepped beside Victoria. "I hear your mother is not feeling well, dear."

Victoria slowed her pace and lagged behind Nina and Elliot as she spoke with the elderly woman.

Elliot flashed another one of his slow smiles. "You look fetching, Nina," he said in a low voice.

Why did he insist on complimenting her when the Duke of Fernbridge couldn't hear him? She didn't like it.

Or perhaps you like it too much, an irritating voice in her head said. "Thank you, but as I said before, there is no need for you to flatter me, Elliot, when His Grace cannot hear you."

"But I told you, I like the way you blush. Besides, since I situated myself next to you, Fernbridge has glanced at you several times."

She started to look at the duke.

Elliot's gentle touch on her arm stopped her. "Don't look at him, darling. Look at me."

"What?"

He released an impatient breath. "He needs to believe I am the only one winning your regard, and that you are like a ray of sunshine breaking through on a cloudy day."

Nina grinned. "Elliot, please tell me you do not win women's favors with drivel like that."

He set his palm to his chest and gave a wounded look, yet his blue eyes gleamed with mirth. "I thought it sounded like something Byron might have written."

She couldn't help the laugh that worked its way up her throat. "Perhaps when he was drunk."

"What are you two whispering about?" Victoria asked, catching back up to them.

"Byron," Elliot replied.

"Byron? Ha! Now I know you two are up to something. I wish to know what." Victoria gave Elliot a playful push on his shoulder. They had slowed their pace and now trailed behind the others on the path.

Lord Hathaway cleared his throat. "Though an architect designed the Grecian folly, the initial idea of the placement of the Ionic columns was mine." He puffed out his chest and pointed to a hill above the tree line. In the distance, the domed structure could be seen.

As they continued toward it, Victoria pointed to a bush with a profusion of yellow flowers. "I wonder what type of plant that is."

"I have a feeling your cousin knows?" Nina glanced at Elliot.

"Do you, cousin?" Victoria's eyes widened.

"It's a species of forsythia."

Nina smiled.

He smiled back.

"What is going on between you two?" With a not so gentle tug on Elliot's arm, Victoria pulled him to a standstill. "Cousin, I wish to have a word with you."

Elliot frowned but stopped, leaving Nina to walk alone.

The Duke of Fernbridge turned around. He gave her the broadest smile she'd ever seen the man offer, then strode toward her.

Chapter Twelve

As the Duke of Fernbridge walked toward Nina, anxiousness exploded in her stomach. She started to smile; then, remembering Elliot's advice not to appear eager to converse with the gentleman, she simply nodded. "Your Grace."

"Lady Nina."

She glanced at Elliot and Victoria. Most likely, her friend was conducting an inquisition as to what was going on.

Fernbridge followed her gaze. "They are cousins, are they not?"

"They are." It wasn't like her to give such succinct responses. Though not overly chatty, she enjoyed conversing, but she wished to follow Elliot's advice about acting more indifferent.

"Your brother mentioned you enjoy horseback riding, along with hopping hedges. Perhaps tomorrow morning you and I might tackle some of Hathaway's hedgerows."

Goodness, Elliot was a genius. The more indifferent she acted toward the duke, the more he sought her out. "If you wish."

Victoria and Elliot joined them. A confused expression

still clouded Victoria's face. Obviously, Elliot had not confessed their plan to his cousin.

The two men held each other's gazes. Elliot was a superb actor. If she didn't know better, she'd think the duke having joined them truly did agitate him.

Lord Hathaway cleared his throat again and opened his mouth as if he wished to chastise them for lagging. The man's gaze settled on the Duke of Fernbridge, and he pinched his lips into a firm line. One did not go about chastising dukes.

Elliot noticed the pleasure in Nina's eyes. Clearly, Fernbridge had said something that delighted her.

"Shall we say after breakfast?" Fernbridge asked. "Hathaway has some exceptional horseflesh."

So, he'd asked Nina to go riding with him.

"Yes, that would be lovely." Nina glanced at him and Victoria. "We are going hedge hopping tomorrow. Would either of you care to join us?"

"Yes, I'll go," Elliot replied.

Victoria shook her head. "I like riding, but unlike Nina, I'm not fond of jumping hedges."

Fernbridge looked over Nina's head and gave Elliot a deliberate grin. The gauntlet had been thrown.

"Are you going to attempt to draw the temple?" Fernbridge pointed at Nina's sketchbook.

"Attempt?" Victoria wrapped her arm about Nina's waist. "Nina is a remarkable artist. If she draws it, it will look like a mirror image."

The pink on Nina's cheeks darkened. "Not quite."

"May I see your drawings?" Elliot asked.

She bit her lower lip and handed him the sketchbook.

As Elliot flipped to the first page, Fernbridge moved

closer and peered over Elliot's shoulder. Several of the sketches were of an extensive garden. One a closeup of a maple leaf. Another of a fountain. The last sketch was of a small cottage-like structure with a stone base and a glass roof. "Where is this?"

"That's the summer house at our country residence."

Elliot handed the sketchpad back to Nina. "You're quite talented."

"Thank you." Her gaze briefly shifted to Fernbridge as if waiting for his comment like a hungry beggar waited for the smallest scrap of bread.

For a moment, Elliot wanted her to win the man's regard. For her to get everything she wanted. If it had been another gentleman—one who Elliot thought would truly love her—he would have given up his plan to win her over, but Fernbridge was a pompous, self-centered idiot if he could not even give Nina a compliment.

If you win her hand, will you be a better husband? He shoved his guilt away. He was a hell of a lot better than the duke. If Nina wished for a true marriage, a faithful marriage, he would give her that. He would do everything in his power to make her happy, whereas Fernbridge appeared too absorbed in himself to notice the desires of those around him.

They continued down the path and reached the top of the hill.

The Temple of Zeus stood around forty feet high. Round with at least twenty Grecian pillars. An impressive structure.

Lord Hathaway smiled proudly as several members gasped with awe.

Fernbridge flashed an unimpressed look at the structure. "The temple on my property is much larger."

Just like Fernbridge to compare sizes. It made Elliot

recall his boyhood days at boarding school when the lads took a gander at each other's cocks to judge if they possessed any shortcomings.

After they'd toured the structure, several footmen placed blankets on an area of soft grass near the base of the temple. Baskets with sandwiches and fruit were set out, along with bottles of chilled lemonade.

Nina sat on one of the blankets and began sketching.

Elliot strode over to her. "May I join you?"

She glanced at Fernbridge, who chatted with Lord Hathaway. "Yes, of course."

He sat and leaned back against a tree. In only a few minutes, Nina had outlined the structure's dimensions. "Why do you wish to marry him?"

The scratch of her pencil moving across the paper stilled for a short moment, then continued. "Doesn't everyone wish to become a duchess?"

Her response bothered him. Could that be all she wanted in life? Perhaps she deserved to marry Fernbridge. "I don't believe that's why you've set your sights on him."

Again, the movement of her hand stilled. "Why?"

"I don't think you are so shallow. I don't think you want to sit around reading while your husband enjoys hunting and fishing. I think you want a husband who is passionate. One who will make you feel special. He has as much passion as a block of wood. Marrying a cold fish like Fernbridge would be a grave error."

Her pencil moved again, sketching the intricate detail of the temple's roofline. "You shouldn't be talking to me of such things."

He grinned. "Because I've touched on a nerve? I think I was correct when I said you wanted to marry him because he is safe. I know Avalon hurt you, but that is no reason to settle for less than you deserve."

She held his gaze for several heartbeats, then continued working on her drawing.

He expelled a slow breath. "Are you ready to begin our lessons?"

"The Duke of Fernbridge is already showing an interest in getting to know me better. I don't think they are necessary."

He said nothing. Waited. She wanted those lessons. He'd seen the curiosity in her eyes. She was so wrong for Fernbridge. A safe, dull life would lead to a dissatisfied life. He'd seen disappointment in his mother's eyes. He surely didn't want to see it in Nina's.

"Do you even know how to kiss?"

Two bright spots colored her cheeks. "Of course, I do."

He made a sound of disbelief.

She tipped her nose in the air. "If you recall, I was courted last season." A hurt expression flashed across her face. So brief one could have missed its appearance.

"I heard that Lord Avalon kisses like a wet fish."

She gave a small laugh. "No, he doesn't."

"And that his lips feel like mush and his tongue is like a serpent's."

"His tongue?" A small line creased the smooth skin between Nina's brows. "What does his tongue have to do with kissing?"

Had Avalon kissed her like one would kiss a sister? It appeared so. But he'd heard the earl was in love with his mistress, so . . . "If you do not know, it appears you are truly in dire need of a lesson. The first kiss you share with a man should be something he cannot forget. Something that keeps him awake at night. I'll come to your room tonight." He thought she'd say no. He thought she might crack her palm against his cheek.

Instead, she continued sketching and nodded. "Very well. Now go away. You're ruining my concentration."

He was going to do more than ruin her concentration. Tonight, he would show Nina what passion was like. What she would be missing if she married such a cold fish.

Chapter Thirteen

As Nina paced back and forth in her bedchamber, she tried to convince herself that she'd only agreed to Elliot's lesson on kissing for academic reasons. She released a pent-up breath. Who was she kidding? She wanted to know what his lessons would entail. Every time he mentioned them, little sparks of anticipation exploded in her stomach. The same sensation she experienced when a carriage took a turn too fast, or she prompted a horse over an exceedingly tall hedge. Danger and the unknown had always caused a thrill within her.

Over the years, James had called some of her actions reckless.

Her brother was right. Allowing Elliot in her bedchamber to tutor her on the art of kissing proved it.

A memory drifted in her mind. A few months ago, from her bedroom window, she'd spotted Caroline and James kissing on the terrace of their home in Essex. It hadn't been a quick press of lips but had gone on forever. Feeling like a voyeur, she'd stepped away from the window, feeling rather hot and odd.

A soft knock on her door startled her from her thoughts.

She tugged her over-the-elbow evening gloves up higher and opened the door. Her gaze shifted from Elliot's blue eyes to his sensual mouth, then to his clothing. Unlike her, he'd removed his evening attire and wore a casual suit and white shirt.

Without uttering a word, she motioned him inside.

He looked at her, then around the bedchamber, and grinned.

Most likely, he found humor in the fact she'd lit every lamp and candle in the room and wrapped her shawl so tight about her upper body she resembled a mummy.

"Thank God the curtains are drawn, or your bed-chamber window would be a beacon for ships."

Warmth flooded her cheeks.

Casually, he walked around the room snuffing out the candles with his thumb and index finger, never flinching as he doused each flame.

Those unsettling sparks exploded in her stomach as the light in the room dimmed. Why did watching him affect her so? Probably because Elliot possessed confidence as he prowled about her bedchamber, while she felt as taut as an over-coiled spring. Why wouldn't she? It was natu-ral. This was the first time she'd allowed a man into her bedchamber. Whereas, Elliot's confidence reflected his experience.

Once only the bedside and mantel lamps remained lit, he faced her. He seemed even larger than when he'd en-tered the room. As if his shoulders had broadened and he'd grown several inches in the span of a few minutes. Surely, it was an illusion brought about by the weak lighting and the fact that his shadow cut across the rug to touch the spot where she stood.

"Are you cold?" His gaze narrowed on the shawl wrapped tightly about her. Without waiting for a response, he strode to the banked fire, removed the brass poker from its stand, and prodded the embers until the fire sprang back to life.

With casual grace, he took several steps, closing the distance between them. His clean, spicy scent filled her nose. Her heartbeat quickened, and she shifted on her feet like a skittish horse.

"Don't worry, darling. I won't bite you. Not unless you beg me to." He grinned.

"You know you are incorrigible." She should ask him to leave, yet she felt anchored to where she stood. Her gaze shifted from Elliot's eyes to his mouth, and she couldn't deny how much she wanted to feel the press of his lips against hers.

"What should I teach you first?"

Everything.

One side of his mouth turned up as if she'd said the single word aloud. But she hadn't. At times, Elliot appeared capable of reading her thoughts. It had always irritated her, but in this moment in time, she wished he could read every wicked thought in her silly head, so she wouldn't have to voice them aloud.

His warm fingers brushed against her arms as he unwrapped the shawl from her shoulders and draped it over the back of an upholstered chair.

"I don't think you need these either," he said, unfastening the three buttons at the wrist of her left evening glove, then those on the right. The material parted, and he skimmed his thumb over the sensitive skin of her left inner wrist.

The hairs on her nape lifted.

"Now take them off. Slowly."

"Slowly. Why?"

"Because the removal of a woman's evening gloves is sensual if done correctly."

Perhaps she *did* need lessons. How was removing her gloves sensual? "I don't understand."

Without responding, he lifted her hand as if he intended to kiss her gloved fingers.

When his teeth nipped the end of the material at her index finger and tugged, she sucked in a startled breath. He did the same to each finger until her glove dangled off her hand. He slowly tugged it off and let it drop to the rug.

He held her gaze. "Undressing a woman can heighten her anticipation. Undressing for a man can heighten his."

"But I don't intend to undress in front of the Duke of Fernbridge."

"No, but if you are to catch his attention further, your actions must draw his regard. As I said, if done correctly, something as simple as removing an evening glove before dinner can center a man's attention solely on you."

She felt self-conscious, but inch by inch, she rolled her other glove down her arm. Her fingers lightly, sensually traced over her skin as she revealed more of it.

As if riveted, Elliot watched. His eyes grew heavy. Was he becoming as aroused as she was? She couldn't help but ask. "Am I a good student, Elliot?"

"I'll let you know after we complete our lessons."

She removed the glove completely and held it between her index finger and thumb before letting it drop to the floor. She'd believed Elliot would smile, but the look in his eyes was so intense she thought it was melting her because wetness settled between her legs.

He set his finger under her chin and brought her gaze to his. "Now, have you ever kissed a man?"

"You know I have."

"Yes, but there are different types of kisses. There is the type you give a family member. Then there is nothing more than a light brushing of the lips, and then there are kisses that make you want to act recklessly. What type of kisses did Avalon give you?"

She glanced down at the hem of her gown and the Turkish rug beneath where she stood. Avalon's kisses had seemed more like the first type. They'd definitely not made her act reckless. Or even made her contemplate acting recklessly.

Without further thought, she got on the tip of her toes and gave Elliot a quick peck on the cheek. "They were like that."

"Well, thank goodness you didn't wed the man. That's utterly shameful. Avalon should be shot."

Elliot looked so agitated, a laugh bubbled up Nina's throat, but when he skimmed the tips of his fingers up her arm, her laugh faded, and heat coursed through her body.

"A proper kiss should entail more than a quick press of the lips on one's cheek."

"How do I let a man know I wish to be kissed on the lips?"

"There are several signals. The way you look at him. You should hold his gaze but allow your regard to dip to his mouth before returning them to his eyes. If he leans in, tip your face up, and when positive he intends to kiss you, close your eyes."

She nodded and took a slow breath to calm her nerves. She slowly let her gaze shift from the deep blue of Elliot's eyes to his mouth, then back to his eyes.

"Well done." One of his large hands cupped the side of her cheek. The other wrapped around her waist.

The tempo of her heart spiked. Not from fear. No, she

wanted to experience this. Worse, she wanted to experience it with Elliot. That knowledge caused her to tense.

"Relax. I assure you this won't hurt. Not a bit." He smiled.

She smacked his shoulder. "Get on with it, you scoundrel."

"I intend to."

His softly spoken words and the look in his eyes caused her stomach to flutter. "Where do I put my hands?" she asked.

A slow smile turned up his lips. "I don't believe most men are too particular during a kiss. They'll be content with your hands on them almost anywhere."

Elliot stared into Nina's eyes as she slowly slid her palms upward over his chest.

"So this is fine?" she asked, her voice a soft whisper in the quiet room.

"Yes." Elliot heard the raspy texture of his voice and wondered if she noticed it, or that he was a bit more excited than he should be. For God's sake, it was only the prelude to a kiss, but someone needed to tell his cock that.

She stepped closer, looking as if the surface of his chest fascinated her. She flexed her fingers. "Will moving my hands like this get the Duke of Fernbridge's attention, should he decide to kiss me?"

Reluctantly, he nodded. He'd come to her room, hoping to disperse any thoughts of Fernbridge from her head. Yet, she still asked about the man. The idea of Fernbridge kissing Nina while she touched the man caused a fire in Elliot's gut. Perhaps he shouldn't be tutoring her in the way to please a man. Perhaps he should be teaching her to give sloppy-wet kisses that would turn Fernbridge off. Perhaps he should tell her to keep her hands at her sides and stare at his forehead.

"Where will he put his hands?" she asked.

His gaze shifted to the plump surface of her mouth. "If he's smart, he'll have his hand on your cheek, as I do, and when he lowers his mouth to yours, he'll slip it to your nape and hold your mouth close to his."

"And his other hand?"

In response to her question, he moved it to the small of her back and pulled her body tighter to his.

Her breathing, like his, had kicked up a notch. Elliot stared into her eyes.

Nina moistened her lips.

His gaze followed the movement, and Elliot lowered his mouth to hers. He kissed her slowly—brushed his lips against hers—determined that piquing her curiosity about the third type of kiss would be best saved for another time.

"Mmm." Her mouth moved against his.

The little sound of pleasure that eased between her lips and the way her sweet mouth answered his, sent a jolt of lust through Elliot's body. Startled, by how much he wanted to coax her mouth open and tangle his tongue with hers, he gave the plump surface of her lower lip a gentle tug and stepped back.

Her lashes fluttered open. "So, how did I do?"

The kiss, though rather pedestrian by his standards, had left him a bit unsettled. He smoothed out his expression. "You could use a bit more practice."

"You're insufferable. I can tell by the look in your eyes I did quite well. When I opened my eyes, you looked stunned. So, unless I've grown an enormous wart on my face, I believe I surpassed your expectations."

She had. While he'd kissed her, he felt the passion within her. She was so wrong for Fernbridge.

She set her hands on her hips. "Well, what do you have to say to that?"

He wasn't going to say anything. No. Instead, he pulled her tighter—felt the soft flesh of her breasts flatten against his chest. "Perhaps we should move on to the third type of kiss."

Chapter Fourteen

The third type of kiss? The thought of what it would entail caused Nina's palms to grow clammy. Yet the anxiousness within her did not outweigh her eagerness. She'd enjoyed the kiss. Not to mention the feel of Elliot's muscled chest under her palms.

Elliot's gaze shifted to the door, and he pressed a finger to her lips. "Someone's coming."

She listened. Indeed, footsteps moved closer to her door—the last one at the end of the corridor.

Someone tapped on the wooden surface.

Heart beating fast, Nina stared at the door as if the devil himself stood behind it. She'd told Maggie not to wait up for her. Had the lady's maid come anyway?

"Nina, it's Caroline. May I come in?"

Nina gulped a mouthful of air. If Caroline found Elliot in here, it would be better than her brother finding him. But if her sister-in-law told James, he might get one of Lord Hathaway's hunting rifles and shoot Elliot.

"Give me a minute, Caroline." Her gaze darted around the room, searching for a place Elliot could hide. She gave him a push toward the window. "You need to climb out," she whispered.

"Nina, we are on the second story. It's a twenty-foot drop," he replied in a hushed tone.

"Yes, but I'm sure you've had to do it before."

"No, darling, never. I'm not a burglar."

"Well, you need to hide." She pushed him toward the curtains and pulled one of the long damask panels in front of him, leaving the material looking bulky and his feet sticking out. She yanked the fabric back. "Why must you have such large feet?"

He leaned close. His warm breath touched her cheek. "Do you know what they say about a man's feet?"

She didn't, but the gleam in his eyes and the way one side of his mouth turned up clearly relayed it was something wicked. Scowling, she grabbed his hand and pulled him toward the bed.

"Nina, is something amiss?" Caroline asked.

"No, I'm coming."

She pointed to the bed. And mouthed the words, *Get under there.*

"Has anyone ever told you how pretty you look when frazzled?" he whispered.

The man was incorrigible, flirting with her at a time like this. She gave him a hard push. It was like trying to move a brick wall.

As she made her way to the door, she frantically pulled several of the pins from her hair, allowing the dark tresses to tumble down. She glanced back at the large tester bed to make sure Elliot was out of sight, then opened the door.

"Sorry it took me so long. I was removing the pins from my hair."

Stepping into the room, Caroline glanced around. "Are you alone? I would have sworn I heard you talking to someone."

"I was singing."

"Ah, I thought perhaps Victoria and you were chatting."

"No, I'm sure she is snuggled under her bedclothes and fast asleep." Nina feigned a yawn. "Which is what I intend to do."

"I told Maggie she could go lie down. Poor thing has an upset stomach, so I came to help you out of your gown."

"You need not worry about me, Caroline. I told Maggie I would be retiring late, and she didn't need to wait up."

"Well, I'm here, so I might as well help you slip out of your gown."

Goodness, she didn't want to undress with Elliot hiding under her bed. The scoundrel would probably peek. "No need to trouble yourself. I can manage. Besides, you're not feeling well."

"It's no trouble at all, and strangely this late in the day, I feel better." She made a small circular movement with her hand. "Turn around, so I can unfasten the buttons."

"Really, Caroline, I can do it."

"Why should you when I am here?" Without waiting for a response, Caroline stepped behind her and tossed Nina's hair over her shoulder. Her sister-in-law unclasped the topmost button, then the next, and the next.

The gown fell off Nina's shoulders, and trying to preserve some modesty, she folded her arms over her corset.

"Nina, step out of your gown."

Reluctantly, she did as instructed and stood with her back to the bed.

Like a determined lady's maid, Caroline untied and unbuttoned nearly every garment Nina wore until she stood in only her chemise-drawers combination, silk stockings, and flower embroidered garters.

"Thank you." Nina kept her back to the bed as she darted behind the dressing screen to remove her remaining garments and slip her nightgown and dressing robe over her naked body.

She stepped out to find Caroline picking up her gown. "Caroline, I'll put my garments away. James must be waiting up for you."

A slight flush settled on her sister-in-law's cheeks, and Nina knew, in a short time, James would be the one removing Caroline's clothing.

Elliot's words flittered through her mind. *Undressing a woman can heighten her anticipation.* Nina thought about what it would be like to have a husband remove her garments, but as the vision drifted through her mind, it wasn't Fernbridge's face she envisioned, but that of the rascal hiding under her bed. She shoved the image out of her head and took her gown out of Caroline's hands.

"Are you feverish, dear? Your face is flushed." Caroline set her palm against Nina's forehead.

"The room is warm."

"Would you like me to ask James to come in here and open one of the windows?"

James? Here? With Elliot under her bed? "No. Nights are still cold, and I'd have to get up and close it."

"Very well." Caroline pressed a kiss to her cheek. "Night, dear."

After her sister-in-law exited the room, Nina slumped against the door.

Grinning, Elliot lifted the bed skirt and poked his head out.

She opened her mouth, intent on telling him to wipe the grin off his face.

Once again, footsteps moved toward her door.

Nina waved a hand at Elliot to get back under the bed. Goodness, she hoped it wasn't James.

Someone scratched lightly at the surface. Too light to be her brother. She released a breath and opened the door.

Maggie gave a quick curtsey. "Lord Huntington's valet gave me one of his famous tinctures, and I'm feeling much improved, my lady."

Nina's heart sunk into her stomach. "Maggie, I told you that you needn't wait up for me."

"I know, but . . . oh, my!" The lady's maid uttered a sound of displeasure at the pile of clothes on the floor and stepped into the room. "I'll not shirk my duties." The maid plucked the garment from Nina's hands and strode to the armoire. While she hung the gown up, Maggie chatted away.

Nina glanced at the bed, wondering if Elliot might have fallen asleep under there.

"I heard belowstairs that you have an admirer."

Nina knew servants gossiped. "Did you hear who?"

"I only caught the end of the conversation, so I didn't catch his name, but if it was me, I'd want it to be Lord Ralston." Maggie released a wistful sigh. "He's a handsome devil, he is."

That was all Elliot needed to hear. If still awake under the bed, he was probably preening like a peacock.

Maggie put the last item away. "I got the impression he's a bit wicked, miss. Is it true he's a womanizer?"

"Yes, he's a scoundrel." She grinned, wondering if Elliot's ears were burning.

"Sit, miss, and I'll braid your hair."

"No need." Nina quickly divided her locks into three long ropes of hair and braided them. "There, all done."

"Well, good night, miss."

"Good night."

As soon as the maid closed the door behind her, Elliot slipped out from underneath the bed. Grinning, he brushed off his clothes.

"Oh, you devil, wipe that smile off your face and tell me you weren't watching?"

His gaze worked its way down her body, now draped in only her nightgown and robe. He looked at her as if he could see through the cotton of her garments.

He leaned toward her, and his warm breath touched her ear. "I couldn't see a thing, but I never thought I'd get so much pleasure from envisioning one woman being undressed by another."

Nina's cheeks warmed.

Elliot strode toward the door and, without saying anything more, slipped out of the bedchamber.

The following morning, those who wished to partake in an early ride were to meet at the stables.

Once again, his valet moved so slow, Elliot headed there late.

Unfair to place all the blame on Wilson. Elliot had overslept. After the fiasco with him hiding under Nina's bed, he'd thought of her standing before him in her nightgown. The sight of her had caused him to feel restless. One specific thought during the long night plagued him—that it had more to do with her than what she'd worn—leaving him tossing and turning until the small hours.

At the stables, nearly everyone had already mounted their horses. He spotted Nina dressed in a navy riding habit with a crisp white shirt. She sat on a chestnut horse with strong hind legs and a short back. The glint in her eyes and bright smile reflected her excitement at taking the warm-blooded animal out to move across the fields and over the hedges. The duke had positioned his mount next to hers.

As if Nina felt the heat of Elliot's gaze, she peered his way. The pink on her cheeks darkened, and she quickly glanced away.

Was she remembering their kiss? That memory had also played a part in his restless night.

Fernbridge's gaze volleyed from her to him. He said something to Nina, and they trotted out of the courtyard.

A groomsman handed Elliot the reins to a black bay. He swung up and into the saddle.

The morning fog had all but lifted, giving Elliot a view of the field and vale. Lord Hathaway's property boasted several rock fences and taller hedges.

As they reached the open field, the riders loosened their grasp on their reins. The ground reverberated from the sound of fast-moving hooves.

Ahead of him, Nina and Fernbridge leaped over one of the low rock fences. They picked up speed and headed toward a hedge. The duke hopped it first, then Nina. Fernbridge rode well, but Nina hopped the hedge as if she rode Pegasus.

Obviously impressed, Fernbridge smiled at her. Nina's horsemanship would recommend her to the man, since he favored sports above everything else. Well, besides his self-importance.

Elliot increased the pressure on his mount's flanks and jumped the rock fence, then the hedge. Moving at breakneck speed, he caught up to them.

His Grace's smile flattened out. He narrowed his eyes at Elliot.

"How about that one?" Nina asked and pointed to a hedge in the distance. They both nodded and followed her. The sound of pounding hooves filled the air.

This time, Nina took the hedge first. Again, with impeccable skill. Her back straight. Her hold on the reins relaxed, leaving the bit loose.

Elliot and Fernbridge moved across the field, neck and

neck; then Elliot pulled ahead. He'd been riding since knee high. He presumed Fernbridge had as well, but Elliot's mount was faster, and he jumped first.

The glower on Fernbridge's face when he caught up to Elliot relayed he didn't appreciate being bested. The duke was still the same privileged snot he'd been in school, believing his rank and wealth meant other men should allow him to gain the victory. Elliot didn't intend on letting him win, especially when it came to Nina.

Ignoring the duke's glower, he followed Nina as she spurred her own mount toward another hedge.

Tendrils of her hair loosened from her pinned-up chignon to sail in the wind behind her. The sight of her controlling the strong animal with such skill caused Elliot to want her even more. Want her in his bed, both of them tangled in the sheets, their mouths moving over each other's skin.

She glanced over her shoulder and smiled.

For a moment, everything that weighed on his mind seemed inconsequential beside the happiness on her face.

With the same skill she'd exhibited before, Nina jumped the hedge, looking as buoyant as he felt.

"I'm next," Fernbridge said as he drew his horse dangerously close to Elliot's, while flicking a crop toward the face of Elliot's mount—an obvious attempt to cause the animal to shy and veer to the left.

Bloody nitwit. Elliot slowed. Beating Fernbridge to the hedge wasn't worth getting his horse injured if the animal twisted an ankle.

Fernbridge's horse must have sensed the man's recklessness because the animal's hind legs grazed the top of the hedge as if skittish.

As they crossed a field, a gunshot rang out.

The bullet whipped by them and struck an oak. The tree's bark splintered, sending shards into the air.

Good Lord, that had been close. Elliot's stomach clenched and a chill raced down his spine. He had witnessed, firsthand, what the impact of a bullet could do to the soft flesh of a human.

Ears pinned back, Nina's horse let of a snort and reared.

For a terrifying minute, Elliot feared she would be unseated. His heart beat fast.

Tightly, she held on to the reins as the spooked horse landed on all fours.

"Nina?"

"I'm fine." She ran her hand over the animal's withers. "You're all right, boy." She spoke in a calm, reassuring voice.

"By God, why would Hathaway allow hunters in the forest so close to where we ride?" Fernbridge asked.

Shielding his eyes from the sun, Elliot looked toward the woods. Whomever it was had moved deeper into the trees, away from them, causing birds to scatter into the sky.

"I think it best we move away from the woods. That fool might aim this way again."

As they rode back to the stables, Fernbridge kept glancing at Nina as if waiting for some delayed reaction, or some form of hysterics. Elliot knew there wouldn't be any. The more time he spent with Nina, the more he realized how strong she was. Yet, her independent nature railed against her desire to be what she thought her family wished of her.

After returning their mounts to the stables, Nina went to her bedchamber to change, while Fernbridge and Elliot went in search of Lord Hathaway. They found him talking with several guests in the drawing room.

"Might we have a word with you, Hathaway?" Elliot asked.

The man's gaze shifted from Elliot to the duke. As if sensing the tension, he stood and motioned to the doorway. "Of course."

They followed the man out of the room and into the corridor.

"Yes, what is it?" Hathaway asked, a thread of nervous tension in his voice. One did not want a houseguest to be displeased, especially a duke.

"Is your gamekeeper hunting in the woods to the west of the riding fields?" Ralston asked.

"No. Of course, not." Hathaway pulled out his pocket watch. "He's out exercising the hounds."

"Poachers," Fernbridge hissed.

Hathaway's cheeks turned red. "What happened?"

"While we were riding, a shot rang out. A stray bullet came close to where we rode."

"Good God!" Hathaway pressed the tips of his fingers to his lips. "I'll get some men over there. And by God, if they find the rascal, I'll have him strung up."

During dinner, Elliot watched Fernbridge and Nina at the other end of the long table. He was sure Fernbridge had requested Nina be seated next to him.

Fernbridge said something and smiled.

Nina returned the expression.

An uneasiness settled over Elliot. A disquiet that might have more to do with jealousy than he wished to admit.

"Lord Ralston?"

He peered at Lord Chambers, who sat across from him. "Forgive me, Chambers, did you say something?"

The earl glanced up the table. His old gray eyes settled on Nina, and his lips twitched. "Never thought I'd see the day."

He frowned at Chambers. He knew what the man implied. That Elliot was besotted over a woman who was clearly looking for a husband, not a widow looking for nothing more than an affair. If he knew of Elliot's finances, he'd understand.

Is that all that attracts you to her? Her dowry?

If he answered truthfully, no. He enjoyed Nina's company. And the kiss they'd shared was etched into his brain. When Talbot had first mentioned Nina's name, something inside Elliot had sparked. Desire. Lust. Was there any difference between the two? In his mind, yes. He'd lusted after women—felt a physical yearning to join his body with theirs—but desire implied more. Something deeper that did not always include sex. He could have easily approached Penny Granger. The American had shown an interest in him, yet he'd wanted Nina from the start.

He glanced back up the table. Nina's brows were pinched together, and he realized he was frowning. Of course, of all the people in the room, she would be the one astute enough to notice something bothered him—to see right through the carefree façade he tried to erect. Unsettled by his own admission, he forced a smile and began a conversation with Chambers.

An hour and a half later, the gentlemen retreated to the smoking lounge, while the ladies went to the drawing room.

Elliot took a slow draw on his brandy.

Fernbridge approached. "The way Lady Nina handled her horse was truly remarkable today. I don't think I've seen a finer horsewoman."

Elliot nodded. On this point, he and Fernbridge agreed.

"I think it only fair I let you know I intend to pursue her. She would make a fine duchess."

Somehow, Elliot had known that was coming, but he hadn't expected the duke to be so forthright. Fernbridge's words were quite telling. He'd said a fine duchess, not a fine wife or companion. He wanted to tell him to stay away from her, but that would only cause the man to try harder.

"Though she told me she doesn't enjoy the hunt, I'm sure I can get her to appreciate it. She seems born for the sport." Fernbridge blew on his signet ring and brushed it against the lapel of his coat, polishing it.

Already the pompous arse wanted to change her—to bend her toward what he took pleasure in instead of accepting her for the enchanting woman she was. Elliot tried not to scowl. Briefly, he contemplated telling Fernbridge of Nina and his scheme. The man would walk away. He'd not like to feel he was being manipulated, but Elliot couldn't deceive Nina that way. He wanted to win her hand, but he'd not resort to anything so low.

The men started exiting the smoking room.

Fernbridge set down his glass of brandy and headed out of the room, obviously intent on wooing Nina.

Elliot drained his dry and followed.

Chapter Fifteen

As soon as the Duke of Fernbridge reached the drawing room, the man strode over to Nina.

Elliot watched as a beatific smile lit up her face. The duke's attention pleased her, but once Fernbridge won this game and the challenge was over, Elliot was positive Nina would shift to nothing more than a trophy wife—a pretty bauble Fernbridge could show off. Then he'd go back to his hunting and sports, and the light in Nina's eyes would dim. That's what had happened to Elliot's mother. He didn't want that to happen to Nina. In truth, neither he nor Fernbridge were good enough for her.

As he started to move toward them, Victoria stepped in front of him.

"What is going on with you and Nina?" His cousin emphasized the question by jabbing her index finger against his chest.

"As I told you before, nothing."

She pursed her lips. "Something is going on."

"I suggest you ask her." It was Nina's place to divulge the plan they had made, especially since Elliot's plan was different.

"I have. She says you are friends."

"We are." Elliot glanced at where Nina and Fernbridge stood talking.

Victoria followed his gaze. She touched his arm, and her smile fell away. "You're not planning on ruining her, are you?"

"Of course I'm not. I'm offended you would even ask such a question."

"Then whatever you're planning is honorable?"

Nina laughed at something Fernbridge said.

Since when had the duke gotten a sense of humor?

"Victoria, if you'll excuse me." He strode toward Nina.

As he joined her and Fernbridge, Nina smiled at him. "His Grace was just telling me a story he heard down at his club about a gentleman whose massive bloodhound has taken over the gentleman's bed, forcing him to sleep on the floor."

Elliot blinked. That *idiot* was him, and he'd only fallen on the floor once. Was the duke aware it was Elliot? He'd only told Talbot.

A smirk lifted one corner of Fernbridge's mouth, revealing he was quite aware of the man's identity.

Damn that sod Talbot. He'd probably told everyone at their club.

The twinkle in Nina's eyes revealed she possessed a strong inkling about the man's identity as well, since she'd met Zeb.

Elliot forced a carefree expression. He was going to kill Talbot when he got back to London.

"What type of idiot gives up his bed for a dog?" Fernbridge held his gaze.

"I think it reflects that the gentleman has a soft heart," Nina replied.

"Or he's soft in the head." Fernbridge's smirk broadened. Elliot ignored the comment and turned to Nina. "I haven't seen much of your brother and sister-in-law." Not that he missed Huntington's deadly glares.

"Yes. Caroline has been unwell."

"I hope she feels better soon."

Without commenting on the discussion, Fernbridge offered his arm to Nina. "Will you take a stroll about the room with me?"

She nodded. "I'd be honored."

Elliot watched them walk away, his gut tight over the thought of how the light in Nina's eyes would be diminished over time if she married Fernbridge.

That night after an evening of musical entertainment, Maggie helped Nina remove her gown. As soon as the lady's maid left the bedchamber, Nina slipped on a simple cotton dress in case Elliot came to her room tonight. He hadn't said anything about continuing their lessons, but that would have been difficult since the Duke of Fernbridge had spent most of the evening by her side.

With regard to the duke, everything was working out the way she'd hoped. She released a long sigh and sat on the edge of her bed. If that was the case, why wasn't she more elated? She stared at the door. Perhaps she *should* be asking herself why she hoped Elliot would come to her room. She buried her face in her hands.

A soft knock sounded on her door.

Her heart skipped a beat, and Nina strode to the door. She pinched some color into her cheeks before easing it open.

Elliot still wore his dark formal attire, but he'd removed his tie and undone several of the buttons at the top of his shirt. The corners of his sensual lips turned upward.

Her foolish heart, which had returned to its normal cadence, fluttered.

He held out his hand. "Will you come with me?"

Her gaze shifted from his outstretched hand to his blue eyes. Oh, how she wanted to go wherever he would take her, but she needed to act smart. She could not go running off with Elliot because he wished it, even though she wished it as well.

"Where?"

"Take my hand, Nina, and you will see."

She set her ungloved hand in his. His fingers curled around hers, causing warmth to travel through her digits and palm, and up her arm. Holding hands with Elliot was nearly as pleasant as kissing him.

Like two thieves in the night, they crept quietly up the dim corridor to a narrow door. Elliot removed a key from his trouser pocket and slipped it into the lock. Light from the gas sconces in the hall highlighted the first few steps in a stairwell—the space so narrow it would be impossible for two people to move up them side by side.

As if noticing her hesitation, Elliot squeezed her hand. "Do you trust me?"

Mouth suddenly dry, she nodded.

He pulled her inside and closed the door behind them. Darkness swallowed them as if they'd entered the mouth of a whale.

His breath touched her cheek. "There are fifteen steps," Elliot whispered. "I'm on the first, so there are fourteen more to go. Be careful as you climb them and don't let go of my hand."

She had no intention of letting go. She tightened her grip.

"Does the dark frighten you?" he asked as they climbed the threads.

"Not normally, but I cannot recall ever being in such complete absence of light."

"Don't fret. We are nearly there."

She'd been counting the steps in her head and knew he spoke the truth.

Ahead of her, Elliot stopped, and the sound of metal scraping against metal drifted in the air as he pushed a door open. Moonlight spilled into the stairwell, and she realized beyond the door was the night sky, with stars scattered in it like pixie dust on black velvet.

"We're on the roof."

"We are." Smiling, Elliot pushed the door completely open. "During a new moon, one can see even the lightest stars in the dark sky and the constellations."

"You brought me up here to stargaze?" She stared at him.

"Yes. I thought you would enjoy it."

With her hand tucked in his, they strode toward the thick balustrade that ran around the perimeter of the roof. They were on the rear of the house, where there were urns every ten feet or so on broad square columns, set between the thick spindles.

She didn't like heights, and the closer they moved to the edge of the roofline, the more her heart quickened. When they were only a few feet away, it felt as if the pounding organ within her might leap from her chest.

Her steps slowed.

"You're shaking. Are you cold?" The smile on Elliot's face dissolved.

"No, I'm a bit skittish about heights."

He cocked his head to the side. "You jump hedges."

"That's different. When I sit on a horse, I feel like I'm one with the animal. My stomach can get a bit queasy as the animal starts to leap, but a sense of euphoria takes over. But up this high . . ." She shook her head. "I cannot explain it. It's like crossing a high bridge. If I'm in a carriage I will not glance out the window."

"Then we don't have to move any closer to the railing. We can leave if you want."

"No, I don't want to leave. I just wish to stay a safe distance from the roof's edge." She turned. A blanket and pillows had been spread out, and a brass telescope stood on a wooden tripod. "Where did you get that?"

"I spotted it in Lord Hathaway's library."

The man would give birth to a bird if he noticed it missing. She opened her mouth.

He held up a hand, halting her words. "Don't worry. I'll return it before anyone ever realizes it was gone."

"How is it you seem to always know what I'm thinking?"

"You have lovely, expressive eyes. Especially when agitated." With his index finger, he stroked one side of her jaw.

A wave of heat sifted through her.

"Have you ever used a telescope?"

"No. Never."

"Then you are in for a treat." Still holding her hand, Elliot led her to the telescope. He adjusted the legs of the tripod, so the eyepiece was at her level.

Closing one eye, she pressed the other to the telescope. The stars appeared brighter, their distance closer, as if she could reach out and touch them, and there were more of them than she'd seen with her naked eye.

"Tell me what you see?" Elliot stepped behind her.

"So many stars I cannot count them."

Standing behind her, he adjusted the telescope's angle. The warmth drifting off him caressed her. "Look here and tell me what you see."

Trying to keep her voice even, she said, "Is that the Big Dipper?"

"It is." His breath tickled the back of her neck.

The fine hairs on her nape stood on end and she fought

the urge to run her hand over them to force them down. This close, she not only felt embraced in the heat of his body, but his masculine scent, a pleasant mixture of shaving soap, clean skin, and the starch on his white shirt.

"Now if we angle it this way, what do you see?"

The hard surface of Elliot's chest pressed against her back. His hands covered hers as he moved the direction of the telescope.

"Is that Libra?" she asked.

"Yes."

Suddenly the heat from his body was gone.

She glanced over her shoulder. He was staring at her with those blue eyes of his. He rubbed at the back of his neck and drew in a slow breath. Was he feeling as hot as her, as if there wasn't enough air in this open space to cool off her skin?

He sat on the blanket; bracing his weight on his forearms, he leaned back and crossed his stretched-out legs at the ankles.

Somehow, peering through the telescope didn't seem as appealing without him standing behind her. She looked through the eyepiece again. When she turned around, Elliot lay on his back, one arm folded behind his head. His eyes were closed. Her gaze drifted over the powerful angles of his body, then centered on the patch of skin where his shirt lay open. She wondered what his skin tasted like.

"Nina?"

His voice caused her to jump like a child caught doing something wrong. She snapped her regard to his face. Thankfully, his eyes were still closed.

"Have you ever slept under the stars?" he asked.

It seemed such a fanciful idea, especially coming from him. She smiled. "Never, but I've danced under them."

Elliot opened his eyes. His lips tipped upward into an amused smile, and she knew he realized she spoke about their dance on Lord and Lady Pendleton's terrace in Richmond.

She sat next to him and wrapped her arms about her knees and stared at the sky. The world around them was quiet, and they didn't seem to need words to fill the void.

He shifted up onto his elbows and pointed to a space in the sky. "There's the group of stars called the kissing couple."

"The kissing couple?" She searched for the stars he talked about. Not seeing them, she glanced at him.

One side of his mouth turned up.

She gave his shoulder a push. "There is no couple."

"What? You don't see them?"

"You're fantasizing. They are not there."

"Nina, if I was fantasizing, it would not be about a couple in the sky. Not when there are warm-blooded things to romanticize about."

She let her gaze drop to his sensual mouth. A mouth that knew how to do things. Things she wanted to learn. But Elliot was not the man for her. He would not be faithful. If she gave in to her desires, he would not want to marry her. Worse, if he did, he would not remain faithful. Ignoring the sparks his nearness caused, she settled against one of the pillows and stared at the stars.

What seemed like only a minute later, a warm finger trailed over her cheek. "Nina, darling, wake up."

She opened her eyes. Elliot sat next to where she lay. She blinked at him, then the sky above. "Was I sleeping?"

His laugh was low, the tone rich with amusement. "Yes."

She touched her chin, hoping there wasn't drool on it. Thankfully, it was dry as desert sand. "Why didn't you wake me?"

"Because everyone should sleep under the sky at least once in their life, and now you have." He scrambled to his feet and offered her his hand.

Nina placed her fingers in his warm grip and stood.

Their eyes locked.

She fought the urge to shift closer to the warmth radiating from his body. She forced herself to step back and reached for one of the pillows. "I'll help you return these to where you got them."

"No need. After I walk you to your door, I'll come back for them."

"No, really. I can help."

He tipped her chin up, so their eyes met. "They are from my bedchamber, darling."

"Oh." She set the pillow down.

"Let's get you back to your room." He took her hand in his and led her to the stairs. At the bottom of the steps, Elliot opened the door an inch.

"Is the coast clear?"

He nodded and released her hand. They stepped into the corridor and made their way to her door.

The way Elliot held her gaze, she thought he might kiss her, but he mouthed the words, *Good night, Nina*, and strode away.

The following morning, Nina awoke late and made her way downstairs to the dining room. Either Caroline and James had already breakfasted or they were still in their bedchamber or on the terrace. Unfortunately, Amelia Hampton and her cousin Priscilla were at the table.

Amelia scrunched up her face as if forced to sniff at refuse.

Nina bit back the urge to ask the woman exactly what bug had crawled up her . . . nose. Instead, she stepped onto the terrace.

Not seeing her brother and sister-in-law, she walked over to Victoria's great-aunt, who sat at one of the wrought-iron tables. "Good morning, Mrs. Darby. Is Victoria still in her room?"

Behind her thick glasses, the elderly woman blinked several times as if trying to draw Nina into focus. "No, dear. She's gone to watch the Duke of Fernbridge and Lord Ralston play tennis."

"Thank you." She'd heard the duke mention he enjoyed playing tennis early in the morning, but since Elliot had been up late on the rooftop with her, she'd not expected him to be the man's opponent.

Nina headed down the flagstone path to the grass courts. As she neared them, grunting and exclamations drifted into the air. It sounded more like two men engaged in fisticuffs.

She stepped into the clearing, shaded her eyes against the morning sun, and peered at the court. Ralston wore linen trousers, beige canvas shoes, and a white shirt with the sleeves rolled above his elbows. At one time, he must have worn a jacket, for one was tossed onto the grass adjacent to the court. The duke sported a sand-colored sweater, tan trousers, and the same tennis shoes as Elliot.

Elliot tossed the ball in the air. She thought he'd lob it to the Duke of Fernbridge, but the muscles in his neck and arm tightened as he smacked it hard with his racket. It flew at His Grace like a cannonball shot at close range.

To his credit, the duke returned the serve with a grunt, but with such force, it sailed beyond the line.

Elliot grinned.

"Nina," Victoria called from where she sat on a concrete bench.

"How long has this been going on?" Nina settled beside her friend.

"Too long. They are like bucks fighting over a doe, and you, my dear friend, are that doe."

How many times had she wanted to tell Victoria that Elliot was just playing a game of sorts, wanting to prove his point about men and competition? The whole plan, and the fact she'd agreed to it, now seemed too terrible to admit to. Along with the fact that perhaps she hadn't agreed to it to garner the Duke of Fernbridge's attention, but because of Elliot's promise of lessons.

Victoria gazed at her with her liquid blue eyes. "You've fallen for my cousin Elliot, haven't you?"

No. Of course, she hadn't, but there was no denying she liked him more than she should. She thought of them on the rooftop. Of the pleasure she'd witnessed on his face as he pointed out the constellations. How he'd looked sprawled out on the blanket. A potent male who made her heart flutter. She glanced at him as he dashed after a ball and sent it flying back over the net.

Last night, they'd done nothing more than enjoy each other's company. She'd felt so at ease, she had drifted off to sleep. Had she wanted him to kiss her when he'd walked her back to her room? Definitely. And that realization had kept her awake for a long period of time after she'd climbed into bed.

"I do find him handsome and charming, but . . ."

"Go on."

"Elliot is not interested in me."

Victoria motioned with her index finger to the spectacle going on. "I think you are mistaken."

They both glanced at the court. The Duke of Fernbridge grunted as he returned another near-lethal serve. It flew by Elliot's head and landed once again beyond the chalk line.

Nina cringed. "One of them is going to get hurt."

"Yes, that might be what they are going for."

"Game," Elliot said.

"No, that landed in!" Fernbridge replied.

"I'm not going to watch this." Nina stood and strode away.

"Wait for me." Victoria stepped beside her.

Fernbridge slammed his racket against the net like a two-year-old child taking a tantrum and drew his forearm over his sweaty brow. "I said that ball landed in!"

Seeing the duke acting like this only reinforced Elliot's belief that the man was not worthy of Nina.

Elliot cocked a brow.

"I want a rematch." Fernbridge set a hand on his hip.

When the duke had asked him to play tennis, Elliot had believed it would be entertaining, not like a gladiator's battle in the Colosseum. The first serve Fernbridge had whipped his way had possessed the velocity of an arrow aimed at a target. Elliot had immediately realized this was not to be a friendly match at all.

And when Elliot had said, "Game," he'd thought the duke about to challenge him to a duel. If a hundred years earlier, he was almost sure the man would have.

"I think we've played enough." He reached out to shake Fernbridge's hand.

"That ball was not out!"

The ball had landed almost two feet out of bounds, but he was not about to argue with the man. Elliot lowered his hand and turned to walk away.

"You're worried if we have a rematch you'll lose. You're a coward, Ralston."

Coward? Elliot pivoted around. "How about if, when we get back to London, you and I go a couple of rounds at Clapton's Boxing Club instead?"

The challenge caused Fernbridge to snap his mouth closed.

"Well?"

"The seam in one of my boxing gloves needs to be repaired."

What a sad excuse. "There are plenty of pairs there."

"Mine are custom made."

Of course they were.

"If you change your mind, send me a note." Elliot walked away.

"You can disregard my title all you want, Ralston," Fernbridge called out, "but others won't."

Insufferable prig. Elliot kept walking.

"My estate is only a two-hour drive from here. I'm going to plan a day trip for Lady Nina to visit my estate. Once she sees my country home, she will be easily swept away, especially after visiting my stables. How could a horsewoman not be impressed with the fine horseflesh I own?"

Elliot turned around.

A self-satisfied smirk lifted one side of Fernbridge's mouth.

"I don't think Lady Nina is the type of woman who can be won over because of your wealth."

Fernbridge gave a haughty laugh. "You haven't seen Fernbridge Hall."

Elliot wanted to wipe the smug expression off the man's face.

"Don't worry, Ralston. I'll invite you to come along, and I'll prove you wrong about Lady Nina. Every woman wants to be a duchess."

That statement made Elliot tense, especially since he'd heard Nina say the same thing, though he'd not believed her.

When they visited Fernbridge Hall, Elliot wondered if he would learn that he'd been wrong.

Chapter Sixteen

As the cherrywood mantel clock in Victoria's bedchamber chimed the midnight hour, Nina sat on the hearthrug and rubbed at her eyes. A planned excursion into the village in the morning had caused most of the guests to retire early. Nina would not be going. She and Victoria had accepted an invitation from the Duke of Fernbridge to visit his estate instead. He'd also invited Caroline and James, but Caroline was still casting up her accounts in the mornings and they had declined the invitation.

"If you don't tell me what is going on with you and Elliot, I might burst," Victoria said, breaking into Nina's thoughts.

Nina pulled her knees toward her chest and wrapped her arms about them. "He's helping me."

"Helping you?" Victoria's head flinched back.

Nina bit her lip, then told Victoria about Elliot's plan.

"You're kidding me." Victoria's mouth gaped.

"I actually didn't believe it would work, but . . ." Heat crept up Nina's face. Perhaps she shouldn't have told Victoria what was going on with Elliot and her, but she was as persistent as a woodpecker after insects in a soft-barked tree. Thank goodness she hadn't mentioned the lessons, only that Elliot had told her that a sportsman like the duke thrived on competition.

"Did my cousin suggest this plan?"

Nina nodded.

A soft knock sounded on the door.

"Who could that be at this hour? My great-aunt retired hours ago." With a bewildered expression, Victoria scrambled to her feet and opened the door.

Amelia stood at the threshold.

"Ah, good, you are not asleep," Amelia said. "This house party is as dull as dirty bathwater, so I've invited several guests from the younger set to meet in a half hour at the maze. . . ." Amelia's voice trailed off when her gaze veered past Victoria to Nina. Instead of her normally sourpuss expression, she smiled brightly at Nina. "Oh, you are here. Saves me from having to walk to your room to invite you."

Quite baffling that Amelia had eagerly invited her.

"Hope to see you in half an hour, ladies. Ta-ta."

Victoria closed the door.

"Do you think she's been drinking?"

Victoria chuckled. "Why? Because she invited you?"

"Yes." Laughing, Nina stood and brushed off her skirts. "Do you want to go?"

Victoria shook her head. "No. I'm too tired to trek down there. What about you?"

Would Elliot visit her room again? "I should probably retire as well." She brushed her cheek against Victoria's and strode out of the bedchamber.

Nina had just stepped back into her own bedchamber when a firm knock sounded on the door. Startled, the muscles in her abdomen knotted. Elliot? No. He wouldn't knock so loudly.

She opened the door. The solemn set of her brother's mouth made her heart skip a beat. "James, what's wrong?"

"I've decided that tomorrow morning Caroline and I will return to London."

"Is she feeling worse?" Nina set her hand on James's arm.

"No, she says she is fine to stay, but I'm concerned about her and the baby."

"So, Caroline told you she thinks she is with child?"

"She did, but I realized it last week when she retched two mornings in a row."

"You must be thrilled." Nina hugged him.

"I would be if Caroline wasn't looking so pale."

She patted his arm. "She did this with her last pregnancy. Hopefully, it will pass in a week or two."

"I hope, but she feels utterly terrible she is not properly chaperoning you, and I do not want her to feel stressed. I'm sure it isn't good for her or the baby."

"I will pack my belongings."

"No need. I've sent word to London. Grandmother should be here sometime tomorrow evening."

Grandmother at a house party? Nina frowned. "I'd rather return home with you and Caroline."

James grinned. "She's not that bad."

"She's a dragon."

He laughed. "A dragoness, dear."

She wanted to punch James in the arm. It wasn't funny. Grandmother was cantankerous, critical, and outright mean at times.

"We will see you in the morning." Her brother kissed her forehead.

"Tell Caroline I hope she feels better."

"I will. Sleep well." He walked out of the room.

Nina strode to the window and parted the damask curtains. Outside, the cloud-covered moon barely lit the Kent sky. From her room, she couldn't see the walls of the maze, formed from tall yews that had been planted over a hundred years ago.

Would Elliot be there? She shook thoughts of Elliot out of her head and forced herself to think of the duke. Each day, he seemed more content to stay by her side. Today, he'd chatted about all the dull things couples who followed the unspoken rules conversed about—weather, the season, more weather—but he'd also talked about horseback riding, something she did enjoy.

However, over the last few days, the only time she'd truly laughed while in the Duke of Fernbridge's company was when he'd relayed the tale about the bloodhound who'd taken up residence in a gentleman's bed. She suspected the gentleman was Elliot and the bed-hogging dog Zeb.

Lord Elliot Ralston was a puzzle. She'd thought him nothing more than a debonair cad. A man who didn't worry about anyone but himself, but the expression on his face when he spoke about his sister and this story about the dog, even his knowledge about the stars and flora, revealed a man more complex than she'd thought.

A movement on the lower terrace caught her attention. Two people stepped off the back terrace and made their way down a winding path. Fingers pressed to the glass, she tried to see who they were, but the dark night hid their identities. Was that Elliot and someone else heading to the maze? Biting the inside of her cheek, Nina strode to the armoire and pulled out her shawl. She should go just in case Fernbridge was going.

On almost silent steps, Nina made her way down the corridor. A door to her left opened, and Millicent Stiles stepped out of a room. The young woman's eyes widened. "Are you going to the maze?"

"Yes."

"Shall we walk there together?"

"I'd like that." Though she'd only met Millicent at this house party, she seemed amiable enough.

As Nina took a step toward the main staircase, Millicent touched her arm and motioned to another corridor. "Come this way."

They moved down the hall; then Millicent stopped and pressed on a panel. It popped open, exposing what many of these country homes possessed: a hidden back staircase that the servants used.

Nina didn't ask how the woman knew about it. Obviously, she'd used the hidden passage before, and she could only imagine why. Many gossips whispered that house parties were rife with bed hopping and wife swapping. She was starting to believe these tales were not solely chin-wagging.

"After you." The woman motioned with her hand.

Nina peered into the dim stairwell, then, holding the handrail, moved down the steps until she reached a landing with two doors.

"Use the one to the left," Millicent whispered.

She turned the handle and pushed the door open. Cool air and moonlight drifted over Nina. Startled, she glanced over her shoulder at the woman. "It leads to outside."

"Yes, only a short distance from the maze."

Nina pulled her shawl tighter about her shoulders as they traversed a path that cut through a copse. They emerged only yards from the maze, its evergreen walls so monstrous Nina couldn't see over the exterior ones.

The sound of low voices drifted in the night air. To the left, she spotted Amelia and several other women, including Lady Constance Hibbs. Nina glanced around, looking for the latter woman's husband. Was he here as well?

Amelia didn't hide her shock when Nina walked up to them with Millicent. Was it her presence with the other woman, or her presence in general? Had she invited her not expecting her to come?

A group of three men stepped out of the same path Nina and Millicent had taken. Joshua Little, Phillip Winston, and Lord Hibbs. The latter glanced at his wife but said nothing to her.

Nina stared at the path. Where was Elliot? She gnawed on her lower lip, realizing the sole reason she'd come here had nothing to do with the Duke of Fernbridge and everything to do with him.

"Now," Amelia said, "these are the rules. The men will enter from the west entrance to the maze. The ladies from the east. We all know the other rules of this game."

"I don't," Nina said.

"You need to reach the fountain without being tagged."

Nina glanced at the path again.

Following the direction of Nina's gaze, Amelia said, "Some of the gentlemen are already waiting at the west entrance for the game to commence."

Did she mean Elliot?

Amelia's catlike grin widened. She waved her hand in the air. "Then off you go, gents. We will give you five minutes before we enter the maze."

As the men made their way to the other entrance of the maze, there was a lot of shoulder clapping and laughter among them.

"Ladies, shall we move toward the entrance?" Amelia asked.

Chapter Seventeen

The layer of dew on the ground brought out the earthy scents of moss and soil. As Nina moved to the maze's entrance, excitement bubbled up in her.

"Time for the fun to begin." Amelia turned and smiled at them before she dashed into the maze.

Once they were inside, the warren of tall yews absorbed the moonlight, making it harder to see, but not impossible. Amelia, in front of Nina, seemed to know the way to the fountain. There was no hesitation in her steps as she immediately turned left at the first opening instead of continuing straight.

Lifting her skirts, Nina followed.

The woman's guffaws echoed in the thick night air.

Nina couldn't help her own laughter.

Amelia glanced over her shoulder and, spotting Nina, picked up speed.

They passed several openings in the yews. Millicent turned into one of them and disappeared.

Nina contemplated whether she should follow her.

No. Her instincts told her to follow Amelia, but as Nina turned back, she realized the other woman had disappeared. Ahead were two openings. Unsure which one

Amelia had turned into, Nina released a slow breath, then went left. After a minute, she felt as if she moved in an endless circle.

"*Drat*," she mumbled. She pivoted around and sucked in a startled breath when she nearly bumped into Lord Hibbs.

His gaze drifted over her, and his smile looked more lewd than friendly. He grabbed her wrist. "Ha! Caught you. Now I'm due a kiss."

No one had mentioned a kiss. She didn't want to touch the man, let alone kiss him, but she had only herself to blame. She should have realized that anything Amelia was involved in was not as it seemed. She tugged her wrist free and gave the man a quick peck on the cheek.

He frowned and grabbed her upper arm. "I'm sure you can do better than that."

Her stomach knotted. "Lord Hibbs, if you do not release me . . ."

His eyes widened; then he laughed. "What are you going to do?"

"I don't think you wish to find out, but I will tell you that you will end up limping back to the house, if you are capable of walking at all."

Making a choking sound, the man stepped back, clearly startled.

"Nina?" Elliot called out.

She spun around to see his tall form moving toward them. So Elliot had been here all along, playing this kissing game with women like Amelia. She should have known. Disappointment settled within her.

"Is there a problem?" Elliot strode up to them, his jaw set at a hard angle.

"Not at all," Nina replied.

Elliot glared at Lord Hibbs as if he didn't believe her.

"Excuse me." Red-faced, the man darted away.

Nina stepped past Elliot.

"Nina?"

"I should get back to my room." She took three steps and turned back around. "Who did you come down here to meet?" She knew she didn't have a right to ask, but she couldn't halt herself from voicing the question.

As if beyond frustrated, Elliot raked his fingers through his dark hair. "I had no intention of coming down here at all until I went to your room and didn't get an answer. And let me give you one bit of advice. If you are ever invited to play a game at night with the likes of men like Lord Hibbs, pass."

Nina realized that. She also realized she'd not come to the maze for any other reason than to see Elliot. She'd not even looked for the Duke of Fernbridge. Not once.

Elliot let out an audible sigh. "I'm returning to the house. Do you wish me to walk you back?"

She nodded. "You went to my room?"

"Yes." He held out his ungloved hand.

She set her palm against his.

His warm fingers closed around her chilled ones. The heat transferred up her arm and through her body, making her feel less chilled.

"Do you have any idea how to get out of here?" she asked.

He didn't say anything. Just nodded.

They made several turns through the maze of evergreens and emerged from the same entrance Nina had entered.

As they strode away, a man yelled, "I got you."

A female squeal drifted through the air, followed by the woman's laughter.

Elliot drew in a deep breath. What had Nina been thinking going down there with that lot? Most of them had lost their morality years ago, especially Lord Hibbs. The man could not be trusted. Several of his maids had left his employment with swollen bellies. His wife was nearly as debauched as her husband. Neither thought anything of carrying on sexual affairs outside of their marriage, and they'd initiated Lady Amelia Hampton into their group. The woman had not been faithful to her husband since the week after she'd spoken her vows. Elliot wasn't a saint, but he would not wish to be associated with any of them.

He glanced at Nina. "Why did you join them? Did you think Fernbridge would be there?"

"I wasn't sure who would be there."

"But you thought I would, didn't you?"

She peered up at him, then, looking away, nodded.

"Nina, I have no interest in associating with the likes of Lord and Lady Hibbs."

"How about Lady Amelia Hampton?"

He released her hand and faced her. "I might not have lived the life of a saint, but I've never cuckolded another man. Never." Elliot started walking toward the house, his long steps causing Nina to take two steps to his one to catch up.

Shivering, she wrapped her thin shawl tighter.

Damnation. He shrugged out of his coat and draped it over her shoulders.

"Thank you, Elliot."

"You're welcome. What did you say to Lord Hibbs?" he asked.

Even in the dim moonlight, Elliot noticed a flush of red settle on her cheeks. She pulled his jacket closer around her shoulders, then fiddled with one of the buttons lining the front. "I threatened a certain part of his anatomy."

Elliot blinked. Perhaps he didn't need to be so concerned about Nina. It appeared the minx knew how to handle men like Hibbs, but sometimes threats didn't stop such men. He opened the door to the servants' entrance and motioned her to precede him.

She stepped inside and handed him his coat. As she moved up the winding steps, her skirts swished as they brushed against the stairway's narrow walls.

He heard her foot slip on one of the worn treads.

Elliot set his hands on her waist to steady her. "Careful," he whispered.

She turned. Their faces even, her breath ghosted across his lips.

As much as he wanted to kiss her, this was not the place for it. Soon some of the other guests who were down at the maze might return. "Nina."

"Yes." Her voice was a throaty whisper.

"We need to get out of here before someone else enters." He released her waist.

Without a response, she turned and moved up the steps.

When Nina reached the hidden wall panel, he reached above her shoulder and gave the concealed door a slight push. "Is anyone there?" he asked.

"No, the corridor is empty." She stepped into the hall.

They moved toward her bedchamber. As they reached the corridor that led to his bedchamber, Elliot knew he should take it and leave Nina to navigate her way to her room by herself. If someone saw them together at this hour, it would be disastrous. Yet he remained by her side. He told himself it was for her protection, but the feel of her breath on his mouth while they stood facing each other would not leave him.

They reached her room, and she looked at him. "Do you wish to come inside?"

Without a word, he followed her and closed the door behind them.

Chapter Eighteen

In her dim bedchamber, Nina stared at Elliot, standing by the door. Why had she invited him into her room? A part of her didn't wish to examine the question. Introspection might reveal too much. She flexed her hand, remembering the warmth of his fingers entwined with hers and the intimacy she'd felt from such a simple act.

As if waiting for her to say something, Elliot remained quiet.

She swallowed and drew in a steadying breath. "I thought perhaps we could move on to lesson three."

He rubbed the back of his neck. "I'm not sure that's a good idea."

She stepped toward him. "You don't want to teach me about the third type of kiss?"

He gave a short laugh, but there was no humor in his eyes. He took several steps away from her, then pivoted around. "It might not be the wisest thing for us to do at this moment."

"Why?" She strode up to him and only stopped when a foot separated them.

He drew the back of his hand softly over her cheek. "It isn't a good idea."

Was it because, like her, he was experiencing the charged

air that almost crackled between them? As he held her gaze, she noticed the blacks of his pupils had expanded, taking over a good deal of the blue. Those intense eyes dipped to her mouth.

She held his gaze, challenging him to do what she realized they both desired.

He released a slow breath. "Very well. Lesson three. Put your hand here." He tapped his index finger over the left side of his chest.

"I thought it didn't matter where I put my hands when I kissed."

"For *this* kiss, it does matter."

She wasn't sure if he meant because this was a different type of kiss, or because of the electrical charge snapping like sparks between them. "So, why this spot?"

"Because you will be able to judge whether my heart rate has increased."

She knew her own heart rate had hitched upward with anticipation. She set her right hand over his lower ribs and skimmed it upward. "There is a problem with this plan."

"Is there?" A raspy tone infused his voice.

"It's near impossible with all the garments you're wearing to tell." She grasped the lapels of his coat and pushed the garment off his shoulders. It landed on the floor with a soft swish. "This is a hindrance as well," she said, unfastening the buttons on his waistcoat.

The widening of his eyes conveyed she'd startled him.

She repeated what he'd said to her during their other lesson. "Don't worry, Elliot. I won't bite you. Unless you beg me to." Nina wasn't sure what was driving her actions or her bold words, but now that she had started down this path, she didn't want to stop. She thought he would grin at her using his own words, but instead the intensity in his gaze notched up.

"I just might ask you to." His low laugh sent a pleasant tingling sensation over her skin.

She placed her palm over the cotton of his shirt above his heart. "It beats nearly as fast as mine."

A slow grin lifted his sensual lips. "Is that an invitation for me to find out?"

Was it? The idea of his hands on her breasts had already caused them to tingle and her nipples to peak. She pressed her body to his and wrapped her free hand around his neck. "I think, this close, you might be able to feel it."

For a brief second, his eyes drifted closed; then, as if she'd broken the last tether of his restraint, he tangled his fingers in her hair and brought his mouth down on hers. The kiss was more demanding than any before. Without preamble, or warning, his tongue entered her mouth and slid against hers.

The sensation was so carnal, so erotic, it caused her to return his passion with the same unrestrained hunger.

Elliot's palm settled on her hip and skimmed upward to capture the weight of her breast. His thumb swayed against her hardened nipple.

She pulled back.

"Forgive me," he said.

Nina didn't want apologies; she wanted more. She worked loose the top buttons that lined the front of her gown.

Elliot watched her, his gaze so scalding, she thought it might make her melt. He'd told her a woman could heighten a man's desire just by the way she removed her gloves. Obviously, removing one's dress took that statement to a new level.

"Nina." There was a warning in his tone, but he didn't step forward to stop her.

She comprehended she was about to cross a line that,

once ventured over, could not be uncrossed, yet she felt almost unable to stop herself. She'd heard women whisper that Elliot was a great lover. Well, the reckless part of her wanted to find out. After unfastening the last button, she shrugged out of her gown. It fell, circling her feet like a coronet.

Elliot's gaze drifted down her length, and then he was standing in front of her, kissing her again with his mouth and tongue while his hands drifted over her body. Neither of them seemed capable of moving fast enough as they tugged at each other's clothing until only her chemise and his trousers remained.

So much for the art of removing one's clothing slowly to heighten desire. They'd already danced around each other for days and they now seemed incapable of restraint. The maelstrom slowed as if the spinning of the world had halted.

His hand molded against her breast. The warmth of his palm filtered through the thin material of her chemise to her skin. She moaned against his mouth.

He responded by increasing the pressure of his hand, while his other one did a slow slide down her back to cup her bum and pull her against him.

Nina understood the hard length in Elliot's trousers. When younger, she'd asked Caroline how a man and woman made love.

Elliot made a primal noise close to a growl, and then they were at each other again, removing what little clothes remained. She'd barely had a chance to examine the beauty of his naked body when he swept her up in his arms and carried her to the bed. As he stretched out beside her, his mouth sought hers and their bodies tangled together like twisted bramble.

He kissed her neck, her collarbone, and then his mouth

moved downward. His lips lightly brushed against the swell of her breasts before his tongue touched the tip of one hardened nipple and drew it into his mouth.

She watched, fascinated by the sight and the feel. Her eyes drifted closed. She centered her mind on the sensations the act drew forth—a restless yearning that grew like a snowball rolling down a hill of wet snow.

His hand slipped over her stomach and lower.

Her skin, already warm, heated under his touch as he slid his fingers over her sex to stroke it.

Wanting more, she arched.

"I know what you want, Nina," he whispered, "but, believe me, you would regret it in the morning."

Her mouth was too dry to respond, but she managed enough strength to shake her head.

"Let me do something else that will bring you as much pleasure." His mouth came down on hers as his finger slipped into her sex, then out again. As he did it again, his palm created pressure on a spot above. A sensation she'd never experienced before grew. It clawed at her.

Shame on Caroline for not explaining this. For not telling her how she would almost want to beg for something that seemed to lie beyond her grasp. She whimpered.

Elliot's body shifted downward. He planted soft kisses against her left thigh, while his finger remained in her. Teasing and tormenting. Then his mouth was on her sex. She experienced the slick slide of his tongue.

She should have been shocked, but she was beyond that point. Carnal need outweighed every other thought she possessed. She clenched at the muscles of her sex, and a wave of sensations raced over her, making her legs almost shake with the intensity. Then she was drifting downward. She opened her eyes to see Elliot peering up at her. He understood what had happened to her body more than she did. He moved to her side and pulled her to him.

Nina set her head on his chest. Below her ear, she heard the *thump, thump, thump* of his heart. She slipped her hand over his thick manhood and stroked him.

The sound of him drawing air between his teeth caused her to glance at him. His eyes were closed. "Might I touch you?"

"It's best if you don't."

"Why not?"

"Because we have completed lessons three, four, and five. If you touch me, we will move on to lesson six. If I give you *that* lesson, tomorrow I will go to your brother and ask for your hand, and you will not marry Fernbridge, but *me,* when I tell him what transpired."

He sounded as serious as a vicar at a funeral. "You're serious?"

"Nina, I want to make love to you more than anything. But I've never taken a woman's virginity. If I take yours, I will feel bound to marry you."

She felt as if her eyes were pried open with toothpicks. She couldn't even blink. She'd not thought Elliot would balk at taking a woman's virginity, but . . .

"Your silence gives me your answer."

She didn't want to stop, but neither did she want to marry Elliot. It wasn't that she didn't care for him. She cared for him more than she should, but Elliot was too much like her father. She feared marrying him would only lead to the type of heartbreak Mama had lived with.

Elliot got off the bed, tugged on his drawers and trousers, and pulled his shirt over his head. His long fingers worked the button before he put on his remaining garments.

"Good night, Nina." He slipped out of the room as quietly as he'd entered.

Chapter Nineteen

The following day, after saying good-bye to Caroline and James, Nina sat with Victoria, Elliot, and the Duke of Fernbridge as they traveled in the latter's carriage to his country residence. Nina hadn't realized Elliot would be joining them today until she'd stepped outside to see him leaning against the duke's carriage, his arms crossed over his chest, looking like he was being forced to swallow a bitter pill.

For most of the journey, the duke had talked about his parklands and horseflesh, especially his Arabians. Elliot had spent most of his time staring out the window as if in deep thought, while Nina tried *not* to spend most of her time thinking about what Elliot had done to her with his mouth and tongue.

The memory of his touch and how it had made her feel caused her body to tingle. She gave an inward sigh. If she were honest with herself, she'd admit how desperately she'd wanted him to kiss her again and bring her to that pinnacle of sensations. The man possessed the ability to make her mind veer to things she shouldn't be thinking about wanting to do again.

She should never have agreed to his plan. Never spent so much time with him. Yet, his plan had worked. The

Duke of Fernbridge's attentiveness to her was undeniable. Yet now it was Elliot who she wished would engage her in conversation.

If the duke asked for her hand and she accepted, there would be no stargazing on a roof or sleeping under the stars.

The Duke of Fernbridge cleared his throat.

She glanced at him. He had an expectant expression on his face as if awaiting a reply. Had he spoken to her? "Forgive me, Your Grace, did you say something?"

"I asked if you brought your sketchbook."

"Oh, I had not thought of it." No, she'd been too preoccupied thinking about last night.

"Well, I'm sure a member of my staff can find you a sketchbook once we arrive. There are dozens of things you will wish to draw. As I said when we visited Lord Hathaway's folly, my property contains one even larger."

Elliot finally pulled his gaze away from the window. He peered at the Duke of Fernbridge, though his countenance gave nothing away as to what he was thinking.

Silence settled over the carriage.

Victoria, sitting next to her, glanced up from the book she was reading, and set it on the seat. "Let's play a game. I will say a word and you must say the first word that comes to your mind. I will start, then Nina, Elliot, and you, Your Grace."

Fernbridge looked bored with the suggestion, and Elliot maintained his unreadable mask.

Nina didn't care—anything that would distract her from Elliot would suit her.

Victoria tapped a finger to her cheek. "Carriage. Now your turn, Nina."

"Horses," Nina added.

Elliot's gaze finally shifted to her. "Straddle."

The way he watched her, along with his word choice, made her stomach flutter with awareness.

Fernbridge scratched the back of his head. "Hunt."

"Hounds." Victoria almost bounced on the seat.

"Foxes," Nina added, trying to ignore the way Elliot peered at her.

The carriage grew quiet.

"Elliot, it is your turn." Victoria waved a hand at him.

"Caress," he said.

The duke's gaze jerked to Elliot.

Victoria giggled.

Nina's body warmed. Everywhere.

"Elliot," Victoria chastised. "I don't think you understand how this game is played. How did you get caress from foxes?"

Thankfully, his heated gaze shifted to Victoria. "Cousin, you said I should say the first thing that came into my mind."

"Yes, but . . ." Victoria's voice trailed off as the carriage took a turn and swayed. They drove through two stone pillars and an open wrought-iron gate.

Ahead on the gravel road, Fernbridge Hall came into view. An English Baroque monstrosity larger than Blenheim Palace.

Victoria made a cooing sound.

The Duke of Fernbridge puffed out his chest. "What do you think, Lady Nina?"

Both Elliot and the duke stared at her, waiting for her response.

The massive residence seemed cold. Cobbles and gravel abutted the front of the home. There were no bushes or shrubs to soften the hard angles of the structure. Though she couldn't tell the duke that. "It's lovely."

He nodded and grinned.

Several servants rushed forward to assist them out of the carriage.

A thin, prune-faced butler with thinning gray hair bowed as they strode to the front door. "Your Grace," the servant said in a monotone voice.

As the butler opened the door, the Duke of Fernbridge acknowledged him with a nod.

They stepped into the entry hall, and Nina's gaze immediately lifted to the domed ceiling that sported a fresco of cherubs playing violins against a blue sky with white intermittent clouds painted on it.

Beside her, Victoria snapped her fan open and fluttered it at her face as if the beauty of it might cause her to swoon.

"Exquisite, isn't it?" the duke asked.

"Breathtaking," Nina replied.

Bloody hell. Elliot tried not to gawk at the domed ceiling soaring thirty feet above them, or the dozen wall niches containing marble busts of haughty-faced men. Since they looked as pretentious as Fernbridge, they were probably his deceased relations.

Nina and Victoria stood with their heads tipped back as they stared at the ceiling. His cousin's mouth gaped like a fish's on dry land.

This elaborate residence was the type of country house Nina had grown up in, yet even she seemed awed by the opulence. Elliot's run-down estate could never compare to this. What difference did that make anyway? He'd all but proposed to Nina, and she'd not accepted. Yet, he'd foolishly held on to a sliver of hope. Now, it whittled away as he listened to Fernbridge boasting about his residence and horses and all the duchy possessed. The sinking feeling in Elliot's gut had turned rock hard.

"Does it make you think of another work of art?" Fernbridge asked Nina.

"Yes, Correggio's *Assumption of the Virgin*."

"You are familiar with painters?" Fernbridge glanced over his shoulder to cast Elliot a smug twist of his lips.

Still staring at the fresco as if trying to memorize every detail, Nina nodded.

"Then we should start our tour in the Baroque room. I have a couple of Rubenses, a Gentileschi, and others you will enjoy." He held out his arm, and Nina placed her hand on it.

Victoria sidled up to Elliot and wrapped her arm around his. "Don't give up," she whispered.

"Give up?" he echoed lamely.

"You might have Nina fooled, but I see the way you watch her. You're not doing this to win some point. You care for her."

He did, but what Victoria didn't know was that Nina had already made her choice and it hadn't been him.

"She's not as materialistic as Fernbridge might think."

No. He didn't think she was, but he also didn't believe she would wish to live in a home with warped floors, faded wallpaper, and over fifty years of neglect. Opulence was one thing. Simple creature comforts a completely different thing.

The tour of Fernbridge Hall's interior took over three hours, and they hadn't even completed a quarter of the residence before they luncheoned alfresco, then headed to the stables.

In front of the carriage house, several stable hands lowered the top of the landau they'd rode over in and harnessed fresh matching bays to the vehicle.

"I thought perhaps we'd tour the grounds after the stables. The sun has warmed the air, making an open carriage ride pleasant. We could visit my folly," Fernbridge said.

The exemplary meal they'd been served curdled in Elliot's stomach.

Victoria gave him a sorrowful look. "You need to invite Nina to your country residence. Perhaps give a grand ball."

Victoria was related to him on his mother's side. She'd never visited the barony's country residence. She was unaware of its dilapidated state.

If Nina married Fernbridge, she would host grand parties at this residence and be the envy of others. But surely, she wanted more out of her marriage. He glanced at the smile on her face as she talked with Fernbridge and wasn't convinced. Not a single soul would envy her if she married Elliot, a man they thought would not remain faithful—a man who possessed not one but two residences in need of repairs.

They climbed into the carriage and crossed a stone bridge.

"There it is. The Temple of the Gods." Fernbridge pointed to the roof of the folly as it came into view above a row of towering evergreens.

The vehicle took a turn in the road and the folly, which resembled the Temple of Hephaestus with its six immense columns under a pediment, stood before them. The magnitude of the structure hit Elliot like a punch to the gut. The duke hadn't exaggerated when he'd said it was larger than Lord Hathaway's. It made the other man's folly look inconsequential.

"It's magnificent," Nina said.

Victoria leaned forward in her seat as if so anxious to tour it, she couldn't contain her excitement. "Oh, Nina. I wish you had brought your sketchpad."

"Dash it all." Fernbridge frowned. "I forgot to get a member of my staff to get you something so you could draw it, but you will have other opportunities."

Elliot's gaze snapped to the man. Had he just informed

them that he intended on asking for Nina's hand? He glanced at her. Her face gave nothing away, except her hands, which were clasped together in her lap, tightened and then relaxed.

Fernbridge stepped out of the carriage and offered Nina his arm. She set her hand on it as the duke led her away and up the broad stone steps.

"Did he imply what I thought?" Victoria's eyes widened.

"I believe so." Elliot released a slow breath, trying to ease the tightness in his chest.

"What do you intend to do about it?" Victoria asked.

"Do about it?" Elliot echoed. "Why, nothing. This is what Nina wants. Her wish to be a duchess is about to come true."

"I don't think this is what she truly wants. I think it is what she believes her family wants, but if you were to offer first . . ."

Elliot's gaze shifted from his cousin to where Nina and Fernbridge stood under the roof of the folly. The duke chatted away as Nina appeared to listen intently to the windbag.

The knot in Elliot's stomach tightened. With a tip of his head, he motioned to them. "I think you are mistaken, Victoria. She looks quite content."

They arrived back at Lord and Lady Hathaway's after the sun set. Tonight was the last night of the house party, and there was to be a ball.

Victoria and Nina headed to their rooms to get dressed.

Fernbridge tossed Elliot a smug smile. "Lady Nina was almost speechless at times. I knew once she visited my residence it would tip the scales in my favor."

The urge to wipe the arrogant expression off the man's face grew strong. Elliot drew in a calming breath. "I'd best get dressed as well."

He'd taken two steps when Fernbridge spoke. "I know the truth."

Elliot stopped in his tracks and pivoted around. Did Fernbridge mean Elliot and Nina's plan to get his attention? "I'm not sure what you refer to."

"Your finances."

Elliot's heart beat fast. "My finances?"

"Let's not dance about the subject. You don't have a pot to piss in."

The man's choice of words was as shocking as the revelation that he knew about Elliot's lack of funds.

"I had my man of affairs do some digging. He even visited your estate when he claimed his horse had thrown a shoe. Shame on you, Ralston. I hear you have your crippled sister working as a maid."

Elliot wasn't exactly sure when he had stepped up to the duke and planted a facer on the man. Just that he must have because Fernbridge was on the ground touching his bloody lip. The man scrambled to his feet and gawked at the blood on his cream-colored leather gloves.

"If you ever call my sister a cripple again, I'll do more than plant a facer on you." Elliot turned and walked away.

"You'll regret that. You're no better than an East End piece of rubble," Fernbridge called after him. "Lady Nina deserves someone better."

I bloody well know that. Better than either one of us.

Chapter Twenty

Nina returned from the Duke of Fernbridge's residence to find Grandmother had arrived from London. As they strode toward the ballroom, the old woman lectured her ad nauseum about bringing Fernbridge up to snuff.

"Remember you have a responsibility to get the man to offer for you before any gossip ruins your chance for a good match."

But as they stepped into the ballroom, it was not the Duke of Fernbridge Nina's gaze searched for, but Elliot.

At dinner, he'd chatted a great deal with Millicent Stiles. Though perhaps that was because the woman had been seated next to him. If he was trying to make her jealous, it wasn't working.

Balderdash. Who was she kidding?

Eager to escape Grandmother's nagging, Nina searched the room for one of the dowager's cronies. "Oh, Grandmother, look there is Lord Pendleton. I shall leave you to converse with him."

Grandmother's hand latched on to hers like a lobster claw. "Remember what I said."

Nina forced a smile and strode to Victoria, who'd entered the room with her great-aunt.

"Mrs. Darby, I'm sure my grandmother would be pleased if you sat next to her once she finds a seat."

The woman nodded and strode toward Grandmother.

"I don't think your grandmother cares for my great-aunt." Victoria pinched her lips together.

"Really? I'm sure she does."

"I'm sure she doesn't. You did that on purpose. Is she being tiresome?" Victoria smiled.

"My grandmother graduated from being tiresome two decades ago. Now she is cantankerous." Nina pinched her lips together and watched Victoria's great-aunt cross the room. "Now I'm feeling guilty."

"For being uncharitable toward your grandmother?"

"No, for sending your sweet great-aunt to sit next to her."

Victoria snorted, then covered her mouth. "She is hard of hearing, so your grandmother's sarcastic barbs and the intonation in her voice will be lost on Great-aunt. So, tonight is our last night here." There was a questioning look in Victoria's eyes. "Do you think the Duke of Fernbridge will pay a call on your brother when we return to London? I presume that was what your grandmother was hounding you about."

Would he? The idea should have made her feel giddy with excitement, but it didn't. Though Grandmother was right on one count—it would stop any unfavorable gossip. It would also make her brother happy to see her settled with a steady type of man. Whereas, if she were to marry someone like Elliot, it might cause James to suffer some malady. He'd think she'd gone quite mad after what had happened with Avalon.

"I'm not sure," she replied distractedly as she watched the entrance. Neither Elliot nor the duke had entered yet.

"Do you truly care for him?" Victoria asked.

She blinked. Not sure if Victoria meant Fernbridge or Elliot. "Who do you mean?"

"The Duke of Fernbridge."

He seemed nice, but did she really know him? Surely, he did not make her stomach flutter, and he was a bit of a braggart. *He's safe*, a little voice in her head chanted. *Yet, it's Elliot you desire*, the voice added.

Elliot strode into the ballroom.

Think of the devil and he doth appear.

Though all the gentlemen were dressed in nearly identical black evening attire, he stood out. Even the light from the chandelier seemed to cast all its luminescence on him, as if it thought him too handsome not to highlight.

His blue eyes met hers. And there it was—that unsettling yet euphoric sensation in her stomach. Like what she experienced whenever she leaped over a high hedge.

"I still think my cousin is smitten with you," Victoria said, pulling Nina from her thoughts.

The fluttering sensation in Nina's stomach knotted as he made his way to a group of men. She forced a laugh. Though it sounded cheerful, it had taken a great deal of effort to produce.

"As you can see, he has no interest in me now that his plan has caused the Duke of Fernbridge to single me out." That wasn't completely true, but telling Victoria that she'd offered herself up to Elliot and he'd plainly stated if he bedded her, he would wed her wasn't something she felt comfortable sharing, even with her dearest friend.

Holding two champagne glasses, Amelia Hampton slinked across the room like the snake she was and joined the group of men Elliot stood with. Standing next to him, she offered one of the crystal goblets to Elliot.

Elliot had said he didn't engage in liaisons with married

women, but Amelia was trying her damnedest to make him break that rule.

The thought of them together made Nina's stomach grow queasy.

The Duke of Fernbridge walked into the ballroom. Upon seeing her, he headed to where she and Victoria stood.

"What do you think happened to his lip?" Victoria whispered.

One side was swollen and red. Nina's rascal brother Anthony had gotten into a few scuffles that had made his lips look similar, but she couldn't imagine His Grace fighting. "Probably a shaving accident."

"Ladies. You both look stunning," the duke said, stepping up to them.

"Thank you, Your Grace." Nina felt the heat of her grandmother's gaze and glanced over to see the older woman nodding her approval.

The violin player drew his bow across the strings of his instrument, and couples started moving toward the dance floor.

"Lady Nina, might we stroll about the room?"

She didn't want to *stroll*. She wanted to waltz and become swept away in the music.

His Grace offered her his arm as if he would not expect her to say no.

"Of course." As soon as they moved away from Victoria, Elliot crossed the room and said something to his cousin.

Victoria smiled and nodded. Then they joined the others on the dance floor who waited for the music to start.

Amelia stood watching Elliot, looking as if she were

sucking on an over-salted herring. Obviously, she'd wanted him to ask *her* to dance.

As the Duke of Fernbridge led Nina around the perimeter of the room, the first strains of a Venetian waltz drifted in the air. She tried not to stare at those moving around the dance floor, especially Elliot, who danced so sublimely. She wanted to be in his arms, moving to the music, while drawing in the heat from his body. Her mind drifted back to them lying on her bed, his wicked mouth between her legs. The memory caused a heartbeat to pulse on the nerve-filled spot his tongue had touched.

"When I return to London," the duke said, pulling her from her wicked memory, "I will be visiting Tattersalls to buy some new horseflesh. Mounts that are accustomed to a woman who rides sidesaddle."

Nina forced a smile. Yet another hint that implied he intended to ask for her hand.

She should feel jubilated. Instead, she felt numb.

As the evening went on, Elliot couldn't keep his gaze from drifting to Nina. The material of her lavender gown flowed with her as she danced with Lord Pendleton.

Throughout the night, he'd avoided Nina for his own self-preservation. He wasn't exactly sure when he'd fallen in love with her, but he had, and there was nothing he could do to stop her from accepting the Duke of Fernbridge's proposal. Elliot was one hundred percent sure the bastard intended to offer for her. Why else would he have sent a man to Elliot's country home? The duke's hateful words about Meg kept replaying in Elliot's head. The impulse to drag Fernbridge outside and give him a thrashing nearly overwhelmed him.

As Pendleton led Nina off the dance floor, Elliot could not stop himself from moving toward her. There was only one waltz left, and he wanted to dance it with her, even if it was to be the last time he ever did so. Once she married Fernbridge, he would not ask her. He'd be too tempted to take their relationship to another level. And he would never cuckold another man—even a bastard like Fernbridge.

He'd made it partway across the room when the Dowager of Huntington stepped in his path and pinned him with her steely gray eyes.

"Lord Ralston, take a walk around the room with me."

It wasn't a question but a command.

He contemplated picking up the disagreeable woman and placing her to his right or left, or out the window. All three options would have him asked to leave the house party. He forced a smile and offered the woman his arm. "Of course, my lady."

Like a stray cat who'd just been adopted by a fishmonger, she smiled—a clearly forced expression. A deception for those in the room to witness. "Let us cut to the chase. You are obviously interested in my granddaughter, but I wish you to step aside." With a jerk of her chin, the old bat motioned to Nina and Fernbridge, who were now standing together with several other guests. "I want her to marry the Duke of Fernbridge," the dowager continued. "The alliance between the two families is well matched."

"Is that all that is important, my lady? An alliance?"

"What else is there?"

"Love." That he'd spoken the word out loud startled him.

The Dowager of Huntington gave a sharp laugh. "I doubt a black-hearted devil like you believes in love."

"That might have been true at one time, but not now."

"Until some pretty widow comes along and distracts you?"

"Your opinion of me is quite low, isn't it?"

"I have always found it hard to believe a leopard could change his spots."

"Do you truly think Nina will be happy if she marries Fernbridge?"

The Dowager glanced around the room. "I believe if my granddaughter marries him, she will bear his heir. The *next* Duke of Fernbridge."

But that isn't love. Not the emotion that keeps one up at night. That makes the heart beat a bit faster when they're near that person. His own thoughts made him laugh.

The old woman's gaze jerked to him. "What do you find so humorous?"

His Byronic thoughts. That Nina had managed to turn him inside out. And the crystalline truth. That he *did* think of her when apart. That those thoughts *did* keep him awake. He removed the dowager's hand from his arm.

"Lord Ralston, don't you walk away," she hissed in a low voice.

Without giving the old woman another look, he strode toward Nina.

As Elliot stepped up to the group Nina and Fernbridge conversed with, he noticed the slight grin on his cousin Victoria's face. He also noticed the narrowing of Fernbridge's eyes, and the man's bruised lip, which looked inflated with air.

Next to him, Nina blinked, then gave a tentative smile.

"Lady Nina, might I have the honor of the last dance?"

Her lips turned up into a full smile. "Yes. I'd be honored."

They stepped onto the dance floor.

"You've been avoiding me," she said, as the music started, and he led her into the first steps.

"I thought it best I give you some space." That was a lie. He had needed the space.

"I don't want things to become awkward between us."

As if someone reached into his gut and twisted it, he experienced a sharp pain. "Has Fernbridge proposed?"

She glanced away. "No."

"But you expect him to, don't you?"

"I believe so." Her voice was low, almost a whisper.

They continued the dance in strained silence, but as the last note whispered in the air, Elliot said, "I hope you will be happy together. I wish you all the best."

Then he forced himself to walk away.

Chapter Twenty-One

Someone shuffling around in Elliot's bedchamber, along with the sun seeping through his eyelids, caused Elliot to blink.

Wilson stood by the windows, drawing the curtain panels open.

The bright light streaming through the window made Elliot's head feel as though a villain poked it with a sharp object. After leaving the ballroom last night, he'd gone to the library and indulged in an excess of Lord Hathaway's fine whiskey.

Wilson slowly shuffled over the wine and navy Turkish rug as if glue were smeared on the soles of his shoes, making each step difficult. The valet's rheumy eyes stared at him through thick glasses. "Do you wish to take breakfast downstairs, my lord, or in your room? Many of the guests are breakfasting on the terrace before departing for the train station."

His tongue felt coated with sawdust. He dragged his hands over his face. "I'll join the others."

"Very well, then. I'll have the staff bring up a bath."

"Thank you, Wilson."

An hour later, anxious to be on his way home, Elliot

strode toward the dining room. When he arrived back in London today, he would confirm that the inventory had been completed at Langford Teas' East End warehouse, and then he'd send a letter to his stubborn sister. He'd promised she could stay for a month, but perhaps she was growing weary of playing maid and would want to return to school.

Once again, he thought about what Fernbridge had said about Meg. The bastard. Guilt more extreme than normal settled over Elliot.

He entered the dining room. No one sat at the long cherry table. Instead, the three sets of French doors that lined the back of the room were open, allowing guests to take advantage of the mild weather and dine alfresco on the flagstone terrace. He stepped outside and stopped. His gaze searched those seated at the wrought-iron tables for Nina. He had expected to find her sitting next to the duke, but he saw neither of them.

Lady Pendleton, who sat at the table directly in front of him, gasped, lifted a trembling hand, and pointed to the roof. She released an ear-splitting scream.

Elliot looked up to see one of the stone pots, which ran between the balustrade on the roof, teetering like a nicked lawn pin about to topple.

"Good God, Ralston, move!" Lord Pendleton yelled.

Elliot had only taken a few steps when the stone vase crashed to the terrace with an explosive noise and landed only a foot from where he'd been standing.

Shards of stone and soil exploded in the air like lit dynamite buried into a rocky hillside.

A collective scream rang through the air, along with several gasps.

Lord Hathaway bounced up from where he'd been

sitting at one of the tables and rushed over. The man's complexion was the color of Wiltshire chalk. "Ralston, are you hurt?"

Elliot brushed off the dirt and stone that had flown at him with a volatile force. "No, I'm fine."

"I have no idea how that happened. Those urns have stood there for nearly a century. One has never fallen before." Hathaway rubbed at the back of his neck as he stared at the other urns lining the roofline.

Elliot peered up. When on the roof with Nina, he hadn't noticed anything wrong with the urns. They'd looked perfectly centered on their stands—none too close to the edge—but he couldn't say for sure.

As he brushed off his clothing, Elliot glanced at those gathered around. He still didn't see Fernbridge. *You'll regret that.* The duke's threat after Elliot had struck him in the face repeated in his head. Maybe the vase falling wasn't an accident. Elliot's thoughts shifted to the Dowager of Huntington. Nina's grandmother had warned him away from Nina, but he doubted the woman would resort to paying someone to split his head open.

Christ. He was letting his mind run wild with a conspiracy theory. He realized Hathaway was still talking to him.

"Ralston, perhaps I should call the local doctor. You've got several cuts on your face."

Did he? He hadn't noticed the stinging until the man mentioned it. He touched his cheek and looked at the blood on the tips of his finger. "Scratches. Nothing more. No need to call a physician."

A crowd gathered around him.

"That was a close call, Ralston," Lord Pendleton said.

"Are you sure you don't wish me to summon the

doctor?" Hathaway repeated, appearing more shaken than Elliot.

"No. I'm fine."

"At least come inside, so your cuts can be examined. My housekeeper has an assortment of salves she keeps belowstairs."

"I'll just go to my room and change."

"Yes, of course." Hathaway was so nervous he cast spittle into the air as he talked. The man followed him inside. "First a bloody poacher endangers the Duke of Fernbridge. Now a fallen urn. No one shall want to come next time I have a house party." The man looked like he wanted to weep.

To hell with Fernbridge. That stray shot had nearly caused Nina to be thrown from her horse. "Did you ever find the poacher?"

"No, but my men could see tracks in the dew-covered soil near the woods."

Without commenting, Elliot jogged up the steps. Inside his bedchamber, he stood before a dresser with a mirror hanging above it and viewed his reflection.

Damnation. He looked as if he'd engaged in a fight with a feline and lost the battle. Several scratches and small cuts dotted his face from where shards of stone had struck him.

Thankfully, his trunk remained in the room. Elliot stripped down to his drawers and shoved the soiled garments into a compartment in the trunk and tossed clean clothing on the bed. He poured water from the ceramic pitcher into the matching basin, splashed it on his face, and dabbed at the cuts with a towel, then dressed.

A soft knock sounded on his door.

"Hathaway, I told you I don't need . . ." He opened it to find Nina.

"Oh goodness," she exclaimed and gently touched his cheek. "I heard what happened and wanted to make sure you are all right."

"I'm fine."

"You don't look fine." She scooted by him.

He reluctantly closed the door. She shouldn't be in his room. Hathaway might send a servant with the ointment he spoke of or Elliot's valet.

Nina walked over to the basin and dipped one corner of the cloth into the water. She brushed the wet material over his cheek, then combed her fingers through the hair at his forehead. "You have a cut here as well."

He couldn't remember anyone ever tending to him. He'd always been on his own after his parents had decamped to their separate houses. Meg with Mother. Him with Father. Then he'd been shipped off to boarding school. Even before his parents' separation, he couldn't remember his mother ever tending to him—only disinterested servants who cared for him because they were paid to do so. Yet, Nina was here washing his face, and he thought his heart might explode from the tenderness he saw in her eyes.

Thank God, she'd not been standing next to him. He didn't want to think about what could have happened to her.

"There," she said, smiling up at him. "All cleaned up, and the cut on your cheek isn't bleeding any longer."

"Thank you."

She strode to the basin and rinsed out the cloth, then took an inordinate amount of time folding it before draping it over the washbowl's edge. Still standing with her back to him, she cleared her throat. "When I heard what happened to you, my heart beat so fast I thought it might snap one of my ribs."

He stepped behind her, pulled her back against his chest, and tangled her fingers with his. Holding her felt so right. Like they were the last two pieces in a puzzle.

She relaxed against him, then turned, and slipped her arms about his neck. Her gaze drifted to his mouth.

By God, he'd taught her well. Without hesitation, he lowered his mouth to the soft texture of Nina's lips.

She made a sound of pleasure.

His undoing. He coaxed her lips open and deepened the kiss. Another sound of pleasure. This one his as he pulled her tighter to him.

A loud knock on the door froze them like pillars. "Ralston, it's Hathaway. I brought you the ointment I mentioned."

The color drained from Nina's face. If found here, she'd be ruined. For a brief minute, Elliot contemplated strolling to the door and opening it—all but sealing Nina's fate. That bastard Fernbridge did not deserve her. He reminded himself, neither did he.

The earl knocked again. "Ralston?"

"Quite unnecessary, Hathaway."

"Are you sure?" the man asked.

"Yes, forgive me, but I'm changing."

"Very well. If you're sure . . ."

"I am."

The sound of the man's footfalls grew lighter as he walked away.

Nina stepped out of his embrace and strode toward the door.

Was she leaving?

He caught her delicate hand in his. "Don't marry Fernbridge."

"He hasn't asked."

"He will."

She gnawed on her lower lip.

"Marry me."

A lump moved in her throat. "Elliot, what's between us isn't love. It's lust. I want something that will last. Lust doesn't. It sparks, then burns out. I saw what that type of marriage did to my mother. I don't think I could take that."

"So, your alternative is to marry a man you have no strong emotions for at all? *I* saw what that did to my parents. That type of marriage is not charitable either."

"I might grow to love him."

"You could also grow to hate him. And there you'd be for the rest of your life, bound to a man you never loved. Then you might turn into your father."

As if baffled, she stared at him with her brows pinched together. "What do you mean?"

"Maybe it won't be Fernbridge who strays. Perhaps it will be you."

"I would never."

"You're in my room. You returned my kiss. Passionately."

"I came to see if you were all right."

He cocked one brow.

"If Hathaway hadn't knocked . . ." With a wave of his hand, he motioned to the bed. "Maybe we would have ended up there."

Heat crept up her neck to her cheeks, causing two flaming red spots.

Nina set her hands on her hips. "I'm not married yet. If I was, I wouldn't have come here."

"No?"

Elliot drew a finger over her cheek. "I'm in your blood, Nina. Like you're in mine. Sometimes lust is more. I will not lie and say I don't want you in the physical sense. Good Lord, woman, the thought of making love to you keeps me awake at night, but it is not an exclusive emotion. Just because we lust after each other does not mean we cannot love each other." He fisted his hand over his heart. "I love you. Is that so hard for you to believe?"

"You only think you do." She walked over to the bed and started unfastening the row of buttons lining the front of her blue traveling dress.

"What are you doing?"

"Join me in your bed. Then, after you get what you want, tell me you still love me."

Damn her and her beliefs. Her opinion of him ran as poor or equal to that of her brother's and grandmother's. In her eyes, he was no better than a rutting dog. One fuck and he'd be relieved of the pain in his cock.

He *was* capable of love. He would give his life for Meg. Not because of what had happened to her, but because he did love her. He stared at Nina as she worked the buttons loose. He'd give up his life for her as well.

God knew he wanted her. He was half tempted to take what Nina offered and let her believe him so heartless. To make love to her until she cried out his name, but he would hate himself afterward and she would, as well. Because she could end up carrying his child, and he'd not allow that bastard Fernbridge to raise it. So he *would* go to her brother and tell him what had transpired between them, and Elliot did not want her to marry him for that reason alone.

"Go on, love. Climb into my bed naked, but I will not join you." He strode to the door and walked out.

Nina's hand on her buttons stilled as if filled with concrete. She stared at the door Elliot pulled closed behind him. Its wooden surface blurred under the tears filling her eyes. Brushing them away, she sat on the edge of the bed.

He'd walked away—left her standing with the front of her dress gaping open.

What had she expected? She wasn't sure, but not this.

Her heart ached as if the air in her lungs expanded and pressed on her heart. She felt worse than when she'd found out Avalon had a mistress. No, not a mistress, but a woman he truly loved.

How could this feel worse? It shouldn't. She'd thought herself in love with Avalon. She didn't love Elliot. Did she?

Nina stared down at her gaping bodice. What had she been about to do? Prove something to him or to herself? The possibility it might have been the latter made her want to weep. Had she wanted to sleep with him because *she* needed to get him out of her system? Not the other way around? What had she thought? One quick tumble with Elliot would cleanse her desire for him? As if he were something she could wash off her hands like dirt. No wonder he'd walked out of the room.

Idiot. She stood and fastened her buttons. Thank goodness they were leaving in a few hours. She couldn't face him.

She stepped into the corridor and stopped. Elliot was leaning against the wall, his arms crossed over his chest. The hard look in his eyes made her want to cringe.

"Don't worry. I wasn't hanging about contemplating whether I wanted to return so I could soil you. I need to lock my trunk; a footman should be coming for it shortly. I'm riding to the train station with Lord and Lady Pendleton. I need to get my hat and gloves. Good-bye, Nina."

"Elliot?"

He opened his bedchamber door, then closed it behind him.

She had a feeling he hadn't just been waiting for her to leave to lock his trunk. He'd also not wanted anyone to enter *his* room and find her there. Everything he said and did made her opinion of him change, but her fear of making a grand mistake—again—kept her from knocking on his door.

Chapter Twenty-Two

Since returning from Lord and Lady Hathaway's house party, Nina had spent the last week avoiding any gatherings by claiming she felt unwell. The thought of running into Elliot held as much appeal as entering a ballroom naked, but she could not hide away forever.

She stepped out of her bedchamber and made her way down the stairs to join the family for breakfast. As she entered the dining room, all conversation stopped as everyone's gazes centered on her. The whole family sat at the table except Caroline and James's son, little Michael, and Anthony. The latter probably wasn't home. Most likely the scoundrel remained in some woman's bed or was sleeping off a night a cavorting.

"Feeling better, dear?" Caroline asked, her tone concerned.

"Yes, much improved." Nina forced a cough.

As she sat, James reached over and gave her hand a squeeze. "You had us worried. If you weren't feeling better today, I was going to insist Dr. Trimble be called."

"No need," she replied, stepping up to the chafing dishes and placing an egg and a bacon rasher in her dish. Taking her seat, Nina felt the chill of Grandmother's icy gray eyes on her.

Last week, as they traveled home from the Hathaways', the dowager had stared at her like an owl would a field mouse after Nina had refused to talk about the Duke of Fernbridge. Once again, she'd lectured her about how Nina would be a fool not to accept His Grace if he proposed.

A footman offered her orange juice. She nodded, and the servant filled her glass.

"So, Nina, now that you are feeling well, will you be attending Lord and Lady Fitzwilliam's ball tonight?" Caroline asked.

Nina's fork, with a piece of egg on the tines, stilled midway to her mouth. Would Elliot be there? She couldn't avoid him for the rest of her life. "Yes, I'll attend."

"I will accompany you," Grandmother said. "That way, Caroline can rest now that she is increasing again."

Caroline's mouth gaped and her eyes grew round. Obviously, she hadn't told Grandmother she was with child. "You know?"

Grandmother squared her shoulders. "Dear girl, you've been looking nauseated for weeks. I'm sure everyone knows."

"She looks lovely." James leaned over and kissed Caroline's cheek.

"None of that at the table. I'm trying to eat." Georgie scrunched up his face. "It's yucky."

James grinned. "One day, young man, you won't think so."

Her youngest brother scrunched up his face further.

Caroline and James could have lain on the table naked for all Nina cared. She was still absorbing the fact Grandmother would be accompanying her, along with the knowledge she might see Elliot.

The butler stepped into the room and cleared his throat.

"What is it, Menders?" James asked.

"A messenger just delivered a note for Lady Huntington."

"Thank you." Caroline held out her hand and opened it.

"What is the matter, darling?" James asked.

"Yesterday, at the newspaper, Mr. Finch informed me he will be retiring to the Lake District at the end of next month. I guess he was not sure whether I would be in the office today. This is his official notice stating he intends to resign."

Grandmother set her fork down and wiped her mouth. "Mr. Finch?"

"He is the illustrator at my newspaper."

"The one who does those political caricatures?" Grandmother's mouth twisted in distaste.

"Yes." Caroline smiled. "Aren't they fabulous?"

"Pish. Radical, I say. Good riddance to bad rubbish."

Caroline flicked Grandmother a reproachful look. "I need to hire someone else. Mr. Finch is beyond extraordinary. It will be difficult to find a replacement."

Nina took a bite of egg. She'd done a few caricatures, but she'd never shown them to anyone in her family. Perhaps she would apply for the position. Working at the newspaper would be her small way of contributing to the suffragist's movement. And a job would distract her from thoughts of Elliot.

She glanced at James. He still had his hand over Caroline's as they chatted. What would he say if Caroline hired her? Though he was more open-minded than most, perhaps it was best not to say anything. She would just go to the *London Reformer* and apply for the job.

Before noon, Nina strode down the stairs. In the entry hall, the sound of Grandmother's cane thumping against the floor drifted closer.

Blast it. Hoping to avoid one of the old woman's inquisitions, Nina dashed toward the front door. She'd just wrapped her fingers about the handle when the dowager stepped into the entrance.

"Where are you off to?" the matriarch asked, her tone sharp.

Nina's shoulders sagged, all hope of avoiding an interrogation gone. Grandmother was like a prized guard dog. "I'm going to see Caroline at her office."

"You're going to the *London Reformer*? What for?"

Think fast, Nina. Think fast. "I'm to meet Caroline, so we can go out for tea and refreshments."

"Perhaps I should accompany you."

Goodness. A rare event when Grandmother accompanied them for tea. She probably wished to talk about the Duke of Fernbridge again. Worse, she'd not approve of what Nina wished to ask Caroline. "Then, afterward, we are going to Liberty to look at fabric."

"Liberty? I hope you aren't going there to buy some god-awful fabric to make a dress like Lady Westfield did. Those rational gowns she wears are hideous. I cannot understand how her husband allows her to socialize wearing such garments."

Husband allows? For a woman who'd favored herself her own husband's backbone, and who wanted to decide what everyone else should do, her grandmother had set ideas when it came to a husband's rights. "Her husband should *not* control what she wears. Lady Westfield's Pre-Raphaelite garments are quite becoming on her."

"Bah! They are an abomination to good taste. Next, women will be going about without their corsets."

Nina didn't have the heart to tell Grandmother some women already were. She might suffer apoplexy if she learned that.

Grandmother continued to stare at Nina as if still undecided about whether she should accompany her.

"After Liberty, we are going to Harrods."

"That monstrosity?" Grandmother frowned. She hated large department stores. "I don't think I'll go." She waved her hand as if Nina were a pesky fly flittering in her face. "Go off then."

Releasing a relieved sigh, Nina stepped outside as Dawson pulled up to the front of the town house with the family's carriage.

The coachman jumped down from his perch and opened the door for her.

"Thank you, Dawson."

As soon as they pulled away from the town house, Nina unbuttoned her blouse and slipped out the sheets of paper she'd hidden with her caricatures. She laid them on the cushion and ran her hand over them, hoping to remove some of the wrinkles.

The clopping of the horses' hooves slowed as the carriage pulled up to the brick façade of the *London Reformer* on Bishopsgate.

"Whoa, boys," the coachman called out.

Nina stared at the building. She nibbled on her lower lip and brushed her damp palms on the skirt of her dress. She wasn't sure what her sister-in-law would say to her proposition. Without waiting for Dawson to open the door, she stepped out of the carriage and marched inside the building before she could change her mind.

The strong smell of ink from the printing presses tickled her nose. To the left of the entrance, the sound of the machinery churning out the newspaper resonated in the air, along with several men's loud voices.

Nina stepped into the offices on the right of the wide corridor.

The copy editor, Mr. Day, glanced up. The man's fingers were always covered with smudges of ink, as was his nose.

Seeing her, he stood. "Lady Nina, how are you?"

"Well, and yourself, Mr. Day?"

"Splendid." He peered over his shoulder to where Caroline sat in her office, which was visible through a window in the wall. "Is she expecting you?"

"No, but I hope she won't mind me visiting." Nina skirted around the man's desk and knocked on the door.

Without looking up, Caroline said, "Yes, come in."

"Hello, Caroline."

Her sister-in-law smiled. "Why, Nina dear, what brings you here?"

"These." Nina placed the somewhat wrinkled sheets of paper on the desk.

"What is this?" Caroline picked them up.

Nina didn't respond, just waited for Caroline's reaction.

Her sister-in-law looked at one sheet of paper, then the next. Her initial unreadable mien shifted to a broad grin.

"Did you do these?" Caroline lifted the drawings in the air.

"I did."

"My goodness, I knew you possessed an artistic inclination. Your sketches are lovely, but it takes a certain skill to do caricatures."

"You think they are good?" Nina's heart beat faster.

"Good? They are impressive." Caroline stared at the one of Prime Minister Gladstone. "This is excellent." She then looked at the last one again. Caroline's green eyes glinted with mirth. "I don't recall your grandmother possessing a hairy wart on her nose."

"I added it after she agitated me one day." Nina bit her lip to stop her laughter.

"Well, they are quite remarkable. Have you shown them to anyone else?"

"Just my friend Victoria." Nina wiped her damp palms

over the folds in her skirt. "Since Mr. Finch is retiring, I wondered . . ."

"Nina, are you applying for the position?"

"Yes, I hoped you would consider me."

"Consider you? Of course. I can do better than that, I can hire you."

Had she heard correctly? She fought the urge to stick her finger in her ear and wiggle it. "Did you just say you would hire me?"

Caroline set the sketches down, walked around the desk, and took Nina's hands in hers. "I would be a fool to pass up such talent."

"But James? What will he say?"

"He might be startled. Especially if he sees your carica-ture of Grandmother with a hairy wart on her face, but let me talk to him. You must realize he supports women in the workforce. I am an editor of a newspaper."

"Yes, but I thought he didn't have much choice in the matter where you are concerned."

"No, dearest. Perhaps his love for me had something to do with it, but his open-mindedness and progressive views are the real reason. I will discuss it with him tonight, but no matter his opinion on the subject, I will not withdraw my job offer."

Feeling almost giddy, Nina kissed Caroline. "Thank you!"

Chapter Twenty-Three

Unlike at breakfast, the whole family sat at the table during dinner. Nina glanced at Anthony, who looked rather wretched.

After Nina returned from the *London Reformer*, she'd passed James's office, and overheard him railing at Anthony for spending his nights cavorting with members of the demimonde and gambling. The dissipation etched on Anthony's face was troublesome to everyone.

Caroline, sitting across from her, nudged her foot under the table, drawing Nina from her thoughts. Her sister-in-law tipped her head toward James and mouthed the words, *I'm going to tell him about your job.*

Anxious to get this over with, Nina nodded.

"James, darling." Caroline set her hand on his arm. "As you are aware, Mr. Finch is retiring, and I need to hire someone to fill his position."

Nodding, James smiled and placed a piece of asparagus in his mouth.

"I do know an artist who is perfect for the position," Caroline said.

"That's wonderful, dear. You should hire him."

"Oh, I'm so pleased we are in accord because I have."

"Wonderful. What's his name?" James forked another piece of asparagus.

"It's not a man. As you know, I prefer to hire women when I find one suitable for the job. My newest reporter, Ginger Templeton, is exceptional."

Grandmother, sitting across the long expanse of the table across from James, grumbled. "That is all your radical newspaper needs. Another suffragist with farfetched ideas."

Nina peered at the older woman. "I've never understood why a woman such as yourself has not joined the suffragists."

Grandmother turned her steely gray eyes on Nina. "Such as myself?"

"Yes. You've always believed women intellectually equal, yet you continue to disparage the movement."

"I cannot understand this effort because it will never happen. The House of Lords and Parliament will always be a place for men. I have always preferred to influence men of power in private conversation."

"Well, I believe change *will not* happen unless women demand that it does." Nina's own vehemence shocked her. She'd never thought much about politics and the suffragist movement, but she was starting to understand Caroline's passion, especially after the fiasco down at Hyde Park. "Why shouldn't women have license over their own lives? They should be equals in the workforce and in the eyes of the law. They should be able to help make the laws they must live under."

Grandmother snapped her gaping mouth closed and offered Nina a hard stare. "What do you think? That one day a woman will be prime minister?"

"Yes," both Nina and Caroline said in unison.

"Pish, what a fanciful thought. You do not understand. The way for women to change the world is by marrying powerful men and influencing them." Grandmother placed a piece of seasoned potato in her mouth.

Nina set her fork down and held Grandmother's regard. "Why should that be our only option?"

"Because it is the only one we presently have."

Caroline shook her head. "James believes it is only a matter of time until that changes, right, darling?"

"I do."

For a minute, Nina marveled at how Caroline had gotten James to say exactly what she wanted him to say. Words that would make it nearly impossible for him to say anything negative about Nina's new position.

"Even though I'm not quite sure what you are talking about," Georgie said, "if James believes it, so do I."

Caroline's regard shifted to Anthony, who seemed unaware that a heated discussion raged on at the table. "Anthony, I'm curious about your views on this."

"If you believe it will happen, Caroline, I'm sure it will." As usual, Anthony proved that even though he appeared to not be paying attention, he had heard everything they'd discussed.

Grandmother flashed a look that revealed she thought them fools.

James was more open-minded than most, but one never knew how he would react to the idea that not only his wife, but his sister would be working for the *London Reformer*. However, the gleam in Caroline's eyes clearly stated she thought she had set this discussion up so perfectly that only Grandmother could balk at her decision to hire Nina.

Her sister-in-law turned to James. "So, as I was saying, darling. I've hired someone."

"Wonderful, dear." He sunk the tines of his fork into a glazed carrot.

"Yes, I've hired Nina to replace Mr. Finch when he retires." Caroline put a piece of carrot in her mouth and smiled as she chewed.

Everyone's gaze shifted from Caroline to Nina.

James's fork stilled in midair. He looked too stunned to respond.

Grandmother slammed her palm down on the table, rattling several dishes. "No. Absolutely not. Bad enough one of you works there."

Caroline squared her shoulders. "Grandmother, might I remind you that I own the *London Reformer* and can hire whomever I wish."

Anthony grinned. "I say, jolly good job, Nina."

The dowager narrowed her eyes at Anthony, then James. "This is all your fault, James. What man gives his wife a radical newspaper as a gift?"

"Might I remind you, Grandmother, this is not your decision," James said.

"You're going to allow it?" Her gray eyes turned to catlike slits.

"As my wife just said, it is her business. If Nina has applied for the position and Caroline has hired her, then the decision is between them."

Grandmother stood up and pounded her cane against the floor. "What will the Duke of Fernbridge think of this?"

Nina blinked. Odd she'd not thought about the duke or his reaction. The only one she'd thought about was Elliot, and it hadn't been about how he'd react, but how this position would distract her from the foolish longing she felt for him.

"Grandmother, the duke has made no commitment to

me nor I to him, so his opinion on this is irrelevant. And it is something I wish to do!"

Grandmother shook her head and stormed out of the room, her cane thumping loudly against the wooden floor with each step she took.

"Thank you, James," Nina said.

"No need to thank me. If you have taken the initiative, I commend you."

"Nina, you will replace Mr. Finch when he retires. I am beyond thrilled to have you working for the *London Reformer*," Caroline said.

Nervousness and excitement intertwined in her stomach. "I look forward to it."

"You know Grandmother will be almost impossible to live with now," Anthony grumbled as he cut a piece of fish.

Nina laughed. "Do you really believe she could get much worse?"

Georgie set his elbows on the table and cradled his jaw in his hands. "I hope not."

Five enormous crystal chandeliers glistened above the wooden parquet flooring in Lord and Lady Fitzwilliam's ballroom. Women in colorful gowns and gentlemen in black evening attire conversed, sending laughter and the buzz of conversation into the massive space. Footmen wearing white gloves carried silver trays with sparkling glasses of champagne.

Nina glanced around as she descended the grand staircase with Caroline and James.

Thankfully, Grandmother, still irate over Nina's upcoming position at the newspaper, had declined to accompany her.

Nina would have been content to stay home and avoid

both Elliot and Fernbridge, but Caroline had insisted she felt well enough to attend.

As much as she fought against it, Nina couldn't stop herself from searching for Elliot. His height made him easy to track down. He stood with several of his friends, including Lord Talbot. As usual, he looked his urbane self in his dark evening wear that clung to his broad shoulders.

The orchestra tuned up their instruments, and Elliot strode over to Lady Montgomery. The auburn-haired widow was only a few years older than him and quite lovely in both manner and beauty. They crossed the room to the dance floor.

Nina wanted to stride over to him and say yes to his marriage proposal, but her fear of making the biggest mistake of her life kept her away. She glanced at her brother. James would call her mad if she became betrothed to another cad. Her gaze followed Lady Montgomery and Elliot until she forced it away.

She noticed Fernbridge striding toward her.

He greeted her brother and Caroline before turning to her. "Lady Nina, how are you?"

"I'm well, Your Grace." There was no fluttering of her heart. No tingling of her skin. She wished there was—but feared there never would be.

"I am pleased to see you are up and about."

"Thank you for the roses."

"You are most welcome." He smiled. "I went to Tattersalls this week. I purchased a gray Lipizzaner horse."

Was he implying he'd purchased it for her? The thought made her stomach squeeze as if bands of steel clamped around it. She forced a smile. "They are lovely animals."

The Duke of Fernbridge began talking with James about the breed, and while the man conversed with her brother,

Nina could not halt her gaze from scouring the dance floor for Elliot and Lady Montgomery.

The woman was smiling at Elliot as he spoke to her. Nina knew they were friends. She'd seen them dancing together last season. Odd that she would remember that. Or was it? She probably could name every woman he'd danced with.

Caroline was also peering at the dancers, specifically Elliot. Her sister-in-law's regard volleyed to Nina and a worried expression settled on Caroline's face.

Even Caroline, sweet Caroline, who thought the best of nearly everyone, worried Elliot would break Nina's heart.

His Grace's regard shifted back to her. "May I call on you tomorrow, Lady Nina, at three o'clock?"

Her mouth went dry. Did he intend to ask for her hand? She searched her mind for some excuse. Finding none plausible enough, she said, "Of course, Your Grace."

"Will you be home as well, Huntington?" Fernbridge asked James.

There would be only one reason he would wish to speak to both her and James. The sudden queasiness in her stomach edged up her throat.

"We will see you then." James appeared beyond pleased. Of course. This was the type of man he wanted her to marry.

The duke nodded and walked away.

Nina felt like burying her face in her hands.

The visible pleasure on her brother's face dissolved when he glanced at her. "Nina? I thought this was what you wanted."

"I don't know what I want anymore."

Caroline touched her arm. "James, will you excuse us? I wish Nina to accompany me to the retiring room."

Her brother opened his mouth as if he wished to say something, but then closed it and nodded.

Caroline looped her arm through Nina's, and they made their way through the crush as the strains to the waltz ended. Nina heard a laugh and glanced sideways to see Lady Montgomery and Elliot making their way through the crowd as well.

Nina's gaze met his.

For several long seconds, it appeared neither could look away from the other.

He inclined his head slightly, then returned his attention to Lady Montgomery.

I don't care. Really, I don't. Yet, a place near her heart ached.

As they walked into the retiring room, Nina overheard two women talking. Lady Amelia Hampton's and her cousin Priscilla Grisham's voices were unmistakable.

"Lady Nina had barely set foot in the ballroom when the Duke of Fernbridge darted over to her. Do you think he wishes her to be his duchess?" Priscilla asked.

"Pish, don't be stupid! Why would he want to marry her? Even Lord Ralston, after having spent time with her at Lord and Lady Hathaway's, has decided to give her the cut."

Nina's hand clenched. The spiteful shrew was just jealous that Elliot was smart enough not to spare her a glance.

Nina and Caroline stepped fully into the room. The gas lights illuminated both Amelia and Priscilla, along with a seamstress who sat on the floor repairing a torn piece of lace on Amelia's hem.

Priscilla's gaze shifted to the doorway. Her face turned an unflattering shade of chalky white.

"Lord Ralston was probably looking for an easy diversion. Avalon said he could have bedded Nina if he wished. She was more than willing," Amelia said.

Nina felt all the blood drain from her face. Had Avalon

said such a thing, or was Amelia spreading more lies? She strode toward them, trying to control the rage shifting through her, almost causing her to see a red haze.

Priscilla gave a small shake of her head and tilted her head toward Nina, trying to warn her cousin they were not alone.

"What is wrong with you, Pris? You look like you've just swallowed curdled milk and are about to cast up your accounts." Amelia shook her head as if she had little tolerance for her cousin.

"She is trying to inform you I have entered the room." Nina set her hands on her hips, fearing if she didn't keep them there, she might place them on Amelia's shoulders and shake her until the other woman's teeth rattled in her head.

Amelia spun around. Her face flamed red.

"I'm not sure why you persist in gossiping about me, but I do not appreciate it." Nina couldn't help the way her voice shifted an octave higher.

"I believe I know why," Caroline said. "Lady Hampton is clearly jealous."

The red on Amelia's face deepened.

"Is that it, Amelia? Are you jealous of the attention Lord Ralston has shown me?"

"Why would I be jealous of that? Lord Ralston has no interest in marriage. If he is giving you any attention, it is because he wants an affair. Nothing more." Amelia glanced down at the seamstress. "Hurry up with my hem, you cow."

The young woman nodded. "Nearly done, miss."

"Are you such a horrid person you are incapable of treating others with respect?" Nina frowned.

"Pish, I'm the girl's better. Why should I?"

"If you require an explanation, I pity you," Nina replied.

Caroline stepped forward. "Don't you understand words can have lasting consequences? It's not kind to belittle another, and it surely isn't kind to gossip, especially when untrue. Case in point, one of my reporters told me about a noblewoman who was caught stealing a scarf at Harrods. I've not repeated this to anyone except Nina because I didn't want to embarrass the woman, even though she could use a good set-down. However, I'm reconsidering. Perhaps I should start a gossip column in my publications. The first story will be about that sticky-fingered lady. Though I might not publish such a tidbit if the woman retracts her claws and stops gossiping."

"You wouldn't publish such a thing," Amelia said.

Caroline's lips formed a sly smile. "Don't test me. If I hear you are disparaging anyone with your vicious tongue, I will."

"Aren't you done yet?" Amelia snapped at the seamstress.

"You should thank the seamstress," Nina said.

Amelia's lips formed a thin stubborn line. "Very well." She looked at the girl. "Thank you." Then she walked to the door and out of the room.

Her cousin followed, a slight smile on her lips as if she had thoroughly enjoyed watching Amelia put in her place.

"I fear she is not very content in her marriage," Caroline said.

"I realize that."

Caroline squeezed her hand. "Don't marry the Duke of Fernbridge."

"What?"

"You obviously love another. Does he return your affection?"

A sheen of tears blurred Nina's vision. She blinked

them away. "He says he does. But I'd hate to disappoint James. Did you see the pleasure on James's face when His Grace asked if he could call tomorrow?"

"Nina. Goodness, James wants *you* to be happy."

"Yes, but we both know he doesn't care for Lord Ralston."

"It doesn't matter if he cares for him. It matters if you do. James will not be the one sharing the man's life, nor his bed. You will. Do not marry a man you do not care for. Please, Nina."

Elliot watched Nina and her sister-in-law as they moved through the crowd. Even in this crush, he had sensed the warmth of her body when only a few feet had separated them. He'd noticed Fernbridge talking with her and her brother. The bastard had cast him a self-satisfied grin as he'd walked away from them. Most likely over the next month the banns would be read and a grand spectacle of a wedding would follow.

Standing next to him, Talbot cleared his throat. "Elliot you haven't heard a word I've said."

He glanced at his friend. "I'm sorry. What?"

Talbot made an exasperated noise, then whispered, "I said, I cannot wait until we purchase Langford Teas, and my father finds out we are his competition. The man might piss himself." Talbot rubbed his hands together and grinned.

Though for different reasons, Talbot wanted this venture to succeed as desperately as Elliot.

Talbot clapped him on the shoulder. "It's not going well with Lady Nina, is it? What happened at the Hathaways' house party?"

"She got what she wanted all along. Fernbridge intends to ask for her hand."

"Buck up, old boy. There are lots of attractive and

wealthy chits here. I still say, I don't understand why you don't just set your sights on Penny Granger. Her family is near the top of the Upper Ten Thousand. Like all the ostentatious nouveau riche from across the pond, she'll not only repair your properties but guild them with gold."

He didn't want Penny Granger, and he certainly didn't want his properties gilded with gold. Marrying anyone besides Nina held no appeal. Perhaps he could hold off. Wait and see if he could increase the profit margins for the tea company at a faster rate.

"Bloody hell," Talbot grumbled. "Lady Clifton and her daughter Georgiana are staring at me. I'm going to head to the card room. Are you coming along?"

"I'll be there in a minute," Elliot replied.

"Don't stand out here torturing yourself."

Torturing himself? Was that what he was doing? Perhaps. "I'll join you shortly."

Talbot strode away.

Elliot watched as Lord Walden approached Nina. She nodded at the young buck, and he escorted her to the dance floor. Talbot was right. The card room would distract him. He pivoted and bumped into a woman dressed in a frothy cream concoction of silk and tulle, as she walked by.

He set a hand on her arm to steady her.

The woman glanced up.

Good God, Lady Sara. The chit possessed a propensity for laughing whenever she got within two feet of a man. And they were practically touching. Elliot glanced at his hand. They were touching. He lowered his arm.

Before he could utter an apology, she blushed profusely and started to giggle. Yet, even though she laughed, there was a look of absolute horror in her eyes. He didn't believe the fear stemmed from him, but from her inability to stop herself from uncontrollable guffaws.

"Lady Sara." He bowed. "Forgive me."

The pitch of her giggling increased. She clapped a hand over her mouth.

Several people turned and stared. The color on her cheeks darkened.

"How are you?" he asked.

She lowered her hand. "I am"—she swallowed as if trying to control her urge to begin laughing again—"fine."

"I'm pleased to hear it."

She appeared to stop breathing for a minute, then sucked in several deep breaths. "How are you, Lord Ralston?"

"I'm well, thank you."

She let out a loud giggle, then pinched her lips so tightly together they lost their color.

Several men in the room, who'd obviously engaged the woman in conversation and knew her propensity for giggling, gave Elliot a sympathetic look.

She was holding her dance card and he could see it was blank.

Damnation. He shouldn't care. He should just walk away. He thought of Meg. How his sister had said she would feel out of place at a ball. Lady Sara felt the same way. "Would you care to waltz?"

He thought she'd break out in hysterical laughter. Instead, her eyes turned glassy and she nodded. "I would like that very much."

Elliot offered his arm, hoping, for her sake, the laughter would not start up again.

She gave a small giggle but otherwise remained composed.

As they took the first turn, he realized she danced well. "You are an accomplished dancer."

A brief smile flicked across her face before she tensed as if trying to control her emotions. "I've had lessons."

"It shows. With a dance master?"

"I had a male instructor, but he quit because of my, um, problem."

"What problem?"

This time she did laugh. Not a long, drawn-out affair, but a short sweet, girlish laugh. "You are too kind, sir."

As they took the turn, he heard a giggle start to bubble up the woman's throat. A panicked expression took over her face.

Damnation. She was about to start laughing again, and the fear of it happening was evident on her face.

"Lady Sara, close your eyes."

Her gaze narrowed on him. She looked too terrified to laugh. "What?"

"You know the steps well enough. Close your eyes."

"I don't think I can. What if I fall?"

"I won't let you."

She gulped at the air but did as he said.

Leading Sara in the steps, Elliot glided her across the floor. If she tripped, he'd feel terrible, but having her start laughing again hysterically wouldn't be any better. No man attending tonight would ever ask her to dance.

The music came to a halt, and Sara opened her eyes. "I didn't fall."

Elliot released the breath he'd been holding. "No, you danced wonderfully."

A pretty smile lit up her face.

Once off the dance floor, he bowed. "Thank you, Lady Sara, for the waltz."

"Thank you, my lord."

As Lord Walden escorted Nina off the dance floor, she watched Elliot do the same with Lady Sara. Him dancing with Sara was one of the nicest things she'd ever seen anyone do. Most men stayed away from her friend as if she were infected with the plague. If they only got to know her, they would see what a wonderful person she was, minus her nervous laugh.

Nina walked over to her friend and clasped her hands.

"I danced with Lord Ralston." Sara giggled, then quickly evened out her expression.

"I saw."

"He bumped into me. I think he noticed my dance card was empty and took pity on me."

Nina watched Elliot's back and broad shoulders as he moved through the crowd toward the card room. There was so much more to Lord Elliot Ralston then anyone realized, but she comprehended it.

It was about time she admitted to herself that she loved him.

Chapter Twenty-Four

The following day, Nina twisted her hands together as the butler entered the drawing room at her family's Park Lane residence.

Menders inclined his head. "Lady Nina, the Duke of Fernbridge wishes to know if you are in."

With a concerned expression on her face, Caroline glanced up from where she sat on the sofa, reading a children's book to her son, Michael.

Grandmother grinned and leaned forward in her chair. "Did he inform you he intended to call today?"

"Yes." The unsettling sensation that had plagued Nina's stomach throughout the morning and afternoon inched up her throat.

"Do you think he is here to ask for your hand?" Grandmother's pale gray eyes gleamed with pleasure.

Finding her throat had gone dry at the thought, Nina nodded and tugged her lower lip between her teeth.

"Nina, if you gnaw any harder on your lip, you will draw blood," Caroline said. "Do you wish Menders to tell him you are out?"

Grandmother pounded her cane on the floor. The sound echoed in the room. "Of course, she doesn't wish to send him away. She's brought the man up to snuff. Every chit from here to Scotland will envy her."

Caroline drew in an audible breath. "Grandmother, one does not choose a husband because they wish to be envied. Love must play a role."

"Pish." Grandmother accentuated her disgust with another thump of her cane.

On the sofa, little Michael eyed his great-grandmother, then wrapped his tiny arms around Caroline's neck as if the old woman were a witch from a Brothers Grimm fairy tale.

"It's all right, darling." Caroline gave Grandmother a scornful look and rubbed her son's back. "Nina, what do *you* wish to do?"

Nina took a deep breath, attempting to calm the quick patter of her heart. "Menders, please show him into the drawing room. Caroline and Grandmother, will you give us a moment alone?"

"Are you sure?" Caroline asked.

"Of course, she is." Grandmother stood.

Nina nodded at her sister-in-law and rubbed her clammy palms on the skirt of her blue dress.

Hesitantly, Caroline stood and exited the room with her son.

At the doorway, Grandmother turned around. "You might never come to love him, but you will have his ear and that is important," she said and left the room.

Wringing her hands together, Nina paced.

What seemed like an eternity later, but was most likely no more than a minute, the duke entered the drawing room and smiled.

Nina felt nothing when she saw him. Not true—she experienced a great deal of apprehension.

"Lady Nina, how are you today?" the duke asked.

She'd been better. "Well, Your Grace, and you?"

"I am anxious to return to my country residence, which I'm sure you understand, having seen its splendor."

Nina forced a smile. The home had contained a multitude of costly items from the furnishings to the paintings, but it had felt cold. Impersonal. Like the duke himself.

"I wish to ask you something." He motioned to the blue damask sofa. "Sit." He said it like she was one of his hounds.

Please don't. The forced smile on her face made her tight jaw send a shooting pain up the side of her face and into her temple.

Fernbridge sat next to her and took her hand in his. His palm was dry as if he didn't fear the answer to his question would be anything besides a resounding yes—that any woman would be beyond lucky to become his duchess. She didn't feel lucky. She felt nauseous.

He gave her knuckles a perfunctory kiss.

She felt nothing. No longing. No burst of excitement as his dry lips touched her bare skin.

"As you are most likely aware, I came to Town to find my duchess." He paused as if emphasizing the profoundness of his statement.

She needed to stop him. She abruptly rose. "Your Grace, what do you think of a woman who wishes to work?"

"Work?" As if the question baffled him, he stood and blinked.

"Yes, when a woman takes on an occupation." The question shouldn't have needed an explanation.

His gray eyes widened, and he suddenly looked as if someone had squirted sour lemon into his mouth. He drew in a slow breath as if he realized he should take care with his words, since Nina's sister-in-law was not only a journalist but the owner of the *London Reformer*.

"If a woman must work to support herself, as members of the lower classes must do, then it is acceptable."

Only the lower classes? The *thump, thump, thump* of Nina's heart had shifted to a fast trot. She strode to the window, needing to calm herself, fearing she might say something she would regret.

She turned back around. "But what if this occupation brings her pleasure?"

He walked toward her and set his hands on her shoulders. As on the sofa, his touch brought her no spark of excitement. No warmth. No connection.

"A duchess, like her husband, would not need to work. It is the duchy's holdings and wealth that make her part of the elite."

He didn't grasp what she was saying, or he did and still could not comprehend her point.

A knock sounded on the door.

Fernbridge lowered his hands.

"Come in," she said. Relief flooded through her at being interrupted.

The butler stepped into the room and bowed. "Lady Nina, would you care for some refreshments?"

"Your Grace, would you care for tea?" she asked.

"No." There was a wisp of impatience in his voice.

"Menders, I'll take some, please."

The butler exited.

The Duke of Fernbridge motioned to the sofa again. "As I was about to say—"

A crash sounded in the hall.

Nina lifted her skirts, dashed toward the door, and flung it open.

Georgie sat on the corridor floor. The hall table lay on its side next to where her brother sat, gripping his ankle and moaning.

Caroline was squatted beside him, examining it.

"Oh goodness, Georgie, what happened?" Nina asked.

"I twisted my ankle, and when I tried to grab the table for balance, both it and I fell."

"Does it hurt terribly?" Nina crouched next to her brother and ran a hand down his back.

"Phillip," Caroline said to the footman who'd come rushing down the corridor, "will you carry Georgie to his room?"

"Of course, my lady." The footman scooped Georgie up.

"I want Nina to come upstairs with me," Georgie said with a whimper.

Georgie wants me to go with him? Nina blinked. That didn't seem like Georgie at all. He was an independent child who tried to act like he never needed coddling. Something smelled as foul as week-old fish. Confirmation came when Nina noticed Caroline winking at Georgie.

"Perhaps I should return tomorrow," Fernbridge said.

"Your Grace, perhaps that would be for the best," Nina replied.

"The child shall be fine," Grandmother said from where she stood at the end of the hall. "No need to cut your visit short, Your Grace."

"No, it is best I return tomorrow."

Caroline stood. "Thank you, Your Grace."

After the Duke of Fernbridge left, Grandmother thumped her cane. "What is going on here?"

"Georgie took a tumble," Caroline said in a matter-of-fact voice.

The old woman released a heavy breath. "Children his age should be at boarding school."

"He has a tutor," Nina replied, following both the footman carrying Georgie and Caroline.

Grandmother made a disgruntled noise.

After Phillip laid Georgie on his bed and strode from the room, Georgie sat up and grinned. "How'd I do, Caroline?"

Her sister-in-law ruffled Georgie's mop of brown hair. "You are born for the stage."

Nina stared at them both. "He wasn't hurt at all, was he? What is going on?"

Caroline took both of Nina's hands in hers. "After I shooed your grandmother away from where she was eavesdropping outside the drawing-room door, I heard what you asked His Grace about women working. The man had no idea what you were trying to say. And I could tell from your voice you didn't wish him to ask for your hand. Or was I mistaken?"

"No. You are correct. I do not wish to marry him."

Caroline released a relieved sigh. "Thank God. If I'd misread the situation and botched up the Duke of Fernbridge's proposal, I feared you would want me run over by a carriage."

"Thank you." Nina squeezed Caroline's hands, then strode to Georgie and kissed him.

Her brother frowned as if she'd slapped his face with a wet eel and wiped her kiss off his cheek. "Yuck! No need to kiss me."

"So, what are you going to do, Nina?"

"I need to think about it."

If Nina didn't stop pacing, she would wear a path in the carpet in her bedchamber. She forced her feet to stop their perpetual motion and glanced out the window. Outside, the London sky was dark and fog clung to the pavement like a lover reluctant to be parted. A carriage made its way down the desolate street. The clopping of the horses' hooves the only noise outside beside the slight whistle of the wind.

She let the curtain fall back into place and glanced at the clock on her bedside table. Nearly one in the morning. For the last three hours, she'd contemplated doing something rash. Something she might regret. Something that would affect her for the rest of her life, and once done could not be changed. As the French would say, a *fait accompli*.

Now or never. She moved to the armoire and took out her navy cape and draped it over her shoulders, snatched her gloves and silk scarf off her dresser, and walked out of her bedroom.

The house was quiet as well, except for the *tick, tick, tick,* of the longcase clock on the first-floor landing. Everyone was asleep, except Anthony, who was not home.

On the tips of her toes, Nina made her way down the steps and out the door. As she moved through the night's fog, she pulled her cape tighter over her shoulders to ward off the dampness in the air. A man stumbled out a residence and swayed on his legs.

With a shiver of apprehension, Nina moved closer to the building she was in front of so the drunk would not see her.

When she reached Charles Street, she hesitated.

She could turn back, or she could continue. This decision would affect the rest of her life.

Releasing a slow breath, she turned onto the street and headed to Elliot's front door.

Chapter Twenty-Five

Outside Elliot's town house, Nina shifted from one foot to the other, while twisting her gloved hands together. Her lungs felt tight—as if someone had shoved a cork into her windpipe, forcing the air to remain and expand.

Not a single light shone from within the residence. Perhaps he wasn't home. Perhaps he was out and about Town. The nagging uncertainty within her whispered she should turn and go. Yet, as if pulled by the force of gravity, she took the final steps to the door.

Breathe. You can do this.

She lifted the knocker and dropped it firmly against the hard surface, then two more times, harder.

Silence. Perhaps that was for the best. She was about to leave when a light flicked on in the entry hall, sending a yellow glow through the transom above the door to spill into the dark night.

"Who is it?" Elliot's voice was raspy.

She opened her mouth, glanced toward Upper Brook Street. Still time to run away. "It's Nina."

The metal *click* of the lock turning echoed into the air as if amplified, and the door flew open. Elliot stood in a velvet robe—his hair in disarray. A dark shadow covered his jaw. He radiated such primal maleness.

Her gaze dipped to his bare feet, then to where the lapels of the robe met at his chest, exposing the surface of skin near his collarbone. A clear image of what he looked like underneath the garment settled in her mind. The thought of why she'd come here made her mouth feel dry. Her gaze returned to his face.

His blue eyes stared at her as if she were a mirage. "Nina, is something wrong? Has something happened to a member of your family? What is it, love?" He peered beyond her as if searching for something or someone, trying to make sense of why she stood at his door at this time of night.

"No, nothing is wrong." Except she'd clearly gone mad. "Why didn't a servant answer the door?"

He blinked. "Nina, it's past one in the morning. They are asleep and probably didn't hear the knocker."

That made complete sense. Nina wasn't sure why she'd asked the question. It seemed rather inane. She drew another slow, yet deep breath into her lungs. She should have downed a few glasses of wine before coming here.

"Aren't you going to invite me in?" She heard the slight shake in her voice and wondered if Elliot noticed it as well.

Still looking flummoxed, he stepped aside.

Didn't he understand why she was here? Did she need to spell it out? "You said if you took my virginity . . ."

His intense blue eyes stared at her as if she'd sprouted a second head.

With her heart beating fast, she strode past him and started up the stairway, plucking her gloves off as she went. Nothing like the sensual way he'd told her to do it. No. She was too nervous. Halfway up the first flight, she realized he wasn't following her. That fact chipped away at her already feigned bravado, yet she forced her feet to continue.

Damn you, Elliot. Don't make me feel like a complete fool.

"Nina, if you continue with this, there will be no turning back."

Well, at least he was contemplating following her. Maybe she needed to act like Hansel and Gretel and leave him a trail, but of clothing. She continued up the steps and, feeling more emboldened now that she realized it was his conscience that hindered him, she dropped one glove on the step, then the other.

She heard him mumble something. Either she was botching this up completely, or she'd done something provocative. Hopefully, the latter.

The squeak of the treads as Elliot moved up the stairs bolstered her confidence. She unwound the silk scarf around her neck and, holding it in her hand, trailed it over several steps before she let it slither down the stairs. She glanced over her shoulder.

She could see the intensity in Elliot's eyes. The unmistakable desire.

"How am I doing?" she asked.

"You get a gold star."

"Is that all?" She trailed her fingers over the banister with the lightest of touches. He didn't respond. She glanced over her shoulder again.

He smiled.

"No response?"

"I'm saving all my energy to stop myself from taking you on the next landing."

"I think your bed will be better."

"Oh, I agree."

As she reached the landing, she paused. The house

was dark, making it difficult to see into the rooms, but she figured Elliot's bedchamber was one floor up. She started up the next flight.

At the landing, she stood still, and Elliot stepped behind her.

"Don't do this, love, unless you're absolutely sure." His breath was warm against her nape.

She was sure. Elliot was right. They were like a fever coursing through each other, yet it went beyond that. She leaned her back against his chest. "You don't want me?"

"More than words could express, but if we do this, you will be mine and I yours. Our fates will be intertwined. Sealed till our dying days."

"I like the way that sounds. Not the death part but being intertwined."

"So, you have given Fernbridge your answer?"

"No, but I will. I don't want to marry him." She pivoted to face him.

He gently took her chin in his hand and brought her gaze up to his. "Then this can wait until after we marry."

"I don't want to wait." And by the firmness under his robe, he didn't wish to either.

"If you're sure."

She nodded.

Tangling his fingers with hers, he led her into the dim room to their right and closed the door.

Her gaze settled on the massive bed with green velvet drapes hanging at the corners. She could see the bedding was tossed aside. He'd obviously been in it when she arrived. A gas lamp and several leather-bound books sat on an adjacent round table.

"You were reading?"

"I was. I've been finding it more difficult to sleep at night."

"So have I." She noticed Zeb sprawled out on a large pillow on the floor.

The dog opened one of his drooping lids and his tail wagged.

"Hello, Zeb."

"Best not to speak to him," Elliot said. "It took me a protracted amount of time to get him onto his bed."

Smiling, she unbuttoned her cape.

Elliot stepped behind her to help slip it off. Neatly, he draped the garment over the back of a damask chair, strode to the grate, and poked at the glowing embers, drawing life back into the fire. Flames flickered, sending light to lessen the shadows.

She glanced around.

"The house needs updating," he said, obviously noticing the way she took in her surroundings.

"I wasn't thinking that. I was thinking it looks no different than the bedchambers in my family's residence."

"What were you expecting? Red flocked paper? Paintings with Bacchanalian revelry?" There was humor in his voice.

Goodness, no. She laughed. "I'm not sure. I've never been in the bedroom of a bachelor's residence."

"I'm working on fixing the property. To be honest, my uncle dearly neglected the residence." He motioned to a ladder propped in one corner of the room, where freshly applied areas of plaster stood in contrast against the light blue walls.

"*You're* working on fixing it?"

"The doubt in your voice will damage my self-esteem." He grinned.

She returned his expression. "I didn't mean I thought you couldn't do the work. But you have to admit it isn't every nobleman who plasters walls."

"Let us just say I have hidden talents."

The heated expression in his eyes caused her nerve endings to tingle. She remembered how talented his fingers, mouth, and tongue were. A warm flush settled over her body. "You do."

"Flattery will get you whatever your heart desires." His grin broadened and he began unfastening the buttons on the back of her gown. His warm breath touched her nape, while cooler air drifted over her spine as he brushed the gown off her shoulders. He pulled her back against him— one hand wrapped about her waist, the other cupped her breast. Even over her shift and corset, she felt the warmth of his big hand.

For a long minute, they just stood there. Him holding her. Her basking in the warmth.

"Are you sure about this?" he asked.

She peered over her shoulder to look at him. "I am."

He unlaced her corset and removed every stitch of clothing she wore until she stood in only her silk stockings and garters. As he'd undressed her, the tips of his fingers had grazed over her skin, causing a tingling sensation throughout her body. He was correct—being undressed heightened anticipation.

His hot gaze traveled from her face, down the length of her body, then back up.

Gooseflesh scattered over her skin.

"Good Lord, you're perfect." Elliot scooped her up and laid her on the bed. He untied the sash of his robe and tossed the garment aside, leaving him clad in only his drawers.

The light from the lamp highlighted the sculpted surface of his chest. He was beautiful.

"Is it time to move onto lesson six?" She skimmed her hand down his hip.

He flashed a wicked grin and shucked off his drawers, revealing his thick and proud manhood, jutting forward from dark hair. Elliot braced his hands beside her shoulders and leaned over her.

"Nina, my dearest love, we will start at lesson two, work our way through lesson five, and end with lesson six. Then we will do them again, if you wish."

"Is that a promise?"

"It is." He covered her mouth with his.

Elliot's kisses usually started out slow, then built. However, this one was intense. The slow build tossed aside for something more primal. Hungry. Demanding. His tongue tangled with hers as if challenging her to respond with the same frenzy.

She did. Her body grew anxious for things to become more complex, as they had at the house party. Her breasts were already tingling. Restlessness coursed through her, making her want more contact.

As if reading her thoughts, he lay next to her. His hands softly glided over her legs, still encased in her silk stockings. He made an appreciative noise. "God, you feel good."

She watched his face, half cast in shadow, as his hand skimmed over the plane of her belly to mold itself to the pliable flesh of one breast. His thumb gently swayed against her erect nipple. He captured the tip in his mouth. His tongue teased before he gently nipped at it.

Pleasure and pain melded into something she could not explain. She arched her body.

"Do you like that?"

She managed a nod.

His mouth moved to the other breast. The edge of his teeth scraped against it. Not in a painful way, but in a way that made her breathing turn shallow. With his mouth still on her breast, his warm palm skimmed over her inner thigh and cupped where she'd grown wet. He made a noise, clearly stating his satisfaction as one finger slide inside her, then out.

She wanted to whimper at the loss of contact. But then his finger returned. Thicker this time. Perhaps two fingers. The sensation didn't feel intrusive—no, the opposite. She welcomed the slight pressure. She moved her hands to his back and tried to pull him on top of her.

He chuckled softly. "What an anxious puss you are. I want to take my time. Taste every inch of your body."

Taste her body? Yes, she wanted him to do that again. The memory of his mouth on her had left her restless throughout the past several days. But the loss of not being able to talk with him was even more profound.

Tipping her head up, she watched him scatter soft kisses over her skin as he worked his way downward. His warm breath fanned against her sex. His tongue touched, delved, and tasted. The same sensation that had built last time clawed for release.

The heavy weight of his erection brushed against her shin. She moved her leg, stroking him.

The noise he made sounded primal, and she felt its vibration against the nub between her legs. Elliot scooted up beside her, and she ran the tip of her finger over the silky skin of his manhood before she curled her hand around it and stroked him.

He nudged her thighs wide and settled his body between her legs.

The weight of his hard length pressed into her. Wanting more of him in her, she arched.

His mouth met hers with a hungry kiss.

Nina answered back, her lips and tongue moved against his. As they kissed, she felt him slipping farther into her.

Caroline had said there might be pain, but there was none. Just a sensation of stretching to accommodate.

Elliot stilled.

"Are we done?"

"Oh, no, love. We are just getting started. I only wanted to make sure I wasn't hurting you."

She shook her head. "No, it feels . . ." She wasn't sure how to explain it. *Nice* seemed too benign. "Pleasant."

"Well, we have to do better than that." He smiled and pulled back slightly, then pushed closer again. Tighter. The same tiny beat at her sex started again. She slid her palm over his back and set her tongue to his shoulder and tasted his skin.

He made a noise, which revealed he liked her mouth on him. His hips were still moving in rhythmic, slow thrust, drawing her closer to her climax.

It crashed over her with more force than the first time . . . perhaps because, on the last thrust, he'd brought his mouth to her ear and whispered, "I love you."

"I love you as well. With every fiber of my being."

He smiled, then pushed deep into her, and by the way he tensed, she knew he filled her with his seed.

There was no turning back.

Chapter Twenty-Six

Elliot stared at Nina as she slept nestled in his arms. A few minutes ago, the clock on the mantel had softly chimed five times. He pressed a kiss to her lips, and she made a groggy noise. "Nina, love, I need to get you home."

In response, she curled her body tighter to his.

He'd let her sleep ten more minutes.

He drew in the scent of her hair and pulled her tighter to him.

Bang, bang, bang. What seemed only a few minutes later, someone pounded the knocker against Elliot's front door in rapid succession—the sound loud enough to wake the dead in Kensal Green Cemetery.

Who the hell would . . . ? He glanced at Nina snuggled next to him and the light streaming through the crack in the heavy curtains. His gaze jerked to the clock.

Damnation. Ten o'clock. Not a few minutes later, but a few hours. He'd fallen asleep.

He peered at Zeb, fast asleep. Of all the days for the dog not to wake him. He raked his fingers through his hair. Easy to figure out who was at his door. He had a feeling if duels weren't illegal, he'd be choosing his second and meeting Huntington in a secluded area of Hyde Park before noon.

As it was, he wasn't sure if the man would just shoot him dead.

He heard the slow-moving steps of his valet. The man scratched on the door. "My lord, there is a Lord Huntington here to see you. The gentleman is in a highly agitated state."

"Show him to the drawing room and tell him I will be down shortly."

He glanced at Nina; she'd not budged. She slept like a rock. She was the soundest sleeper he'd ever seen. He moved the hair off her neck and nibbled the sensitive skin. "Nina, love. We overslept."

"Hmmm, that's nice." She rolled over and pulled the blankets over her head.

Elliot would have laughed if not for the fact that he might be about to draw in his final breath and meet his maker. He slipped from the bed and dragged his robe over his shoulders.

"I love you," he whispered and pressed a soft kiss to her cheek.

She stirred ever so slightly.

They'd both confessed their feelings to each other several times during the night. Elliot recalled how a tear had trailed down Nina's cheek as she'd admitted she loved him. He wasn't sure if it was fear or joy that had caused it, but he was determined to prove to her during their lives that he would cherish her till he drew his final breath, which hopefully wasn't in a few minutes.

Outside his door, Wilson looked paler than he normally did, as did the housekeeper, who stood behind him.

The valet's gaze veered over Elliot's shoulder to Nina lying in his bed. The man mumbled the Lord's name. Surely a prayer. "Should I see if I can find a constable before you go downstairs?"

"No. But perhaps you should stay up here." He didn't want Wilson or Mrs. Lamb to be hit by a stray bullet if Huntington started shooting wildly.

He descended the steps and stepped into the drawing room to find the marquess pacing back and forth as he rubbed at the muscles in the back of his neck.

"Huntington," Elliot said.

The man spun around to face him. Both worry and agitation etched on his face. "Is my sister here?"

The man's concern for his sister's well-being left Elliot with no option but the truth.

"She is."

"You bastard!" Huntington's keen regard swept over Elliot's robe and bare feet.

Appearing in his robe with not a stitch of clothing on underneath wasn't the wisest way to face Nina's brother while she lay naked in his bed—even if she intended on marrying him.

Like a starved lion spotting its prey, Huntington stalked toward him as if ready to make his kill. "I'm going to bloody well see that you are put six feet under." The marquess swung his fisted hand at Elliot's face.

Better than a bullet to the head, Elliot thought as he ducked the blow. He had only a slim chance of surviving a bullet. And though Elliot had seen the marquess fight at Clapton's Boxing Club and knew him to be an extremely capable fighter, a round of fisticuffs Elliot could handle.

"Huntington, I love your sister and wish to marry her."

The man seemed in too much of a rage to hear him. With a bloodthirsty gleam in his eyes, Nina's eldest brother swung again, clipping Elliot in the ear.

Bloody hell. Elliot might deserve a good trouncing, but he would not let the marquess beat him to a pulp.

"Huntington, I will not stand here like a dunce and let you pummel me."

"I don't want you to. I want you to fight back. That way, I can hit you harder."

Elliot blocked Huntington's next jab, then struck him in the gut.

Air swished out of the marquess's mouth, but he grinned as if relishing the fight. "Come on, you bloody sod."

"Huntington, this won't—" Nina's brother planted a facer on Elliot, halting his words. Pain shot from his jaw to his temple. The inside of his head felt fuzzy.

Elliot stepped back and waved him to come after him. "Come on, Huntington. You want a piece of me, then try to take it. I'm done trying to talk sense into you. If it's a fight you want, I'll give you one."

The left side of Huntington's mouth turned up in a feral grin as he moved toward Elliot.

Huntington favored an aggressive stance, usually putting his opponents on the ropes.

Elliot would not allow him to back him up. He needed to act as aggressive. He struck him with a combination, hitting his jaw, then gut.

The marquess blinked and shook his head as if wishing to clear his vision.

They exchanged several more blows.

The metallic tasted of blood filled Elliot's mouth.

With his sleeve, Huntington swiped at his bleeding nose.

They both were breathing hard when, over Huntington's shoulder, Elliot saw the door inch open.

Wilson hesitantly stuck his head into the room. "My lord, a Lady Caroline Huntington is here."

The man had just gotten the words out when Lady Huntington brushed by the servant and strode into the room, looking out of breath. She narrowed her eyes at them. "Are you two done acting like barbarians?"

Huntington dashed over to her. "Caroline, love, you look unwell. Is something wrong?"

She glowered. "Of course, something is wrong. When I told you it was a possibility Nina was at Lord Ralston's residence, I asked you to wait for me before you came charging over here."

"You didn't walk here, did you?" her husband asked.

"No, I did not walk here. I all but ran. I couldn't wait for a groomsman to ready my carriage. I knew if you found Nina here you would do something like this." She waved her hand to his bleeding nose and disheveled clothes.

"What did you expect me to do, Caroline? Pat Ralston on the back and say, 'Bang-up job, old chum'? 'Hope you had a grand time deflowering my sister'?"

"Of course not. But behaving like this will not settle anything. Is Nina even here?"

The object of their conversation stepped into the room. Though Nina wore her gown, she looked thoroughly tumbled. Her long black hair trailed over her shoulders. Her lips were kiss swollen, and she, like him, wore no shoes.

"What in God's name . . ." She looked at him. "Elliot, you're bleeding." She gave her brother a hard stare. "James, you brute. What have you done?"

"What do you mean what have *I* done? I have a bloody nose, so don't look at him as if I beat him senseless without getting my fair share." Huntington swiped the back of his hand over the blood seeping out of his nostrils.

"Well, you deserved it." Nina set a hand on her hip.

"I came here to protect your honor."

"My honor does not need protecting."

"No?" With a sweep of his hand, he motioned to her

disheveled appearance. "I can see you've already tossed it into the rubbish pail."

Nina's face turned red.

"Watch what you say to my fiancée, Huntington. Or I'll damn well break your nose this time."

Nina turned and smiled at him. "Fiancée. Oh, I like the way that sounds."

"I don't see a ring," Huntington snarled.

Elliot got down on his knee and slipped off his signet ring. "Nina, will you marry me?"

"I will." Excitement glinted in her eyes.

Elliot slipped the ring on her finger.

Huntington folded his arms over his chest. "You really want to marry this bounder?"

"I do."

Elliot wrapped an arm around her waist and pulled her body to his side. "You might not believe me, Huntington, but I love your sister. I will do everything within my powers to make her happy."

"See, he loves her, darling, and she loves him," Caroline said. "And really, isn't that all that matters?"

"Hmmm." Nina's brother glanced around the room pointedly, as if taking in its shabby appearance.

Last week, Elliot had not only worked on the plaster in his bedroom, but he'd repaired the ceiling in this room as well. He'd done a dashed good job, if he could say so himself, but like most of the other rooms in this town house, the rugs were threadbare and the furniture dingy. Elliot realized what Huntington was pondering—the possibility he'd seduced Nina for her dowry. It might have started that way, but he would have walked out of her life if she'd loved Fernbridge. He just wanted her to be happy.

Huntington opened his mouth.

Elliot held up a hand. "Nina, Lady Huntington, will you give us a moment alone?"

"I do not know if we should," Nina said. "If we walk out of this room, are you both going to act rationally? Or are you going to try to knock each other's heads off?"

Huntington released a slow breath. "We will be fine."

Lady Huntington flung her husband a warning glance before she and Nina strode out of the drawing room.

As soon as the door closed, Elliot spoke. "I know what you are thinking. But you are wrong. I love your sister. This has nothing to do with her dowry."

The marquess cocked a brow.

Elliot hated to see the doubt in the man's face. "My uncle did not handle his money wisely. I am not so reckless. I am making repairs. The roof is new, and the bathing room has been updated with running water. I am determined to make this a home your sister will be proud to receive callers in. But more importantly, I will always cherish her."

The door opened. Nina poked her head inside the room. "I don't care about the furnishings. What you just said was the sweetest thing anyone has ever said. And I can help. I will soon be a working woman."

"What?" Elliot blinked.

"I'm going to take a job at Caroline's paper. I will be the illustrator."

"What do you think of that, Lord Ralston?" This from Lady Huntington, who watched him closely over Nina's shoulder.

"Well, it's unconventional, but Nina loves sketching. So, if it pleases her, it pleases me."

"It does?" Nina asked.

"Of course."

Huntington shook his head. "If you are looking for un-conventional, then you have found the right family. But I still don't think it a wise union. Once a scoundrel, always a scoundrel."

"That's not true," Nina interjected. "How about your dear friends Lord Westfield and Lord Adler? Both were notorious rakes and are now happily married."

Lady Huntington stepped over to her husband and poked him in the ribs. "She has you there, darling."

He grunted and rubbed at where his wife had prodded him. "Caroline, I am battered and bruised. Please don't add to my injuries."

She arched a trim brow. "And whose fault is that, dear husband?"

The marquess turned his glare on Elliot. "I want the banns read starting next week."

Elliot looked at Nina. "I wish to acquire a special license."

Nina smiled at him.

"Considering the circumstances, it is probably for the best. If you cannot get the archbishop to agree, let me know." Huntington tugged on the cuffs of his sleeve and straightened his coat, then cast Elliot a hard stare. "I warn you, Ralston—hurt my sister and I'll make you pay."

Chapter Twenty-Seven

In the drawing room of his Charles Street residence, Elliot stood by the mantel and stared at the clock as it ticked the minutes. Hard to believe he was to be married in less than an hour.

He glanced at his sister, who'd arrived in London yesterday. She wore a simple sky-blue gown that he'd purchased for her at Harrods. He'd wanted to buy her something more elaborate, but she'd said it was the bride's day to shine. He had a feeling that wasn't the sole reason. His sister didn't wish to stand out.

"Are you nervous?" Meg asked, grinning. The playful tone in her voice was refreshing after the row they'd had last night. The stubborn girl still insisted she would not return to Mrs. Gibbs's School.

"Anxious more than anything," Elliot replied.

"I can tell. If your foot taps any harder against the floorboards, you might weaken them."

The sound of rain pattering against the panes of glass drew his attention to the window. He walked over and pulled a heavy curtain panel back. The sky had shifted from blue to gray with dark, angry clouds hovering above.

"Hopefully, it will stop before the ceremony." Meg stepped beside him.

He nodded. A black carriage with the Duke of Fernbridge's seal moved slowly down the street. Even with the light rain, he could see Fernbridge's blond hair and the scathing expression on the man's face. Nina had sent a letter to the duke explaining she'd accepted Elliot's marriage proposal.

For a minute, Elliot thought His Grace intended to stop. But it wouldn't be in Fernbridge's nature to concede defeat, and he was sure that was how the duke saw Nina's decision to marry Elliot.

The light drizzle that started before Nina and Elliot's wedding had turned into a torrent of rain by the conclusion of the ceremony. So far, if one disregarded the inclement weather, everything else had gone off without a hitch.

Startling, if Elliot considered the lethal glower Nina's brother James had hurled at him during the ceremony. At one point, he'd wondered if the man contemplated putting a knife in his back. Even her debauched brother, Anthony, was giving him a deadly stare as Elliot and Nina stood in the vestibule, preparing to exit the church.

Elliot's gaze shifted to the Dowager of Huntington. The old woman's countenance was unreadable. Perhaps that was how Nina's grandmother looked while planning someone's demise.

Elliot thought of the urn that had tumbled off the roof at the house party, and, once again, wondered about the old woman. No, a preposterous thought. She was cantankerous, overbearing, but surely not capable of murder. It was an accident. Though it seemed he'd had his share of them.

At least, he'd scraped up enough blunt to have all the wheels on the carriage replaced and the interior reupholstered with navy velvet. He would not have either his wife or sister riding around in an unsafe vehicle.

Nina and Elliot dashed to the carriage and settled inside.

"Husband," she said, talking over the patter of the rain hitting the roof. She smiled. "I've been relishing the thought of calling you husband all week."

Husband? The word seemed odd, yet somehow perfect when she peered at him with her lovely face with no traces of apprehension. The fact that she trusted him meant more than anything else.

"It sounds beautiful coming from you." He touched her cheek, and though it seemed unnecessary with the rivulets of rain slipping over the windows making it almost impossible for anyone to see inside, Elliot tugged the shades down.

In the darkened space, Nina's soft laugh filtered into the air. "What are you up to, Elliot?"

"Throughout the ceremony, all I could think of was making love to you again." He pulled her onto his lap and brushed his lips gently against hers before deepening the kiss.

With a purr of pleasure, she wrapped her arms about his neck and returned his heated kiss.

Having her in his arms with their mouths pressed together felt so right. Perfect. He slipped his hand under the skirt of her white gown, gliding his hands over one of her smooth legs, encased in silk stockings.

She moaned against his mouth and parted her legs slightly.

He found the small slit in her drawers and drew his finger over her already wet folds.

She moaned again.

Damnation. He needed to stop. They were probably close to Huntington's residence and entering the house for the wedding breakfast with a cockstand pressing noticeably against the front of his trousers would surely break some unwritten rule of proper etiquette.

He pulled back. "We need to stop, love."

Nina smiled at him, her eyes a bit glassy from desire, and her breaths, like his, uneven.

She nodded and started to slide off his lap.

"No, stay. Let me hold you for one more minute."

"I'd like that." She rested her head against his shoulder and combed her fingers through the hair at his nape.

The pounding of the heavy raindrops hitting the carriage's roof slowed.

"The rain is stopping." Nina raised her head and glanced at him. "Caroline said rain on a wedding day is good luck. She said it drizzled the day she married my brother."

Elliot wasn't a superstitious man, but he hoped Lady Huntington was right.

The carriage stopped, and Nina slipped off his lap.

Inside Nina's family residence, they greeted the guests.

After the wedding breakfast, which took several hours, they were shown into a large drawing room.

Elliot watched Meg make her way into the room. He frowned. Damp weather sometimes affected his sister's leg, and today was no different, if her limp was any indication. The oppressive guilt Elliot always experienced when he witnessed Meg's pain ratcheted up. He fought the urge to go to her and ask how she felt. She wouldn't appreciate it. She'd told him last night not to treat her differently.

Nina, standing next to him, touched his arm. "All the

chairs are taken. I'll go ask a footman to bring in more, so your sister need not stand."

As she turned to leave, he caught her hand. "I thank you for your thoughtfulness, Nina, but it's fine."

She blinked. "I don't understand."

"Meg doesn't wish for any special treatment."

"Elliot, I would not wish *any* guest to not have the option of sitting, if they desired to."

He motioned with his chin as Talbot walked up to Meg and pointed to a now vacant chair.

Meg scowled at Talbot and limped away.

"See, Talbot was only trying to be helpful, but she's taken offense."

"Aw, I see. She desires others not to offer her special treatment. I can understand that."

"What is wrong with others wishing to help her?" Elliot asked.

"Might I ask what happened? Was it an accident?"

The air in the room suddenly felt scarce of oxygen as if the chimney was blocked, sending smoke into the room. He would eventually tell Nina what had transpired. But he didn't wish her to look at him differently, and if he told her, he feared she might. "Yes, an accident. A terrible accident."

He was relieved when Talbot walked up to them, ending the discussion. Talbot took Nina's hand in his and kissed her gloved fingers. "Might I say, Lady Ralston, you are the loveliest bride I've ever seen."

"Thank you, my lord. You are too kind." She smiled. "If you'll excuse me, I'm going to go chat with my new sister-in-law."

As Nina walked away, Talbot frowned. "I hope she has

better luck than I did. I showed your sister there was an empty chair and she almost bit my head off."

Elliot opened his mouth to respond, but his friend waved off his reply.

"So, you've gone and done it. Gotten yourself leg-shackled."

"I don't look at marriage to Nina that way."

"Yes, yes, I know you think yourself in love. I will admit one thing: Your wife is truly a delightful woman."

"She is extraordinary in every way."

Talbot made a sour face. "Oh, bugger. Am I going to have to hear you wax on poetically about love and marriage?"

"You might." Elliot clapped Talbot on the shoulder. "Wait one day, my naysaying friend, it will be your wedding I'll be attending."

"Won't be for many years. I intend to stay a bachelor until I'm well into my forties. Tell me, what is the status of our acquisition of Langford Teas? Is the inventory matching the books?"

"Yes. Everything is going well. The sale shouldn't be delayed."

"Good."

"I'll be leaving London in about ten days. Nina has asked to see Ralston House."

"Really?" Talbot scrunched up his face.

Elliot nodded. The thought of Nina seeing the rundown residence made him rather apprehensive, but she'd asked to visit, and he would not lie to her or make up an excuse not to go there.

He glanced at Meg, who was smiling as Nina chatted with her. Nina would be a good influence on his sister. Perhaps she'd be able to convince her to return to school.

"Oh, bloody hell, Elliot, you're truly besotted," Talbot said, breaking into his thoughts.

"What?" He blinked at his friend.

"You're staring at your wife as if infatuated. That is why I don't wish to marry. It turns a man's mind to mush."

"You better hope not, if I'm to run Langford Teas and increase the profits." Elliot grinned.

Huntington walked up to them. "Might I have a word in private with you, Ralston?"

"Of course. If you'll excuse me, Talbot."

Elliot followed Huntington into his office. The room was richly furnished with an enormous desk and mahogany paneling covered the walls. They'd already discussed the marriage settlement. He presumed Huntington wanted to threaten him one last time, as he had on several occasions over the last week.

"Have a seat, Ralston." The marquess motioned to one of the two chairs facing the desk.

"If this is going to be another lecture on my need to take care of your sister, I prefer to stand." Elliot was being generous with his wording. Both men knew Huntington had threatened him more than lectured him.

"I don't intend to *lecture* you. This rushed wedding didn't give me much time to have you investigated, but I have come across some rather interesting information." Huntington sat and removed a folder with several sheets of paper from the top drawer of the desk.

He wasn't surprised Huntington had had him investigated. The man clearly loved his sister. Elliot would probably have done the same if the tables had been turned.

"After seeing the inside of your London town house, most of what I found out wasn't that much of a surprise, except for this." Huntington slipped a paper across the polished surface of his desk.

Without picking it up, Elliot could see it was information about Langford Teas. He and Talbot had been careful to not let anyone know of their intention to buy the company. "How did you . . . ?"

The marquess waved a hand in the air as if that wasn't important. "Is this why you married my sister?" Huntington's jaw tensed.

"No. Talbot has the collateral, and I will run the business."

Huntington strummed his fingers on the top of his desk. "I'd be willing to invest in the company."

"Why?"

"Because my sister's happiness is paramount to me."

Elliot slid the paper back across the desk. "I don't need your money, Huntington. You can shove it up your arse."

Instead of looking offended, Huntington grinned.

"Well, if I had known saying that to you would have made you smile, I would have said it a while ago."

"I think you might just prove me wrong, Ralston. And whether you believe it or not, I hope you do, for my sister's sake. And yours."

By the time Elliot, Nina, and his sister made their way to Elliot's Charles Street residence, darkness had settled over the city's sky. Elliot glanced at Nina, who rested her head on his shoulder. Though the two residences were relatively close, Nina had fallen asleep the moment she'd settled inside the vehicle.

Elliot pressed a light kiss to the top of Nina's head.

"You do love her, don't you?" Meg tipped her head sideways and studied him in the dark compartment.

"I do."

Pleasure lit up her face. "I can tell. Don't worry about her family. They will come to realize it as well."

He hoped she was right.

Meg shifted her position, and he noticed how she cringed. Like a puff of smoke, his good mood evaporated, weighed down by his guilt. He needed to make Langford Teas a great success, not only for his wife but for his sister's sake. He'd already decided Nina could use her dowry to purchase whatever she wished, but he'd not touch it, and the remainder would be left for their children. Elliot was sure that if they were prudent and judicious, they could muddle through their tight finances once Elliot and Talbot owned Langford Teas.

"Your month at Ralston House has nearly come to an end. I'm pleased you are going to return to school shortly and finish out the term."

"I don't intend to return to Mrs. Gibbs's School." His sister squared her body like a ram about to butt heads with another equally stubborn ram.

"Why the bloody hell not?" he asked in a low voice that still conveyed his agitation.

"Don't you growl at me."

"Why do you not wish to return?" he asked, attempting to keep his voice calm.

"I can be of more help at Ralston House. Wait until you see what I have done."

"I don't want you to scrub floors and walls. You are a baron's sister."

Meg didn't answer—just avoided his regard by staring out the window.

"Don't you want to attend the London season?"

"No," she replied, her gaze still centered outside.

Elliot tried not to grind his back teeth together. "Why not?"

"I'll end up being a wallflower. Don't you understand?"

"Is that what you think? Meg, you are a lovely young woman."

Silence stretched between them.

Perhaps, it was best not to argue with her. Hopefully, Nina would know what to do. God, he hoped she would, since he was at a complete loss. He'd also have to admit what had happened to Meg.

The carriage's wheels slowed as the vehicle pulled in front of their town house.

Meg motioned to Nina. "She's the soundest sleeper I've ever seen besides Camille Edgerton, who slept like a rock at school."

His sister's mood appeared to have shifted back to less defensive.

The coachman opened the door and assisted Meg as she stepped out of the carriage.

"Nina, darling. We are here." He drew his finger over his wife's cheek.

A slight smile curved up one side of her mouth, but, otherwise, she didn't move. He lifted her into his arms and tried not to curse when he conked his head on the roof of the carriage as he carried her out.

"How romantic, Elliot. You're going to carry your bride over the threshold," Meg whispered.

He grinned. "I don't have much of a choice."

"Oh, I think you would have done it anyway," his sister said.

True. Though he'd hoped his wife would have been

awake when he'd carried her over the threshold . . . and when he carried her to their bed. *Their bed.* Good God, he was married, and he would be waking up with Nina beside him every morning. He liked the idea, though he didn't think Zeb would be as pleased.

Meg opened the door and it squeaked, sending a bone-chilling noise into the night.

Elliot glanced at Nina and couldn't help his smile. She'd not even blinked.

Since he'd told the servants not to wait up, no one rushed forward to greet them.

Meg followed Elliot up the stairs.

"Good night, Meg." He kissed her cheek, then carried his sleeping wife into their bedchamber.

Chapter Twenty-Eight

With Nina sleeping and cradled in his arms, Elliot stepped into the bedchamber and pushed the door closed with his foot. Thankfully, the grate was lit, taking the chill out of the room. And, by some miracle, Zeb was fast asleep on his own pallet.

After laying Nina down, he removed her satin shoes and draped a woolen blanket over her. He strode over to Zeb and ruffled the fur behind his floppy ears before patting his head. "Be a good fellow and stay here throughout the night. That's a special lady lying over there."

Elliot stepped into the adjoining bathing room. One of the first improvements he'd made upon taking residence in this town house was to modernize the bathing room. He turned on the hydronic pump, sending warm water up from the kitchen to the copper tub, then stripped off his clothes and lowered himself into the crystalline water.

The hinges on the door squeaked.

A sleepy-eyed Nina stood at the threshold. "Why didn't you wake me?"

"Oh, I tried." He laughed. "My sister says you sleep more soundly than one of her old school chums."

An adorable shade of red crept over her cheeks. "Please don't tell me I snore."

"Then I won't tell you."

"Goodness, do I?"

"No." He grinned.

Nina released a heavy breath. "You are a tease."

He wanted to tease her even more, but in a different way. He crooked his finger and held out his hand. "Why don't you join me?"

She stepped closer. As she did so, her hands were already unfastening the pearl buttons on the front of her dress. The fabric parted and she slipped it off her shoulders and arms. It fell and billowed around her feet.

His cock grew hard and thick.

While holding his gaze, she removed her other garments and stood completely naked except for her silk stockings and lace garters, which were adorned with beads and stitched blue flowers.

"I heard in Lancashire they believe a bride should wear something blue on her wedding day." She traced the tip of her nail over the blue flowers.

Elliot's gaze settled on her finger, which was moving gently over the garter on her thigh. He wanted to remove the silky scrap of embroidered material with his teeth.

Nina pulled the small stool in front of her and set one foot on it, giving him a perfect view of her sex, nestled below the triangle of curls. While glancing coquettishly at him from her lowered lashes, she slowly unrolled the first stocking.

He nearly climaxed. Holding his body in check, he swallowed hard and grabbed on to the side of the tub, forcing himself not to pull her into the water, stockings and all.

She lifted her other leg and rolled down the second

stocking with the same deliberate slowness. What an adept pupil his wife was.

"If you don't get in here soon, I might drag you in." Once again, he held out his hand.

Taking it, she stepped into the tub.

"Sit on my lap, love, and let me bathe you," he said huskily.

Nina glanced down at the water and his engorged cock. A small lump moved in her throat. His sweet wife knew what he wanted. She slipped into the water, placing her knees on each side of his body, and sucked in a breath as she lowered herself onto his hard length. "I don't think I can take you all the way in at this angle."

"You can," he said. "Just relax." He licked her nipple before taking it into his mouth.

Nina's eyes drifted closed, and she lowered herself, sheathing him completely with her tight, wet warmth.

Unable to stop himself, he bucked his hips.

Her eyes opened and she smiled. "Do that again."

With his hands on her bum, he moved as she rode him. Her rhythm matching his. Shortly, they would both find their pleasure. He cupped the back of her head and brought her mouth down to his and tangled his tongue with hers.

Her sex clenched against his manhood.

"Come on, love. That's it." He placed his hands on her perfect derrière again and squeezed.

Nina's breaths were short and shallow. Her body stilled and she tipped her head back as she reached her climax.

The sight of his wife with beads of water glistening on her naked skin as she orgasmed was the most erotic thing he'd ever seen, and Elliot toppled over the edge with her.

* * *

In their dark bedchamber, Nina snuggled closer into her husband's embrace. His heart beat steadily under her ear. She shifted and realized the sheets below the counterpane were tangled about their legs. After she and Elliot had made love in the bathtub, they'd washed each other. Her soapy hands had glided over the hard planes of his body as his had traveled over the softer curves of hers.

She smiled as she remembered his wicked words about there being so much more a couple could do once married.

Elliot's arms tightened about her. "What are you smiling about?"

She lifted her head off his chest.

He watched her with the same intense gaze as last night.

"I think I'm going to like being married."

Smiling, he arched a brow. "You just think?"

"Well, I've only been married less than a day," she teased.

"Perhaps there's something I can do to make you say you are enraptured with being married."

"You're doing it right now."

"Am I?"

"Yes, this room is dashed cold. So, I'm enjoying you holding me."

"I know a better way to make you warm besides just holding you."

"Ah, you're willing to get up and revive the fire?" She laughed.

"What a killjoy my new wife is." Elliot grinned and kissed the tip of her nose. "Your wish is my command."

Naked as the day he was born, her husband slipped from the bed and padded across the dark room to the cooling grate. Missing the warmth of his skin against hers, she pulled the blankets tighter around herself as she watched him. He seemed so at ease with his body. It made her think of when she'd undressed for him. She'd acted confident, but inside she had felt anxious, her stomach a bit queasy, but the look of appreciation as she'd removed her clothing had bolstered her confidence.

As he squatted before the grate, her gaze drifted down the breadth of his shoulders and to his bum. Elliot possessed a beautiful body.

He stood and turned around.

She tried to keep her gaze on his face and not on his manhood and the crop of dark hair around it as he strode back to the bed. "Aren't you cold?" she asked.

Elliot glanced down at his erection. "Not in the least." He slipped into the bed and pulled her close to him. "Good lord, woman, your feet are like icicles." He tossed the blankets over his head and made his way under them to her feet.

"What are you doing?" She laughed as his hands rubbed at her feet.

"Warming you," came his disembodied voice from under the blankets.

She lifted the bedding and peered down at him.

"Get back up here." She smacked his naked arse.

Laughing, he pulled her back into his arms and held her tight to him. "Night, wife."

"Good night, husband."

Nina had learned from her lovemaking with Elliot that the human mouth could do so much more than consume food. Yet, even in her groggy state, she questioned Elliot's desire to wake her up in the morning by licking at her cheek with robust enthusiasm.

She opened her eyes and almost screamed at the bloodshot eyes staring at her and the large snout only an inch from her face. She might have contained her yelp, but her hand squeezed Elliot's thigh as she realized she lay sandwiched between him and Zeb.

"Well, aren't you frisky this morning, Nina?" Elliot mumbled, slipping a hand over one of her breasts.

"Not exactly," she replied, staring at Zeb, who, in turn, stared at her as if she were an interloper. "Elliot, it appears we are not alone."

"Not alone?" he echoed. Then he jerked upward into a sitting position and stared at Zeb. "Damnation, Zeb. Even on my wedding night, you don't possess the decency to stay in your own bed."

The dog sat up and bowed his massive head and gave what Nina could only describe as a whimper.

"Oh, Elliot, you've hurt the poor dear's feelings."

Next to her, Elliot flopped onto his back and released a long weary sigh. "Fine. If you want him to invade our bed so be it, but one morning you could end up on the floor."

Our bed? Nina stopped patting the dog's head and peered at her husband. "Am I to share this bedchamber, Elliot?"

"I had hoped you would, but it will be bloody crowded with Zeb in it as well."

True. And after spending a night snuggled up next to Elliot, there was no place else Nina would rather be. "Zeb," she said, in the sweetest voice she could muster, "you need to return to your own bed."

"Good luck with trying to get him to do so," Elliot grumbled.

But he'd no sooner finished talking than the dog slowly slipped off the bed to make his way to his pallet on the floor.

Elliot blinked as if watching a mirage. "I'm not sure how you spoke to him differently than I have a thousand times before, but I should reward your genius."

"And how do you intend to do that?"

Slowly, he trailed his finger over one of her breasts before he lifted the blankets and climbed under them, and this time it was not her feet his wicked hands stroked.

Chapter Twenty-Nine

Several days later, as the sun rose beyond the heavy curtain panels, Nina snuggled tighter into her husband's embrace. With her head resting on his chest, she listened to the beat of his heart. A few minutes ago, after their round of lovemaking, the *thump, thump, thump* had slowed to a smooth cadence.

They'd fallen into a pattern of lingering in each other's arms in the morning, even when they had not made love. Nina relished the act of making love with her husband. The glorious joining of two bodies evoked a pleasure difficult to describe. But holding each other afterward was glorious as well—a wonderful calm to an act that was sometimes primal and all-consuming.

"What are you thinking?" She lifted her head and peered at Elliot, wondering if he was feeling the same way about just lying together.

A wicked grin turned up one side of his mouth. "That in a few minutes, I'll be ready to make love to you again."

Well, it appeared her solitary thoughts were just that. "I was thinking how I like snuggling with you. Don't you enjoy it?" She heard the almost wistful tone in her voice.

"Always." He wrapped his arms tighter about her.

Smiling, Nina rested her head back on his chest. "Today,

Meg and I are going to begin packing up all the books in the library. The painters will be arriving in two days."

Elliot released a slow breath as he grappled with the fact that it was Nina's dowry that paid for these repairs. Though she had initiated it, not he. He was impatient to get the sale of Langford Teas settled and try to grow the business.

"After my meeting with Talbot, I'll help pack and carry the books into the attic."

"Meg wants to bring several crates of books with us to Ralston House."

The room grew quiet. Nina glanced at him. "Elliot, are we still leaving in three days?"

"Yes. After my meeting with my solicitor."

"I cannot wait to visit our country home. Perhaps we can hold a family gathering there in a few weeks."

A gathering? Elliot cringed. He'd been dreading the moment his wife laid eyes on the interior of Ralston House. "Nina, the property was neglected. It needs a great deal of work."

She patted his chest. "I'm sure it isn't quite so dreadful."

No. It was bloody well worse than she could imagine. A money pit that would suck up a great deal of her dowry if she allowed it. He only hoped it didn't rain. If it did, the sound of water landing in the metal pails in the east wing would echo through the house. A *plop, plop, plop* almost capable of driving one mad.

"I'm excited about tonight." She ran the tip of her finger down the center of his chest.

Under the bedding, his cock twitched, coming to life again.

"You haven't changed your mind about accepting

James's invitation to join him and Caroline at the theater, have you?" Nina peered at him with her warm, honey-colored eyes.

Truthfully, the thought of sitting in Huntington's box at the theater with the man glowering at him held little appeal, but for Nina's sake, he would try to get along with his brother-in-law. "Of course not. I'm looking forward to it."

One side of her sweet lips turned upward into a disbelieving grin. "I think that's balderdash, but I thank you for agreeing to go."

"Do you really wish to thank me?" He slipped his hand between them to palm one of her breasts.

With a giggle, his wife slipped from the mattress and dragged her silky robe over her shoulders. "Though I'd love to stay in bed, we need to get up. Already, I wonder what your sister and the servants must think of us, lolling around in bed so late every day."

Elliot rolled onto his back, letting the absence of his wife's warm skin cool his fervor. "They think we are newlyweds."

She looked at him, her expression serious. "Is it always like this, Elliot?"

"Like what, darling?"

She averted her eyes and fiddled with the sash on her robe. "You know."

"Do you mean the lovemaking?"

"Yes, and the feeling of contentment in one's marriage."

With a grin, Elliot folded his arms behind his head and stared at his beautiful wife. "As far as the first part of your question, definitely not."

Even with her face cast downward, he could see a slow smile turn up her lips. He was telling her the truth. He didn't want to think about past lovers, but making love to Nina was different. It had been since the first time he'd kissed her. Sex was one thing, but adding love to the equation shifted it to something completely unmatched. He'd never wanted to lie around in bed afterward. No, he'd wanted to go. Sex had been an act solely based on physical release and pleasure with little, if any, emotional connection. He had wanted it that way. Not now.

"And what of being married?" Nina asked with an inquiring expression.

He chuckled. "I've never been, but if my parents' and grandparents' marriages are any indications, this is very different." He extended his hand, and she placed hers in it. Her fingers were cool, and he rubbed his hands over them to warm the skin. "Love makes it different. Without it, it can be strained. My grandparents' marriage was arranged. They never loved each other, nor did my parents, for that matter. But we chose each other."

"We did, didn't we?"

"Yes." He gave her a playful smack on her luscious bum. "Now, you better move away before I pull you into this bed and keep you all to myself for the remainder of the day."

"Don't you have a meeting with Talbot this afternoon?"

"I do."

"Care to tell me what it is about?" She tipped her head to the side and studied him.

"Our future, my love. Our future."

Nina carried a small empty wooden crate into the library. While Elliot attended his business meeting, she and Meg filled several crates with books to be carted up to the attic, so they would not get paint splatters on them. Meg marked the boxes she wanted brought to Ralston House. Her new sister-in-law had revealed that some rather ravenous bookworms had caused a great deal of destruction to the collection there.

Releasing a slow breath, Meg gingerly lowered herself into a chair and rubbed at her left leg. She glanced up, and seeing Nina, the girl quickly pulled her hand away as if reluctant to have anyone see her massaging the area, which obviously ached.

Nina opened her mouth to ask Meg how she felt, but snapped it closed as she remembered Elliot warning her away from inquiring. Instead, she set the empty crate down and plopped into the chair next to Meg. Perhaps if she sat as well, the girl would rest a bit. "My mouth is parched and my nose itches from the smell of these musty books and the dust motes. What do you say we have some tea?"

Meg's sideways glance conveyed she knew what Nina was about.

For a moment, Nina thought Meg would be stubborn and not accept the offer, but she nodded.

In truth, Nina's mouth was dry. She stood and rang the bell pull.

Meg laughed.

Startled, Nina spun around to find her new sister-in-law grinning broadly. She gave her a questioning look.

"I hate to say this, but it might be quicker, even with my sore leg, if I go and get the tea."

Elliot's sister admitting her leg plagued her seemed like a breakthrough. Nina glanced at the door to make sure Mrs. Lamb hadn't entered the room. "I've noticed both the housekeeper and valet are rather like turtles."

"Uncle Phillip asked Elliot on his deathbed to keep

them on, along with Zeb. I don't think Elliot would have tossed them out anyway."

Nina didn't think so either. Her husband worked at giving a devil-may-care attitude, but there was so much more to him. And as far as the dog, Elliot might act like he resented Zeb, but deep down he truly cared for the bloodhound.

Mrs. Lamb shuffled into the room—the soles of her shoes making the same *swish, swish, swish* the valet made when he walked.

"Mrs. Lamb, will you bring us tea?"

The housekeeper pulled out her hearing trumpet. "What, my lady?"

"Tea," Nina repeated in a louder voice.

"Yes, my lady." The elderly woman turned around and moved slowly out of the room.

"Meg, tonight Elliot and I are going to see a play. I know he asked you to attend with us and you told him no, but is there anything I could say that might sway you to change your mind?"

The girl drew her bottom lip between her teeth.

It was evident her sister-in-law wanted to go; she just needed a push. "The newspapers are proclaiming *Robinson Crusoe* extremely well done, and the performances far superior to any other play in London."

"I've never been to the theater. What would I wear?"

"We are close in size, and I have a canary-yellow gown that would look divine on you." Nina reached for Meg's hand and squeezed it.

Meg lifted her solemn face to Nina's. "Are you sure you wouldn't mind if I went?"

"I would be overjoyed. Please say you will attend." Nina pressed her hands together as if praying.

Still looking unsure, Meg nodded.

"Wonderful!" Nina exclaimed and wrapped her arms about her sister-in-law.

Elliot could hardly believe Nina had been able to convince Meg to join them at the theater. His wife was a miracle worker. He glanced at his sister. She looked beautiful and so grown up in the yellow gown that Nina had lent her.

Meg's already large eyes grew wider as she walked around the theater's circular balcony and peered up at the soaring ceiling of the rotunda.

"Are you anxious to see the play?" he asked, leaning closer to her.

A smile spread across Meg's face. "I am."

"Have I told you how pleased both Nina and I are that you decided to join us?"

"At least a dozen times," she replied, her smile broadening.

With a chuckle, Elliot glanced at Nina. She wore a violet gown with a low neckline. He wanted to pull her into the next alcove they came across and kiss her senseless.

Ruddy hell, he was a randy bastard who couldn't seem to get enough of his wife. Thankfully, she didn't seem to mind. In fact, she equaled him in her desire.

As if reading his mind, she grinned at him.

"I must be the envy of every other gentleman in attendance, since I am accompanied by the two loveliest women in all of London."

Meg giggled.

Startled by the sound, Elliot's regard shifted to his

sister. He squeezed his wife's hand. She really was a miracle worker.

"Lord Ralston, how are you?" a gentleman to his left asked.

He glanced to his side to see Lord Hampton. Thankfully, Elliot didn't see the gentleman's wife, Amelia. The woman had implied at Lord and Lady Hathaway's house party that she'd be open to a liaison with Elliot. She was trouble with a capital T. Hampton had gotten himself a young bride, but she was not a faithful one. Poor bastard.

"Well, Hampton, and yourself?"

"Jolly good. I hear felicitations are in order." He smiled at Nina. "Lady Ralston. Brava on getting this rascal to settle down."

Elliot cringed. Living down his bachelor ways would take some time, but having other men remind Nina of the fact that'd he'd been a cad wasn't helpful.

"Thank you, my lord." Nina's smile dimmed when Amelia stepped beside her husband.

"You both know my wife, Amelia, don't you?"

Next to him, Elliot felt Nina stiffen, though she said hello, as did he.

"And who is this lovely young lady?" Hampton asked, peering at Meg.

"Lord and Lady Hampton, may I introduce you to my sister, Margaret Havenford."

Greetings were exchanged.

Nina had grown uncharacteristically quiet, and Elliot felt relief when, at the top of the wide staircase, the Hamptons went to the left and they turned to the right.

"You don't care for Amelia?" he inquired in a low voice.

"Not particularly."

"I don't either," he whispered.

That seemed to release the tension in her body.

As they made their way down the narrow corridor that led to the boxes closest to the stage, a door opened ahead of them, and the Duke of Fernbridge stepped out.

"Your Grace." Nina smiled tentatively at the man.

His gaze roamed over Nina as if she were an odious offering from a costermonger selling day-old fruit.

Elliot's hand clenched.

The duke's narrow-eyed gaze shifted to Elliot, and a sneer twisted the man's mouth. Then, without a word, Fernbridge brushed past, giving them a direct cut.

Nina's face paled. "I did not think he would be so angry."

Elliot squeezed her hand.

"Who was that rude gentleman?" Meg asked, frowning.

"No one of great importance," Elliot replied.

They stepped inside Nina's family box. Lord and Lady Huntington were already seated. Thankfully, Nina's ill-tempered grandmother wasn't in attendance. The woman was probably still sulking over Nina's and his marriage.

James stood and greeted Nina with a kiss before welcoming Meg. He shook Elliot's hand in a tight grip.

Elliot forced a smile. "Huntington, thank you for the invitation."

Releasing a frustrated breath, Lady Huntington gave her husband an elbow in the ribs.

A surprised *oof* escaped the marquess's mouth, causing him to release his attempted-bone-crushing grip.

Elliot grinned at his new brother-in-law. "You'll have to do better than that, Huntington."

A devious smirk settled on the man's face. "Want to meet at Clapton's Boxing Club tomorrow?"

"No," Nina said, scowling at them. "I will not have my husband and brother brawling."

Lady Huntington hugged Nina and greeted Meg, who stared cautiously at Huntington. "Don't let my husband's lack of civility scare you, Meg. His bark is much worse than his bite." She turned to Elliot. "I am beyond pleased you could join us."

"Thank you, Lady Huntington," Elliot replied.

"Lady Huntington?" she echoed, arching a brow. "We are family—you must call me Caroline. And your new brother-in-law, James. Right, darling?"

Huntington made a noise that sounded more like he had indigestion than was agreeing.

Ignoring the man, he said, "Only if you will call me Elliot."

"Very well." The woman's green eyes smiled.

They took their seats. Throughout the performance, Elliot enjoyed the pleasure on both Nina's and Meg's faces. At the end of the act, the curtain closed and the lights in the theater grew brighter, announcing intermission, while the orchestra played the entr'acte.

"Would anyone care for a refreshment?" Elliot asked, standing.

A round of chatter started as everyone requested their beverage choice.

Huntington unfolded himself from his seat. "Do you need help?"

The last thing Elliot wanted, besides a bullet to the brain, was Huntington accompanying him and making those grunting noises he made while in Elliot's company. But he needed to try to make peace with the man. "Thank you, Huntington."

"James," his brother-in-law grumbled.

"James," Elliot repeated with as much enthusiasm as the marquess had said it.

Several minutes after Elliot and James left the theater box, Meg whispered, "Is there a water closet?"

"Of course." Nina stood. "Caroline, we will be back shortly."

After exiting the public loo, Nina asked Meg if she wanted to meet James in the Grand Salon.

The expression on Meg's face reflected her uncertainty.

Her sister-in-law's limp didn't seem as distinct, but perhaps Meg worked hard to make it less obvious. "If you do not wish to, we can return to our seats."

"No, I'd like to see it."

"So how are you enjoying the play?" Nina asked as they made their way.

"I am so glad you and Elliot invited me." The girl's face beamed with pleasure.

Nina interlocked her arm with Meg's. "We are exceptionally pleased you decided to join us."

The room was crowded. Nina scanned the bar area and didn't see Elliot or her brother.

"Perhaps they have already returned to their seats," Meg said.

Nina perched on her toes. She was about to suggest they leave when she spotted James at the bar area and Elliot behind him talking with that shrew Amelia. Her stomach knotted as the woman placed the flat of her palm on Elliot's chest.

Chapter Thirty

Elliot narrowed his eyes and jerked back as Lady Amelia Hampton set her hand on his chest. Good God, anyone who saw the contact would assume they were lovers. He was tired of trying to just ignore the woman. It wasn't working.

"Madam," he hissed through gritted teeth. "We need to get one thing straight. There shall be no liaison between us. Not now or in the future. I love my wife."

Startled by the vehemence, Amelia's eyes flashed blue fire and her lips puckered as if he'd shoved a piece of salty, raw eel in her mouth.

"Have I made myself clear?"

Red-faced, she spun on her heel and stormed away.

Releasing a breath, Elliot glanced around the room. His gaze stopped on Lord Hampton. The old man looked irate. Had he witnessed his wife placing her hand on him? Did he think they were lovers?

Hell and fire. He was tempted to go up to Hampton, but what would he say? *Put a leash on your wife, you old fool, she's after anyone with two legs and a cock?* Probably best to not say anything.

Still holding the two glasses in his hand, Elliot turned to see if Huntington had collected their other drinks. If he'd thought Hampton's gaze angry, Huntington's was feral. He stared at Elliot as if ready to rip his head off.

Jesus. The last thing Elliot wanted to do was explain to the man he was not bedding Lady Hampton.

Huntington's attention traveled to a point beyond Elliot, and his new brother-in-law's mien shifted from barely contained rage to one of concern.

Elliot glanced over his shoulder. Nina and Meg were both staring at him.

The devastated look on his wife's face made him feel as if someone had slashed a blade across his heart.

Damnation. It was like he'd built a house of cards and someone was fanning it with a bellow and any moment it would topple down.

Nina spun around and strode from the salon.

Meg, nibbling on her lower lip, looked unsure if she should go after her or stay. His sister shot him a disappointed expression and strode after Nina.

Several people, witnessing Nina quickly weaving through the crush, eyed Elliot, obviously wondering what was going on.

Christ. Elliot started after her and caught up to Meg, her limp more pronounced.

"Be careful, Meg," he said, fearing she was trying to move so fast she might fall.

His sister turned her stormy eyes on him. "It is not I who needs to be careful."

He gritted his teeth. If he could not even get his sister to believe him, he was doomed. "It's not what it looked like."

"You are not carrying on with that woman?" she asked in a harsh whisper.

"No, of course not," he replied in a low voice. "Do you believe me?"

She released a relieved sigh. "I do, but it is not me you must convince."

His sister's belief in him was like a balm to his bleeding heart. He glanced over his shoulder to see Huntington making his way toward them.

"Go catch up to your wife, Elliot, and explain. I shall stall her brother by asking him to assist me with making my way back to his box."

With a nod, Elliot strode ahead and caught up to his wife in the corridor near Huntington's box. "Nina, wait."

She turned. Her jaw was clenched so tight it probably sent a sharp pain into her head. His heart bled a little more when he noticed the glassy sheen reflecting in her lovely eyes.

He set the glasses he was holding down on a mahogany hall table and took her hands in his. "That wasn't what it looked like."

"I didn't think it was."

Her response startled him. He blinked. "You didn't?"

"No, I trust you. But I needed to leave before I did something rash."

"Like?"

"Take the two glasses you were holding and dump them over Amelia's head."

Elliot's bark of laughter had two people farther down the hall turning to peer at them.

"Why, you little minx. I was concerned you thought—"

"No. I'm not blind, Elliot. I witnessed how Amelia looked at you at Lord and Lady Hathaway's house party, and your shocked expression revealed you did not initiate the contact. It took nearly everything I possessed to leave the salon without confronting her. I didn't want to cause a scene. God knows my grandmother would never have let me live it down, and the vision I had of Amelia with champagne dripping down her face was rather tempting."

"Thank you." He squeezed her hand.

"For what?" Nina tipped her head to the side.

"For trusting me."

She smiled.

Huntington and Meg were walking toward them. Meg's face reflected her concern. Huntington appeared ready to put a bullet in Elliot's skull.

"Ralston," Huntington said in a deadly, low voice. "I wish to have a word with you."

The lights in the corridor flicked, announcing the play was about to resume.

Ignoring the man's demand. Elliot studied Meg. Her leg probably ached, and most likely she wished to sit.

"Not now, Huntington," he replied, in a voice as steely as his brother-in-law's.

As the carriage moved past a gas lamppost, light highlighted the interior of the dim compartment. Since they'd started on their journey home, Nina had been quiet. Elliot hoped she wasn't thinking about Lady Amelia Hampton.

Elliot glanced at his sister, sitting across from them. Meg's eyes had drifted closed only a minute after they'd settled into the equipage. She'd obviously found the theater both exciting and overwhelming. All evening, he couldn't help wondering how her leg felt, but refrained from inquiring.

With a cautious smile, Nina twisted on the seat and peered at him. Her warm-colored eyes looked darker in the dim space. She skimmed her gloved hand over his chest. "What did my brother say to you outside after we left the theater?"

The man had railed at him until Elliot had thought they'd come to blows. Well, at least he'd wanted to plant a facer on Huntington. His brother-in-law, once again, informed Elliot if he hurt Nina, he'd regret it. The rage visible on Huntington's face was understandable. Elliot wasn't sure how he would have reacted if Meg was married and her new husband was seen with another woman touching him as if they were more than acquaintances. The most important part was that Nina trusted him.

He pulled Nina closer to his side. "Nothing of importance."

"I told him Amelia is just an unhappy and unpleasant person, but my brother is overprotective."

"You think?" he asked with a low chuckle.

"He will come around. I promise. Give him time." She bit her lip. "What does it mean to bugger yourself?"

The question startled Elliot, and he coughed as if a piece of food were lodged in his throat. "Where did you hear that?"

"From you."

"Me?" He cocked an eyebrow. "When?"

Nina snuggled closer to him and ran a finger over the edge of his jaw. "When you and my brother were talking outside the carriage."

He kissed her forehead. "Were you eavesdropping?"

"Ha! You were both talking quite loudly. And do not try to change the subject."

He leaned close and allowed the warmth of his breath to ghost over her ear. He loved the way goosepimples scattered over her skin when he did that and regretted not being able to see them in the dim compartment, but he felt her slight shiver and heard the way her breathing quickened. He whispered what it meant.

"Oh, that's . . ." She tipped her head to the side. "Quite physically impossible."

"It is," he replied, a grin tugging up the edges of his mouth.

The carriage came to a stop and swayed to the side as their coachman lowered himself from his perch. The man opened the door.

Elliot helped Nina out. "I'm going to carry Meg inside. She won't admit it, but I'm quite sure walking around the theater made her leg ache."

"You're a good brother, Elliot." Nina ran a hand over his arm.

The smile on his face felt as if someone had attached lead weights to his cheeks. He was not a good brother. He'd caused Meg all the pain she contended with every day, and *nothing* he could do would ever change that fact.

Inside, Elliot was nearly at Meg's room when her eyes fluttered open.

Looking dazed, his sister glanced around. "Put me down, Elliot. I'm quite capable of walking!"

He ignored her complaints until they reached her bed-chamber door and lowered his sister to her feet.

She smacked him in the chest. "You big ape, I told you I could walk. You are so stubborn."

"And you aren't?" Elliot bit back, tossing a wink at his wife, who was grinning at them.

"I'm not as stubborn as you," Meg replied. "What do you think, Nina?"

Nina laughed. "Oh, I'm staying out of this discussion."

Smiling, Meg clasped Nina's hand and hugged her. "Thank you so very much to both of you for inviting me to attend the play. I enjoyed it tremendously." On her tiptoes, Meg pressed a quick kiss to his cheek, then entered her bedchamber.

With his fingers intertwined with Nina's, Elliot led his wife down the corridor and into their bedroom.

Zeb glanced up from his pallet. The animal had returned to sleeping there. Most likely, the dog had concluded there wasn't enough room for him. Though occasionally he still tried to join them in the mornings.

"Hello, you handsome fellow," Nina said, patting the dog's head. "Did you miss us?"

Zeb made a whining noise as if he'd been sorely neglected.

Nina reached into her reticule, unwrapped something, then set it on the floor in front of Zeb.

Why, the sly little minx. "Good lord, woman. Have you been bribing him all along?"

"I have."

"You're a genius."

Grinning, she strode to the fire and rubbed her hands close to the heat.

For a moment, Elliot could do nothing more than take in the beauty of his wife as the glow from the grate sent wisps of light onto her face. "I have an idea as to how I could warm you," he said.

"Do you now?" she replied. The low, sensual texture of her voice caused his manhood to grow hard.

"Definitely." He stepped behind her, pulled her back against his chest, and nuzzled her neck.

Her head lolled to the side, giving him better access, as she let out a contented sigh.

"I think my lovely wife needs a refresher course in lesson four."

Nina giggled. "I think we covered lessons four, five, and six last night."

They had, but tonight, Elliot wanted to pull the bedding off the mattress and place it on the floor before the hearth, so he could make love to her in front of the fireplace and watch the light dance across her naked skin.

Zeb's low growl, followed by a gruff bark, pulled Elliot from his thoughts.

Nina turned around. A slim line formed between her brows. "What do you think that's about?"

"He probably heard a cat."

Zeb bounded toward the door and scratched at the surface.

"Do you think Wilson forgot to take him out? Perhaps your lessons should wait. Better to let Zeb out now than in the middle of the night."

Having had to do that several times, Elliot silently agreed. He nuzzled Nina's neck one more time. "When I come back, I'm going to finish what we started."

"Is that a promise?"

"Most definitely."

As soon as Elliot opened the bedroom door, Zeb dashed down the stairs as if on the scent of a fox. Elliot couldn't remember seeing the hound move so fast.

After stepping out the French doors that led to the terrace, the bloodhound sniffed at the ground.

"I hope this isn't going to be an hour-long process, Zeb," Elliot grumbled.

The dog ignored him and continued sniffing while walking toward the shrubs at the side of the yard.

Elliot stepped off the terrace and moved down the flagstone path. At the rear of the yard, he noticed the wrought-iron gate in the brick wall was wide open. He strode toward it.

Moonlight glinted off the metal lock, broken, lying on the cobbles beyond the gate.

Elliot strode through the opening and crouched to pick it up. A shadow darkened the ground in front of him.

The fine hair on Elliot's nape lifted. He glanced over his shoulder to see a short cudgel lifted above his head. The weapon came down hard, striking the side of his skull.

Chapter Thirty-One

The unexpected impact of being struck in the head sent Elliot to the cold pavement.

Damp and gritty cobbles pressed against the side of his face. A buzzing filled his ears, and pain seared his skull like a branding iron pressed to the back of his skull.

In the dim light, he saw his hooded assailant lift his weapon, intent on striking him again. Acting fast, Elliot stuck out his foot, hitting the bloke in the shin with as much strength as his foggy brain could muster. His heel slammed against bone and flesh. Not hard enough to break the bastard's leg, but with enough force to send his attacker off balance to stumble backward several feet.

The blackguard landed on his arse and uttered an *oof*.

Elliot tried to scramble onto his hands and knees, but the grayness closing in on his vision and the way his surroundings listed sideways made it almost impossible.

His attacker stood and moved toward him.

Forcing all his resolve and strength into his arms, Elliot pressed his hands to the pavement to lift himself to his feet. His body shifted sideways as he tried to gain his equilibrium.

His assailant drew the cudgel back several more inches

as if hoping to strike a final blow that would split Elliot's skull open like a soft-boiled egg cracked against the edge of a plate.

The man was nearly upon him when from the corner of his eye, Elliot saw Zeb barreling toward them, uttering a low, menacing growl.

The hooded fellow cursed and took off down the mews.

Zeb started after him.

"Stay!" Elliot commanded, knowing Zeb's bark was worse than his bite, and if his assailant struck the old dog with his cudgel, it might do the dog in.

As his attacker moved farther away and into the dark night, the clap of his shoes pounding against the cobbles receded until they could not be heard.

Zeb whimpered and nudged Elliot's hand with his snout.

Wincing, he reached out and patted the dog's massive head. "Good, boy."

The door to the carriage house opened, and Rigby, looking as though he'd hastily dressed, stepped out.

"My lord," the man said, rushing over to him. "Were you set upon?"

Elliot gingerly touched his throbbing skull and grunted his reply.

"Let me help you inside, then I'll go fetch a doctor and constable?"

"I can get myself inside. And there is no need to fetch either a doctor or a constable," Elliot replied, his voice gravelly.

"My lord, are you sure?"

"Yes." A constable would ask him questions, and Elliot wondered if his assailant had been looking to get into the house to rob it or if it was something more sinister. The attack had seemed personal. Hard to discount this was the second incident. Third, if he included the episode with his carriage. A constable would ask if anyone had threatened him lately. Nina's brother's face flashed in his mind. James had been livid at the theater. Could he have hired some lackey?

"At least let me help you inside," the coachman said.

"No, I'm fine."

The man gave him a dubious look but nodded.

Feeling as if his brain was swathed in fog, Elliot made his way back to the house and stepped through the French doors, Zeb trailing him. The hound's big brown eyes peered up at Elliot as if he was as doubtful as Rigby as to the state of Elliot's health.

As he stepped into the entry hall, the room began to spin. Gritting his teeth, he braced a hand on the entry table, attempting to gather his equilibrium. Under his weight, the table wobbled. The green vase on it toppled over. With an explosive noise, it slammed against the tiled floor, sending shards of pottery across the surface.

A crashing noise downstairs echoed throughout the town house as if wishing to wake everyone within its walls. Chest pounding against her ribs, Nina flung open the bedchamber door and rushed down the stairs.

As she made her way, she saw the vase from the hall table broken—its pieces of green pottery scattered across the tiled floor. Then Elliot, his back facing her, came into view. One of his hands cradled his head. The other held on to the edge of the hall table with a white-knuckled grip.

More than once, Nina had witnessed her brother Anthony in his cups. If she didn't know better, she would have thought Elliot drunk.

"Elliot?" she called out, taking the last step and setting a hand on his back.

A bright drop of red blood dripped onto the table to contrast with the white marble surface.

She gasped and swallowed the bile working its way up her throat. "You're hurt. What happened?"

"I'm fine," he said, his voice rough and low. He glanced at her. A slow line of blood weaved its way from his hairline to his cheek.

The acidy taste of bile filled her mouth. She grabbed the hall chair and pulled it toward him. "Sit, before you collapse."

"Nina, love, are you wearing your shoes? I knocked the vase over. Be careful the shards of broken pottery."

"Goodness, Elliot, don't worry about me. I have my shoes on. Sit and tell me what happened?"

He lowered himself onto the chair.

"The gate to the mews was open. When I went to close it, I noticed the lock on the ground. I bent to pick it up, and someone cracked a cudgel against my skull."

"Goodness! Zeb must have heard him. That was why he wished to go outside." Nina took a quick glance at the dog, who sat at the rear of the hall, looking concerned.

"Elliot," Meg cried, leaning over the railing of the stairs, her blue eyes wide with fear.

"I'm fine, Meg. Go back to bed."

Limping, Meg made her way down the stairs and to his side. Thankfully, the girl had slippers on. "What happened? Did you fall?"

"I think someone tried to rob him," Nina said.

"In the house?" Meg glanced around.

"No, he was outside with Zeb. Don't worry the dog scared the man away."

"I'll go get some ice from the kitchen." Meg darted toward the stairs.

"Meg, slow down," Elliot mumbled, wincing.

Nina crouched in front of him. "We need to fetch the doctor."

"No, I'll be fine."

"But you're bleeding."

"Just a scrape." He stood and slipped his arm around her shoulders, and they moved up the steps.

Inside their bedroom, Nina dragged the counterpane down, and Elliot sat on the edge of the mattress.

"Should we wake your valet?" Meg asked, dashing into the room with ice wrapped in a cloth.

"God, no." Elliot gave the slightest shake of his head, as if anything more would cause him unbearable pain.

"Are you sure you do not wish us to send for a physician?" Meg plucked nervously at the fabric of her sleeve.

"Positive, Meg. Now go to bed," Elliot replied.

Meg twisted her hands together.

"Go on, Meg," Nina said. "Don't worry. I'll take care of him."

Meg hesitated, then, with a nod, exited the room.

"We should fetch a constable." Nina helped Elliot remove his clothes.

"I didn't see my attacker's face." Elliot rested against the pillows and placed the ice-filled cloth to his head.

Nina nibbled her lower lip. Uneasiness settled in the pit of her stomach. Why didn't he want to send for a constable? Did he think he knew his attacker? Goodness, did she believe it was someone her brother hired?

"Nina, stop gnawing on your lip, darling."

"I still think I should send for a doctor."

"I'm already feeling better." He lifted her hand and kissed her fingers. "Come warm me in bed. That's all I need."

* * *

The following morning, Nina stormed into her family's Park Lane residence.

"Lady Nina," the butler said, stepping into the entry hall. The look on his face clearly betrayed the servant sensed her agitation.

"Is my brother in his office, Menders?"

"Yes, my lady. Should I announce you?"

"No, need." She strode past the man and into James's office.

He glanced up. The smile on his face dissolved, and he stood up so fast his high-backed leather chair nearly toppled over. "What is the matter? Has Ralston done something to upset you?"

"No. But I fear someone else might have." All night, she had wondered if James had had a hand in what had happened to Elliot.

A line formed between her brother's brow. "I don't understand."

"Did you have Elliot attacked last night?"

Her brother's eyes widened. "Nina, what are you talking about?"

"Nina?" Caroline said, stepping into the room. "What would make you think something so heinous?"

"Caroline, you didn't see James's face yesterday in the corridor at the theater. He looked ready to kill Elliot, and someone attacked him last night."

Looking truly shocked, James stepped around his desk. "What?"

Nina told them about the incident.

Caroline gasped. "Is he injured?"

"Sore, but he says he is fine."

"Surely you do not think James responsible." Caroline pressed the tips of her fingers to her cheek.

"He was livid with Elliot."

"True," Caroline said, "but I explained to James how Amelia has been trying to get Elliot's attention and is jealous of you. He now understands your husband does not encourage the woman's advances."

James had grown quiet. He rubbed the back of his neck. "I love you, Nina, but I would never have your husband attacked. That you could even think me capable of such an atrocious act . . ."

The hurt expression on her brother's face was enough to make Nina regret coming here. "James, forgive me for accusing you."

"I was angry, but wanting to kill a man and actually doing it are not the same thing."

"Yes, I know. It was probably a thief, but what of the incident at Lord and Lady Hathaway's house party?"

"What incident?"

"That's right. You had already left. Grandmother didn't tell you how one of the large urns on the Hathaways' rooftop fell and nearly hit Elliot."

"Good Lord!" James leaned back against the corner of his desk. "Amelia's husband, Lord Hampton, saw the way his wife placed her hand on Elliot's chest at the theater, but I do not think he would have Elliot attacked."

"I don't believe so either. He is such a sweet man, and he was not at the house party to see how his wife eyed Elliot," Caroline said.

"Yes, but people talk, and Hampton is beginning to realize his wife has no compunction about cuckolding him. The old fool should never have married the woman." James shook his head. "And then there is the Duke of Fernbridge."

"What of him?" Nina tipped her head to the side.

"Rumor has it Fernbridge threw a vase across his dining room when he learned of your marriage. It appears His Grace has more of a temper than we realized." James released a heavy sigh.

"Perhaps it was only an accident at the house party and last night just a thief," Caroline said. "Mayfair has experienced an increase in robberies over the last several weeks."

James scrubbed a hand down his face. "Perhaps. But, Nina, I'd feel better if you and Elliot moved in here."

"No, we are leaving in three days to go to Ralston House. Caroline is probably right. It was most likely a thief last night and the other incident an accident."

Elliot awoke and cradled his throbbing skull. He glanced at the spot next to him. Where was Nina?

The door inched open, and she strode into the room carrying a tray. "How is your head?"

"Fine," he lied, ignoring the icepick-like pain.

"I brought you some tea and milk-toast." She set the tray down.

Her thoughtfulness was appreciated, but the thought of eating milk-toast held as much appeal as going to Clapton's Boxing Club today and engaging in a round or two.

"I called on my brother this morning. He acted shocked when he heard what happened to you. You were suspicious of James, weren't you? That was why you refused to call a constable."

He tangled his fingers with hers. "Getting struck in the head causes a bit of confusion. My head is clearer now. I don't think it was him. It was a botched robbery."

"But what of the incident at Lord and Lady Hathaway's house party?"

He'd wondered about that as well. And the incident with his carriage. Thankfully, Nina didn't know about that. He appeared to be one unlucky bastard, or someone *was* definitely trying to kill him.

"I'm sure it was an accident," he replied, trying to ease Nina's mind.

Three days later, in the dim night, the carriage Elliot hired at the train station rumbled toward Ralston House. His body tensed with nervous energy and he rubbed the back of his neck.

Nina, sitting next to him, touched his arm. "Are you sure your head feels better?"

"Yes, much better." He wasn't lying. The pain had subsided unless he touched the goose egg on his head. The tension he experienced centered on what Nina would think of his estate.

Estate. The word made one envision a place of grandeur, and at one time Ralston House had been that. But now it had loose shingles, peeling paint, and bowing floors.

He thought of the opulence of the Duke of Fernbridge's country residence with its elegant furnishings and stable full of prime horseflesh. Two residences that were like night and day. Worse, Talbot said Lord Huntington's house in Essex, where Nina had grown up, was one of the grandest country homes he'd ever visited.

If he could build up Langford Teas, one day this house would reflect great wealth. He'd make it a home Nina and their children, and Meg and her family, would proudly stay at, but such a day was long off.

Elliot noticed Nina peering at him and realized he tapped his foot nervously against the floorboards. He stilled the movement.

The carriage drove between the two brick pillars. The gatehouse had been vacant for a long time, but it appeared Mr. McWilliams had pulled the wrought-iron gates wide in anticipation of their arrival today.

As they drove closer, Elliot was pleased that the night hid an abundance of sins, but that would only delay the inevitable.

He glanced at his sister. He appreciated the work Meg and Mrs. Newcomb had done to make the place cleaner and more presentable, but in the morning, Nina would see not only the condition of the residence but the threadbare upholstered furniture and curtains, so old they might disintegrate under one's touch. And if one didn't get a spring up their arse when sitting on the sofa, they were indeed lucky. Thank goodness, he'd ordered new mattresses for Meg's bedroom and his after his stubborn sister had refused to return to school. Sleeping on a lumpy bed would not have helped her leg and at least Nina would have a comfortable place to sleep tonight.

"Oh, the flowers are beautiful!" Nina said, peering out the window as the vehicle took the winding road to the residence.

Elliot glanced out. The moon highlighted the pink and white astilbe he and Mr. McWilliams had planted on both sides of the winding drive, sending spikes of featherlike flowers to sway in the slight breeze.

"Elliot helped plant them," Meg said.

Nina turned on the seat and stared at him. "You planted them?"

"With the help of Mr. McWilliams, the groundsman."

Elliot feared the smile on his wife's face would soon be turned upside down. Such splendor could not overshadow the dismal interior of Ralston House.

The rattling of the harnesses and the sound of the gravel crunching under the wheels came to a stop.

Without waiting for anyone to open the vehicle's door, Nina anxiously swung the carriage door wide and stepped down into the front courtyard. Excitement lit up her eyes as she viewed the house.

Though he'd told Nina the house needed a great deal of repairs, she'd seemed to brush his comments aside. She would learn he'd not exaggerated. Elliot assisted his sister out of the carriage.

Mr. McWilliams stepped out of the stables to the right of the house's front courtyard.

Nina smiled at the groundsman as Elliot introduced him. "Even at night, I can see how spectacular the flower-beds are, Mr. McWilliams."

"Thank you, Lady Ralston. Couldn't have gotten them all planted without the help of his lordship."

The housekeeper strode out of the house, the key ring attached to her waist jangling. She bobbed a curtsey to Nina.

"Nina, this is Mrs. Newcomb, our housekeeper."

"Nice to meet you," Nina said.

The woman smiled and curtseyed again, while the driver and Mr. McWilliams removed their traveling trunks and the crates of books they'd brought from London.

Elliot released a slow breath as he offered Nina his arm and they stepped into the entry hall. He blinked. The scent of lemon balm drifted in the air, the hall table gleamed from a fresh coat of wax, and the Carrara marble floor sparkled. From the corner of his eye, he saw the proud smile on both Meg's and the housekeeper's faces.

In the dim light, it looked elegant. He glanced up at the nearly twenty-foot ceiling. Shadows drifted across the surface, hiding all the cracks in the plaster. No amount of polishing and scrubbing would hide the shabbiness in the morning, and the thought that his sister was doing such work still upset him. The girl was beyond stubborn. Hopefully, Nina could convince Meg to return to school. He didn't wish to mull over it now. He had a new mattress to try out with his lovely wife.

Chapter Thirty-Two

As the sunlight filtered around the bedchamber's curtains, Elliot wrapped his arms tighter about Nina's warm, sleeping body, and glanced around. When they'd stepped into the room last night, lit by only the banked fire and a small lantern on the mantel, he'd not noticed the walls were freshly painted. Even the cracks in the plaster were repaired, including the crown molding, running the perimeter near the ceiling.

Elliot blinked to make sure he wasn't dreaming.

His sister's smiling face as they stepped into the house late last night floated to the forefront of his mind. He recalled the way the entry hall had looked as if someone had spent days scrubbing it to a new shine. He'd thought Meg and Mrs. Newcomb had performed a miracle, but the repaired molding meant Meg had hired a skilled workman.

Someone knocked on the door.

"Yes?"

"M'lord, do you want your breakfast served in your room?" a woman asked.

The voice didn't sound familiar. "Is that you, Mrs. Newcomb?"

"No, m'lord. I'm Molly Jenkins. One of the new maids."

New maids? What the blazes was going on? If they'd

intended to stay in this run-down place, he would have asked Mrs. Newcomb to hire a staff, but he had been sure that as soon as Nina saw the condition of Ralston House, she would be anxious to return to their London town house where some improvements had been made. And he'd hoped, with only the housekeeper and gardener about, Meg would eventually wish to go back to school.

His sister had a good deal of explaining to do. Like where the hell she'd gotten the funds to make the improvements to this room and to hire several new maids? Hopefully, Meg hadn't taken up being a highway robber. The idea should have made him laugh, but it was the only explanation that came to mind.

"Jenkins, is my sister up?"

"Yes, m'lord. She's already in the morning room eating breakfast."

"Then we shall join her."

Stretching like a cat, Nina made a contented noise. "Morning."

"Morning." He pressed a kiss to the top of her head.

With lowered lashes, she drew a finger over his bare chest.

He wanted to kiss her and wake her body fully with his own, but he needed to confront his wayward sister and find out what was going on. "Meg is already up and eating breakfast. How about we join her?"

"Sounds wonderful." Nina glanced around. "This is a gorgeous bedchamber. I cannot wait for you to give me a tour of the rest of Ralston House."

Elliot silently groaned.

A short time later, as Elliot and Nina made their way to the morning room, he tried not to gape. Every room they passed was freshly painted with barely a crack in the walls. Perhaps he *was* dreaming and at any moment, he'd wake up.

"The way you described Ralston House had me thinking it was near crumbling, but every room is as stunning as the bedchamber," Nina said.

Well, it *had* looked like it was crumbling.

They stepped into the morning room. New curtains hung on polished brass rods, and the old beetle-eaten floorboards at the entrance were gone, replaced with solid pieces of oak.

His sister glanced up from where she sat at the table, then obviously reading his confusion, busied herself slathering marmalade on a piece of toast.

"Meg, might I have a word with you?" Elliot released a slow breath, trying to ease the pressure in his chest.

She motioned to the silver chafing dishes, sparkling on the sideboard. "After we eat breakfast, Elliot."

"It smells divine." Nina strolled to the sideboard and picked up a plate.

"Yes, our new cook is quite talented," Meg said.

New cook? Elliot twisted his head so fast to peer at his sister a burning pain shot up the back of his neck. He didn't remember Ralston House having an *old* cook. Mrs. Newcomb usually did the cooking, though nothing too extravagant. What the bloody hell was going on? He narrowed his eyes at Meg.

His sister glanced away and took an overly robust interest in smearing *more* marmalade on her toast.

Elliot strode over to Nina. She placed scrambled eggs, toast, and strawberries on her plate. She smiled up at him, and he forced himself to return the expression as he glimpsed at all the silver chafing dishes and the assortment of food.

Christ. His sister must have taken up thievery. Nothing else made sense.

He filled his own dish with bacon, eggs, toast, and fried tomatoes, then sat at the table. A movement outside caught his attention. Two workmen, one carrying a ladder, the other a wooden toolbox, walked by the window.

Blast it all. What was going on here?

Red suffused Meg's cheeks as she nibbled on her toast.

"Sister, dear, as soon as we have eaten breakfast, I really must have a word with you," Elliot said.

"I'm sure whatever it is can wait. Didn't you promise Nina a tour of the gardens in the morning?"

"I don't believe Nina will mind waiting a few minutes, would you, darling?"

Nina lowered her glass of orange juice and smiled. "Of course, it can wait."

"The peonies, roses, and cornflowers are all beginning to bloom. It's most spectacular with the morning dew on the buds, surely our talk can wait until after you tour it," his sister said.

Elliot shook his head. "No. We'll have our talk first, Meg."

Forty-five minutes later, after Meg took an extraordinary amount of time eating her toast in an obvious attempt to avoid talking with Elliot, he and Meg entered the library.

This room, like the others, appeared transformed, with new navy damask curtains, along with a brightly colored Turkish rug. The bookcases that lined two of the walls were now in pristine condition, and across from the desk were two high-backed chairs upholstered with the same fabric as the curtains.

Elliot tried not to grind his teeth as he motioned for

Meg to be seated in one of the new chairs. He walked around the desk and braced his palms on the surface. "It appears you have some explaining to do."

"I'll explain, but only if you sit and stop glaring at me."

Releasing a long breath, Elliot lowered himself into the chair. "Is this better?"

"A little, but you are still scowling." Meg folded her arms over her chest.

He briefly closed his eyes and prayed for patience. "Stop stalling, Meg. Tell me how you have paid for all these improvements."

"Promise me you won't get mad."

"Meg, what have you done?"

The way she nibbled on her lower lip made Elliot even more anxious. Maybe his jest about her becoming a highway robber wasn't too far off.

As if gathering her courage, Meg drew in a slow breath. "I've sold Swan Cottage."

"What?" He shot up from the chair and raked his hands through his hair. "I don't understand how that is possible. How could you sell it? You're seventeen and not to take possession until you are twenty-four or married."

"Well, it took some finagling." She twisted her hands in her lap. "I forged your signature on several letters and documents."

Damnation. So his sister was not a highway robber, but a forger. And there was nothing he could do about it without exposing her illegal actions. "My God, Meg! What possessed you?"

She pointed around the library. "This house has been a weight around your neck since you inherited it. It's dragging you down. Papa left the cottage to you. Most men would have sold it to pay for the repairs at their entailed properties, but you are so full of guilt over what happened to me, you wanted me to have Swan Cottage."

"I told you it was yours because I wanted it to be part of your dowry."

"I do not know how many times I need to tell you: I am not getting married." She drew in a shaky breath.

It took him less than five seconds to make his way around the massive desk. He crouched before her and took her hands in his. "Don't cry, Meg."

"I have worked so hard to make this a home you would be honored to call yours. Can't you be proud of me?"

"I am proud. Exceedingly. You have transformed Ralston House." Mr. McWilliams was right. Meg just wanted to prove her worth and capabilities. She was lovely, kind, resourceful, and so much more. It appeared she was also a competent forger of documents.

"You are?"

"Yes, but I'm shocked as well. You have always loved Swan Cottage."

"But I love you more." She sniffled. "Elliot, you should not have told me I could have Swan Cottage. You need to let go of your guilt. I have never blamed you for what happened. You need to forgive yourself."

He didn't believe he would ever forgive himself, especially if Meg spent her life hidden away in this house.

"Have you ever thought that my love for you is the reason I wanted you to have the cottage?" He pulled her to her feet, embraced her, and drew a hand over her back.

"I got an exceptionally good price for Swan Cottage," she said.

"How much did you get?"

She walked over to the bookcases, removed a thick lexicon bound in blue leather, and handed him the document that was folded inside.

Good Lord, he'd not thought the property worth so much. "That's an impressive amount. How much do you have left?"

"Not very much, but wait until you walk around Ralston House. You will be amazed at the repairs."

As Nina and Elliot walked through the garden at Ralston House, Elliot entwined his fingers with his wife's.

"The gardens are enchanting, Elliot. I cannot believe that you and Mr. McWilliams are responsible for them. You should feel extremely proud."

After Mr. McWilliams's guidance and both of their back-breaking work planting flowers, the gardens appeared quite presentable. Even picturesque. Bright bursts of color abounded nearly everywhere the eye looked. Yet, Elliot's mind kept going back to what Meg had done. That she had given up Swan Cottage.

"Elliot?" Nina stopped and set her free hand on his upper arm. "You seem distracted. What is the matter?"

"I'm sorry. I've been thinking about Meg."

"Will you tell me what happened? How was she injured? I know it has something to do with you. I see regret in your eyes every time you talk to me about her." She squeezed his hand.

How astute his wife was. What would she think of him after he admitted what happened? Elliot glanced over her shoulder and stared blindly into the distance before returning his gaze to Nina.

"My parents were not suited to each other." He gave a humorless laugh. "That's a bloody understatement. They fought constantly, but the summer before I was to go away to university, they tried to reconcile. It was a disaster. They argued nonstop and realized their marriage would never work. Each blamed the other, and they had a vicious row. My mother was screaming, as was my father. I needed to get out of the house, so I took my grouse-hunting rifle and marched out to the woods. I was so furious over the constant fighting. I just wanted to blow off some steam. I was shooting at three fallen tree trunks. One to my left, two to my right. All I remember is turning to shoot at the trunk to my left. My finger pulled on the trigger, and then I saw Meg, but it was too late. She was right in front of the trunk." Elliot roughly raked his fingers through his hair. "The bullet hit her leg. Good God, there was so much blood, I thought she was going to die. By the time I ran back to the house, carrying her in my arms, her face was as white as a bleached piece of paper."

"It was an accident, Elliot." Nina stepped up to him.

He had thought he would see repulsion in her face, but Nina set her head against his chest and wrapped her hands around his waist.

"Yes, but if I hadn't been so angry, I would have heard her. I should have heard her, yet all I heard in my head was my parents fighting."

"But she lived."

"Yes, but I fear her limp makes her feel like an outcast, and no matter what I say to her, I cannot get her to understand how lovely she is. Meg's limp doesn't define her, but I believe she is self-conscious and cannot see past it. So, neither can I."

"But I see the way she smiles at you. I do not think she blames you."

"Maybe not, but I fear she will be content to hide away in this house."

Nina pulled back and held his gaze. "There is not much

time left to the school term. Why don't we have her return to London with us?"

"I doubt she will go."

"It will all work out, darling. Trust me."

The confidence in Nina's face lightened his mood. He had a feeling Nina could do anything she set her mind to.

Chapter Thirty-Three

The following day after luncheon, Meg and Nina unpacked the crates of books they'd brought from London, intent on organizing them in the massive floor-to-ceiling bookcases in the library at Ralston House.

"How about if we place all the fiction books on this wall?" Meg removed several thick tomes from a crate.

"That's a wonderful idea. Then we can place the horticultural, reference, and other works here." Nina pointed to the other wall of shelves.

"Yes, that's what I'd thought." Meg smiled.

Nina had thought she would never have a sister-in-law that she would like as much as Caroline, but she enjoyed spending time with Meg just as much. Last night, Elliot, Meg, and she had played cards well into the evening. Both Elliot and his sister had finally relaxed and enjoyed themselves after a tense day between the siblings.

Since her conversation with Elliot yesterday, Nina had been spinning ideas in her head as to how to get Meg to return to school, but with the term nearly over, she decided to settle her energy on getting her sister-in-law to return to London with them, and she had an idea of how she might accomplish such a goal. It centered around the fact that

Meg had done a remarkable job decorating Ralston House. The girl possessed an extraordinary eye for design. Perhaps if she asked Meg to help her decorate the London town house, that would convince her to return with them.

The sound of someone entering the library pulled Nina from her thoughts. Elliot strode into the room carrying another crate of books. He wore a white cotton shirt and rough woolen trousers. The shirt's top buttons were unfastened and the sleeves rolled up, exposing his strong forearms. She presumed that while they sorted the books in the library, he intended to join Mr. McWilliams and work in the garden. He'd spent quite a few hours there yesterday, causing his skin to turn a darker sun-kissed shade.

"This is the last crate." His gaze locked with hers, and a broad smile tilted his sensual mouth.

That mouth had done wicked things to the place between her legs last night until her body had pulsed with pleasure. She felt her cheeks warm at the memory.

As if reading her thoughts, his smile broadened, and he winked.

At times, it was difficult for her to comprehend they were married. That London's most confirmed bachelor had chosen her as his wife, and that she had tossed all her doubts about him away. She loved him, and unlike Avalon, she truly believed Elliot loved her as well, leaving her feeling more content than she could ever recall.

Elliot set the crate down and wrapped an arm about her waist, pulling the side of her body tightly to his. "You're both doing a bang-up job. This looks wonderful."

"All credit goes to Meg. She has a keen eye for design."

"She does," Elliot said.

Nina could see the pleasure on Meg's face over the compliment.

Elliot gave Nina a quick kiss. "I'm off to help Mr. McWilliams with the transplanting of several bushes."

An image of Elliot working in the garden appeared in her mind. Yesterday, she'd attempted to read a book while sitting on a garden bench close to where he worked, but the sight of his muscles bunching and flexing had caused her to spend more time watching him than reading. Who knew observing her husband working in the garden could be such an aphrodisiac?

Elliot strode out of the room.

A broad grin spread across Meg's face. "My brother is completely smitten with you. I do not think I've ever seen him so content."

Meg's words sent a pleasant sensation of warmth through Nina's body. "Really?"

"Yes. It's nice to see him so carefree. He's been so worried lately about . . ." Meg bit her lip as if about to say something she wasn't sure she should reveal.

"What has he been worried about?"

"Things." Meg busied herself with placing several more books on the shelves.

Nina knew one of those *things* was that Meg had left school and was determined to hide away at Ralston House. "Meg, I was wondering if, when Elliot and I return to London, you would accompany us. You are immensely talented when it comes to design, and I could dearly use your help."

As if nervous, Meg rubbed her palms over the skirt of her dress. "I'm sure you could do it on your own or ask your sister-in-law Caroline for her assistance."

"I don't have your keen eye, and Caroline is quite busy with her newspaper." Nina smiled. "And though it is not public knowledge, I do not think Caroline would mind me telling you she is with child."

"Oh, how wonderful." Though Meg smiled, a forlorn and faraway look settled on her face as if she one day wished to become a mother but believed she would not.

The expression wrenched at Nina's heart. One way or another, she was going to get her new sister-in-law to London. As if completely deflated over the prospect of decorating the London town house, Nina released a long sigh and slumped into a chair. "I'm positive I will not be able to do as good a job as you could do." The statement wasn't a lie.

Meg nibbled on the nail of her index finger. "Very well. I will help you decorate the town house."

"You will? Oh, thank you!" Nina bounced up from the chair and gave Meg a hug. A wave of guilt flittered through her, but she tamped it down. She would not regret her performance. London would be good for Meg, and Elliot would be overjoyed when he learned his sister would return with them.

Meg rubbed a cloth over a dusty leather-bound book. "Elliot tells me you are not without your own talents. I hear you are an exceptional artist."

"He said that?" His compliment pleased Nina.

"Yes, he told me your sketches are excellent and that your sister-in-law has hired you to be the illustrator for her newspaper after the current artist retires."

"Yes, I will start in a few weeks."

"How marvelous," Meg said. "I'd like to have an occupation."

"Did you learn anything that interested you at Mrs. Gibbs's School?"

"At school, we were not encouraged to pursue an occupation. We are taught French, poetry, how to watercolor, do needlepoint, and dance. Though they told me I did not have to participate in the latter."

A wave of anger drifted through Nina. No wonder Meg felt like an outcast. They had excluded her—made her feel she was not capable. Nina fought the urge to ball her fist. They would hire her a dancing instructor, or Elliot could teach her.

"Mrs. Gibbs told Elliot they taught geography, math, and astronomy. It was the latter that caused him to enroll me, since he knows I love stargazing, but we barely touched on those subjects."

Perhaps it was good Meg hadn't returned to *such* a school.

"But I did enjoy the other girls. Well, most of them. A couple of them were snotty."

By "snotty," Nina wondered if Meg meant they made comments about her limp. She thought of people like Amelia Hampton who seemed to elevate themselves by tearing others down. Poor Meg.

Wanting to say something to please the girl, Nina said, "After we return to London, we will go and visit the Royal Observatory Greenwich. Have you been there?"

"Elliot took me there a few years ago, but I would love to go again."

"Then we shall make it a priority."

Several minutes later, Meg pointed to a stack of books she'd placed on the corner of the desk. "These books are all reference guides."

Nina picked them up and started placing them on the shelves. The last one was a copy of Debrett's. "This is a recent addition."

"Yes, I didn't realize Elliot owned a copy. I found it on a table in the town house's library."

Her family had a copy at their country house, but it was quite old. Nina opened it up and flicked through, stopping when she reached the page with her family's information.

Her eyes settled on the ink mark that circled her name and the writing next to it.

> *Broken-hearted with a sizable dowry. Perfect for the plucking.*

As Nina stared at the comment, her heart skipped a beat, then pounded against her chest as if it might leap out.

"Is something wrong, Nina? You've lost all your color. Are you feeling ill?" Meg strode over to her.

"No, but I need to talk to your brother." Heart still racing, Nina snapped the book closed and felt the pinch of tears at the backs of her eyes.

"Are you sure you are fine?"

She nodded, even though her stomach clenched, making her want to cast up her accounts. She clasped the book to her chest and walked out of the library. Exiting through the French doors in the drawing room, she stepped onto the terrace. Once at its edge, she set a hand to her forehead to shadow her eyes from the sun and surveyed the gardens below.

A movement caught her attention, and she saw Elliot and Mr. McWilliams digging at the roots of several bushes. On legs a bit unsteady, she walked down the steps, then took the path to where they worked.

As she approached, Elliot glanced up and smiled.

"Might I have a word with you?" Her voice cracked.

"Of course." The smile on his face faltered. He pushed the end of the shovel into the ground, tugged off his thick suede gloves, and tossed them onto a bench. "Is something the matter?"

* * *

The unshed tears turning Nina's eyes glassy caused worry to spring to life in Elliot. Good God, what had happened? Elliot took a step toward her.

She jerked back as if he had leprosy.

"Nina, love, you're scaring me. What's the matter?" A bead of sweat trailed down his back.

She handed him the book she'd been cradling to her chest.

"What's this?" He glanced down at the title and frowned. "Debrett's?"

"Yes, open it to my family's page."

As he did so, a sick sensation tightened his gut. He recognized the book as Talbot's. The image of his friend writing something in it flashed in his memory. The knot in his gut twisted tighter as he flipped through the pages. A dull ache started stabbing at his temple. What the bloody hell had Talbot written? The air in his lungs locked as he glanced down at the page.

Broken-hearted with a sizable dowry. Perfect for the plucking.

Elliot glanced up from the page to see a tear sliding down Nina's check. The sight wrenched at his heart. The last thing in his life he wanted was to hurt her.

"You bastard! Was that all this was about?" She swiped at the tear.

Mr. McWilliams, who only stood a few feet away, set his shovel into the ground and, looking uncomfortable, walked toward the potting shed.

"No. Of course, not, I—"

"All those things you said to me about how we chose each other. They were all lies, weren't they? It was all about my dowry. What an easy mark you must have thought me. Did you laugh at me behind my back at how easily you broke down my defenses and positioned yourself not only in my life but between my legs?"

"Nina, I love you. What we have is not a lie."

Her laugh was sharp, humorless. "I thought you were different than Avalon, but you are worse."

Elliot hated the pain he saw in her eyes. He reached for her hand.

She swatted at it. "Don't touch me. Don't ever touch me again."

"Nina—"

"Just tell me one thing. How long ago did you plan to win my dowry? The day of my family's ball? Before that? Was even your offer to help me get the Duke of Fernbridge to notice me all part of your scheme? Of course, it was. Offer the naive woman lessons. Tempt her with kisses. Tell her how she deserves better than a cold fish like Fernbridge." With trembling hands, she wiped away the tears trailing down her cheeks.

"Darling, let me explain."

"Explain? With more lies?"

"No. With the truth."

"And what truth would that be? The one that I'm mistaken? Or the one that you love me?"

"Nina, I do love you."

"What's going on?" Meg asked, moving down the garden path toward them. "What's happened?"

His sister looked almost as upset as Nina. He knew why. She'd thought herself finally part of a caring family. That this home would be filled with love and laughter. Something they'd never had growing up, and she sensed, as he did, that their rickety house of cards was tumbling down.

"Ask your brother. He'll tell you all about it." Nina took two steps, then spun around. "Does Meg know?"

"Know what? Would someone please tell me what is going on?" Meg's eyes had turned as watery as Nina's.

"Of course, she doesn't." Elliot drew a deep breath into his lungs. "Meg, can you give Nina and me a moment?"

"No need," Nina said. "I don't wish to talk to you. Not now. Not ever." She pivoted and walked away.

"Please, let me explain." Elliot dashed after her.

"Go to the devil," she said and continued up the path.

He let her walk away. He realized Nina needed a few minutes, then maybe she would listen to him.

"What have you done?" Meg asked.

"She needs to realize I love her."

Meg's fingers bit into his upper arm. "I know you do, but something has happened. Tell me what?"

"It might not have started out that way. You know I needed money." Elliot raked his fingers through his hair.

"Elliot, do not tell me that is why you picked her."

"Initially, yes. No. That's not completely true. In fact, I don't think it is true at all. I've always had a soft spot for Nina. Last season, I found my gaze straying to her repeatedly during balls. I loved her smile and her passion for life. When Talbot suggested her because of her brother's wealth and the dowry that would be offered, I readily agreed." He fisted a hand over his heart. "I ended up wanting her more than her dowry. I've not touched it."

"You need to tell her that."

"Don't worry. I'll prove my love to her if it is the last thing I do."

Chapter Thirty-Four

Over the next few days, minutes seemed to move at a turtle's pace. Elliot had tried to talk to Nina, but every time he stepped into a room, she walked out, except during meals.

Meg had said to give Nina more time, but he hated to see the hurt on Nina's face and know he was the cause. He realized loving someone made their pain as acute as your own.

He stared at the door that connected this bedchamber to the one Nina and he *had* shared. She'd said she didn't want him in her bed, so he'd moved into the adjacent room. He strode to the door and tried the handle. She'd locked it, and it remained locked. But every night he tried it, and every night he spoke to her through it, but he feared his words fell on deaf ears.

Zeb, lying on his bed in the corner of the room, made a whining noise. The bloodhound's mood, which had improved since Nina had come into their lives, seemed morose again. He had also been giving Elliot the same disgusted look his sister had favored him with over the last two days.

Elliot set his palm on the connecting door. "Nina?"

She never answered, but he knew she was there.

"I admit my need for funds prompted me to decide to

marry, but it was your spirit, your smile, everything about you that made me want *you*. I have thought you a special person for quite a long time. Last year, I watched you dancing with Avalon and other men, and I wished I were one of them. But I will not lie about this. I didn't want to marry. My parents' tumultuous marriage left a bitterness in my soul. The constant bickering. The fighting over everything. That was my idea of marriage, but once I fell in love with you, I realized a couple can love each other. And a marriage does not have to be that way."

He paused and waited. But she said nothing. He kneaded the stiff muscles in the back of his neck. Avalon had damaged her trust, and Elliot realized he'd snapped it in two. He hoped the break was repairable.

"Nina, please don't let what we have slip away." Elliot prayed he'd hear the *snick* of the lock unfastening. He didn't, but somehow, he knew Nina stood on the other side of the door. He could sense her closeness just like he could feel the limbs connected to his own body.

The following morning, as Elliot tucked his white cotton shirt into his rough woolen trousers, he stared at the door connecting this bedchamber to the one Nina slept in. He hoped during the night she'd thought about what he had said.

Perhaps today Nina would speak to him, and he could get her to believe how much he loved her.

He stepped into the corridor, made his way down the stairs, and outside to help Mr. McWilliams lop several thick tree branches. The early morning sun cast its first rays on the dew-covered plants in the garden, and the scent of flowers and soil drifted to his nose. A year ago, he wouldn't have taken any pleasure in the sight of a garden blooming or comfort in the earthy scent of soil; now, he realized the work it took to bring such splendor to the human eye.

Not seeing Mr. McWilliams in the gardens beyond the terrace, he headed toward the less manicured area of the parkland and the tool shed. Most likely, the gardener was sharpening and oiling his tools.

As he approached the old stone structure, Mr. McWilliams came into view. The gardener was scratching the back of his head as if perplexed.

"Is something wrong?" Elliot asked.

"Aye, I would have sworn I closed the door to the shed last night, but I found it open this morning."

Mr. McWilliams was getting old, and Elliot noticed the man's forgetfulness. He clamped a hand on the man's shoulder. "Perhaps the wind blew it open."

"Aye, the wind," the man said, giving Elliot a sideways look, since they both knew there had been no wind.

They opened the wooden shutters on the exterior of the shed that covered the mullioned glass, sending light into the dark interior of the building.

Inside, Mr. McWilliams removed several hand saws from their hooks. "I sharpened them on the grinding wheel yesterday." He pointed to a long wooden ladder, hanging sideways on the rear wall. "Can you get that, m'lord?"

Elliot lifted it down and they headed toward the first tree that needed its dead growth removed.

After a restless night, Nina stepped into the morning room to find it empty, except for the maid who was setting the chafing dishes on the sideboard. She forced a smile. "Good morning."

"Morning, m'lady." The maid strode out of the room.

Before her fight with Elliot, Nina and he had always arrived after Meg for breakfast, since Elliot and she had enjoyed each other's company in the morning, whether they simply snuggled or made love. Now she always arrived before Meg. Nina's cold, empty bed held little appeal.

Though she got up early, Nina was not the first one up. Elliot rose before the sun was barely over the horizon and went to work in the garden with Mr. McWilliams.

Nina strode to the bank of windows and glanced out. She told herself it was because she wanted to admire the bright burst of colors in the flowerbeds, but deep down she admitted the truth—she wanted to see Elliot. Her gaze traveled through the gardens until she found him. He stood on a tall wooden ladder cutting a branch.

The sinew in his arms flexed as he drew the saw back and forth. He leaned to the right, and the ladder tipped precariously.

Her stomach fluttered and jumped within itself.

One of his large hands reached out to wrap about a branch, and he steadied the wobbling ladder.

With her hand grasping her skirts, she let out a relieved sigh.

Meg entered the room and stepped next to her at the window. "It is obvious you love him, and no matter what he did, he fell in love with you. Can you not find it in your heart to forgive him?"

"I just need a bit more time."

Meg nodded and moved to the chafing dishes to fill her plate.

Elliot climbed down from the ladder. He handed Mr. McWilliams the saw, said a few words to the grounds-keeper, then moved toward the house.

Not wanting him to notice her staring, she strode to

the sideboard, set a single egg on her plate, and sat across from Meg.

Her sister-in-law looked at her dish and frowned. "That's all you intend to eat?"

"I'm not very hungry."

Elliot strode into the room, rolling down the sleeves of his cotton shirt and fastening the button at the cuffs. "Morning."

"Morning, Elliot," Meg replied.

His gaze met hers. "Hello, Nina?"

She normally ignored him, but this morning, she nodded.

As he filled his dish with food, she stared at his broad-shouldered back and the way his body tapered at his waist. When he turned, she jerked her gaze away and stared at the few remaining pieces of egg in her plate.

Elliot sat at the head of the table next to her and Meg, his dish laden with eggs, bacon, and fresh fruit. She could smell Elliot's skin—a mixture of soap and sweat. If she set her tongue to his neck, it would taste salty. Wanting to distract herself, she placed a piece of egg in her mouth.

Like his sister, Elliot frowned at her dish. He reached for a piece of toast from the rack and put marmalade on it, then set it on her plate.

She glanced up at him. "Thank you."

A hopeful smile touched his lips.

"What were you and Mr. McWilliams working on this morning?" Meg asked.

Elliot explained how they were pruning overgrown trees and would soon till the soil in several of the beds and add flower seeds.

When Elliot talked about the gardens, she could hear the excitement in this voice, and whether she wished to admit it or not, she got her own sense of pleasure from his enthusiasm.

* * *

By late afternoon, Meg and Nina finished cataloging and filling the shelves in the library with the books from London. The task complete, Nina gathered her sketchpad and box of charcoals and set out for the garden. She sat on a stone bench across the path from a small birdhouse where two birds fluttered their wings in the water.

Halfway through sketching the birdhouse, she examined her work. Was it truly good enough for the *London Reformer*, or had Caroline only given her the job because she was her sister-in-law? That thought caused an anxious feeling in the pit of her stomach. Sadly, the only person she wanted to share her doubts with was Elliot.

She released a heavy sigh. Each hour, she missed him more. She thought of the concerned look in his eyes when he'd set the toast on her plate. Having him act like he cared made staying angry at him even harder. She wondered if tonight he would talk to her through the door that connected their bedchambers, as he had every night since they'd slept apart.

A noise to her right caused her to peer at the thick shrubs behind her. "Hello?"

She heard rustling again.

"Elliot? Mr. McWilliams?" She stood and parted several of the branches. "Is that you, Zeb?"

Except for the sound of birdsong, silence.

Well, if it had been the dog, the bloodhound had obviously walked away. Nina rubbed at the charcoal smears on her fingers, picked up her sketchpad, and strolled back into the house. As she stepped into her bedchamber, she heard someone in the attached bathing room. Not someone. Elliot. It contained the only tub long enough to accommodate him. She bit her lip while contemplating whether she should leave.

The bathing room door opened, and Elliot stepped out, wearing a navy damask robe with a velvet collar.

He didn't appear to realize she stood in the room. His dark brown hair looked almost black when wet. As he strode toward the door that connected this bedchamber to the one he now slept in, his loosely tied robe exposed slivers of his masculine body beneath the material.

The sight made her own body warm. Before their fight, she would have walked up to him and untied the sash so her greedy hands could travel over the hard contours of his skin. She could almost feel what he would do in response. How he'd cup the back of her head, press his mouth to hers, and coax her lips open, while his palm would seductively skim over her body. The slide of his tongue against hers and his large hand caressing her would have her moaning against his lips.

Just the thought caused her nipples to pebble and wetness to grow between her legs.

As Elliot's fingers curled over the handle to the connecting door, he stopped, and slowly turned as if she'd physically touched him.

His gaze locked with hers.

Before he could say anything, she opened the door and slipped from the room.

Chapter Thirty-Five

Nina blinked awake as the door to her bedchamber squeaked and opened. A tall figure slipped into the room.

Elliot. As much as she wished to open her arms and ask him to join her in their bed, she closed her eyes and pretended she was asleep.

His feet shuffled across the rug, and she could hear his breaths as he stared down at her. In truth, she wanted him to stay more than she wanted him to go. She missed the way he held her while they lay in bed—as if she meant the world to him. As if he cherished her. Elliot was right. No matter how he'd set out to win her, he did love her, and she loved him. With every fiber of her being.

Damnation. She was tired of being angry. Tired of not talking to him. And tired of not having him lie next to her in bed. It was time to let go of her anger.

She opened her eyes and stared into the dark eyes of a stranger, holding a two-pronged weeding fork to her neck. The scream that worked its way up her throat was silenced as the man cupped his large hand roughly over her mouth, the tips of his fingers tight and bruising on her skin.

Her heart pounded so forcefully against her chest, she thought it might explode within her.

The man's lips twisted into an unpleasant grin, and a calculating expression of malice lit his eyes.

"Get up," he whispered in a gruff voice, pressing the points of the garden tool into the soft flesh of her neck, while his other hand still covered her mouth.

The strong scent of liquor wafted to her nostrils as she tossed off her bedding and scrambled to her feet.

"Is your husband sleeping in the next bedroom?" he asked.

She shook her head.

As if he knew she lied, a sneer spread across his face. But instead of moving toward the door to where Elliot slept, he prodded her spine with the sharp points of the tool, and they stepped into the hall and down the stairs.

She contemplated trying to bite him, but the pressure of his hand on her mouth was so tight, she couldn't even part her lips. Her mind raced with swirling thoughts. How to get away. What did he want? Who was he? Was he the same man who'd attacked Elliot outside their town house in London? Each thought bombarded her brain in rapid succession, making her head spin.

They entered the morning room. One of the French doors stood wide open, and he shoved her through it. The tips of his fingers continued their bruising pressure on the skin around her mouth. She was breathing so fast through her nostrils, she was starting to feel dizzy. She tried to calm herself—tried to center her mind on the single thought of how to escape.

The cool night air filtered through the soft cotton of her nightgown, adding to the shivers already coursing through her body, making her feel as if she'd plunged into a bank of snow.

He released her mouth, reached into his pocket, and

removed a stone the size of an orange. He threw the stone at Elliot's bedchamber window, shattering the glass.

A crashing noise caused Elliot to jackknife up in bed. Confused, he glanced around the dim room. His gaze narrowed on the window. Moonlight highlighted a sizable hole in the pane and the shards of glass scattered on the floor.

He scrambled out of bed, scooted his feet into his slippers, and dragged his robe over his shoulders. As he stepped up to the window, broken glass crunched under his soles. The sight of a stone lying on the rug made the hairs on the back of his neck stand.

This was no accident.

Elliot peered outside. Under the gray light reflecting off the moon, he saw a man standing in the front courtyard and, next to him, Nina in her nightgown. The man's arm was wrapped about Nina's throat, forcing her to arch backward, while the blackguard held a two-pronged weeding tool against her side.

Elliot's heart beat as fast as a racehorse's during the last furlong at Epsom Downs.

The bastard dragged her backward toward the horse stable.

Fear as intense as when he'd shot Meg exploded within him, making him feel as if he'd walked into a nightmare. Elliot darted into the adjacent bedchamber's dressing room and removed the mahogany box containing Uncle Phillip's British Bull Dog revolver.

As he loaded the bullets into the chamber, his hand shook. Not from fear of holding the cold metal, but from the fear of what might happen to Nina if he wasn't quick enough to put a bullet in the man's heart.

Exiting his bedchamber, he shoved the gun into the pocket of his robe and raced down the stairs, taking the steps three at a time. He dashed outside, and his warm breaths left white puffs in the frigid air as he raced to the stable.

One of the massive cross-bucked doors was pushed wide open. Without removing the gun from his pocket, he curled his fingers around the weapon's handle and stepped inside the dark space. He could hear the horses shifting in their stalls, but it took several seconds for his eyes to adjust to the dim space.

"Nina?" he called out.

"Elliot!" Though he couldn't see her, he could hear the fear in her voice, and his desire to kill the bastard holding her against her will grew stronger.

The kerosene lamp that hung on a hook up in the loft flickered to life.

Elliot's gaze zeroed in on the man holding Nina in front of him, his arm wrapped tightly around her waist. His other hand holding the tool to Nina's neck. The light highlighted the fellow's face.

It took several seconds for Elliot to realize it was Langford's nephew, Harry Connors.

"What is this about, Mr. Connors?" Elliot asked, trying to keep his voice from ratcheting up.

"Retribution." The slight slurring of the word informed Elliot the man had been drinking.

"For?"

Connors barked out a humorless laugh. "You're about to take what should be mine."

"Yours?"

"Yes, Langford Teas!" Connors's voice was almost shrill in its intensity. "An eye for an eye is only fair."

Damnation. He didn't have a clear shot. He needed to keep the man talking until he did. "That urn on the Hathaways' roof didn't just happen to fall, did it?"

The light from the lantern highlighted the twisting of the man's lips. "If the old woman hadn't screamed, that urn would have left you splattered all over the terrace. I tried that after I missed shooting you while you were out riding. And if you'd been traveling at a greater speed when you lost your carriage wheel, you'd be six feet under as well."

Good Lord. The madman had loosened the bolts securing the wheel and come damn close to getting Nina injured while out riding.

Didn't Langford's nephew realize his uncle would just find another buyer? "And the attack outside my London town house? I presume that was you as well."

"You're like a cat, Lord Ralston, but even a cat runs out of lives. Or his wife does." The man's unpleasant smile broadened.

"Release my wife. This is between you and me."

"No." He jerked violently on Nina's waist, causing her to cringe. "Why should I? Did you think of me when you offered to buy my uncle's business? I should be the one getting Langford Teas, but you approached him with your fancy clothing and smooth words and stole it out from under me."

"You want it. Let my wife go, and I shall back away from the deal."

"Too late. You've turned my uncle against me."

"I don't think I did. You did that all on your own."

Lips pinched tight, Harry Connors moved closer to the loft's edge, where there was no railing.

Nina's eyes grew wide with fear.

"No!" Elliot's heart pumped faster, causing the *swish,*

swish, swish of blood coursing through his veins to reach his ears.

"Pay attention, my lord. I want to watch your face as your wife falls to her death. I want to see your pain. I want you to know what I have felt."

The man was mad. How could he equate a business with a human life? "I'll trade my life for hers."

"Would you do that?" Connors asked.

"Without hesitation."

"How sweet. That pleases me. It makes me realize how devastating it will be for you when I toss her over the loft's edge, and she lands broken and twisted at your feet."

A bead of sweat dripped down Elliot's spine. Though he still didn't have a clear shot, he slipped his finger over the trigger's cold metal, hoping he would get an opportunity before it was too late.

The man twisted Nina's face toward the lantern. "See the fear in her face?"

He did and it made him want to rip the man's heart out with his bare hands. Elliot withdrew the gun and aimed it at the man.

Connors laughed. "Go on and shoot me, but when I fall, I will take her with me."

"If you release her, neither of you has to die."

"You must think I'm a fool, Lord Ralston. Why should I trust you? As soon as I let her go, you'll put a bullet in me." The madman took another step closer to the loft's edge.

"If you toss her over, I'll shoot you for sure. Think of that, Connors."

"I don't care. I have nothing left. You've stolen my future."

A rustle sounded at the door and Meg stepped into the barn. Seeing the man holding Nina, and Elliot pointing the gun, his sister screamed.

Then everything happened so fast. Nina twisted herself loose from the man's grasp. The momentum of her thrusting away, caused Connors to stumble backward. His left hand lashed out and grasped the partial rail as he dangled over the edge. His legs swung in the air like a rag doll's. As the man looked over his shoulder at the stable floor, twenty feet below him, terror filled his eyes.

The wood made a splintering noise as it broke loose from its mooring. Connors tumbled backward, arms flailing in the air, then landed with a *thud*.

Nina, visibly shaking, wrapped her arms about her waist as she viewed the man's twisted, supine body. His legs bent at an odd angle. His chest made a rattling noise as he drew in his last breath.

Meg gasped and brought her fisted hand to her mouth to stifle her scream.

Elliot tucked the gun back into the pocket of his robe and started up the ladder. "It's safe, Nina. Come down."

"I killed him." Tears trailed down her cheeks.

"No, he lost his balance. He was drunk, and liquor will do that to a man."

"But I pushed him."

Elliot was damn glad she had. Better the bastard was dead than her.

"No. He was already losing his balance." The thought that he might have lost her made him want to wretch like a drunkard after downing a whole bottle of gin.

She gave him a disbelieving look as she took his hand and climbed down the ladder. Once they reached the ground, Elliot noticed the uncontrollable shivers that racked Nina's body. He pulled her into his embrace and rubbed his hands over her upper arms and back, trying to stop her shaking.

"Who is he?" Meg asked, her voice barely an audible whisper.

"The nephew of the proprietor of Langford Teas."

"I don't understand," his sister said.

Nina's teeth chattered.

"I'll explain once we get inside. Nina needs to get warmed up, and I need to send Mr. McWilliams into town to get the local constable."

An hour after the constable left, Nina sat in the drawing room with a warm cup of tea cradled between her hands. Though the porcelain held the heat of the hot brew, her fingers still felt chilled to the bone. Her body, along with her brain, felt numb—as if she were floating above and looking down at a horrid dream, instead of being an active participant in everything that had transpired.

Next to her, Nina felt the cushion on the sofa dip. She glanced sideways to see Elliot sitting next to her.

"You look cold. Let me put this more firmly on you." He pulled the heavy woolen blanket tighter around her shoulders.

"Thank you. Where is Meg?" she asked, suddenly realizing her sister-in-law was no longer in the room.

"I told her she should go to bed."

Yes. She remembered that now.

The housekeeper stepped into the room. "Do you wish for more tea, my lady?"

"No, I am fine, Mrs. Newcomb. There is no need for you to remain up."

The woman looked unsure, as if she thought any minute Nina would need some medicinal tonic to calm her fraying nerves.

"No need to worry. I'll take care of my wife, Mrs. Newcomb."

The housekeeper nodded and left the room.

The door had no sooner closed behind her when Elliot took the teacup from her hands and set it on the table. He rubbed her fingers between his warm palms. "Are you sure you do not want Mr. McWilliams to fetch the village doctor?"

She shook her head. He'd asked her that more than once. Physically, she wasn't injured. Mentally was another question. She was sure this incident would linger in her mind for a great length of time. It was not every day a madman wished to kill you, and it surely wasn't every day you pushed him to his death.

"It wasn't your fault, Nina." Elliot tipped her chin up and held her gaze.

Odd. Even when she was trying to gather her frayed thoughts into a semblance of cohesion, Elliot realized what she was thinking.

She nodded.

"I wish I had possessed a clear shot. I would have felt little guilt in sending Connors to the devil. Not after I'd witnessed the fear on your face."

Even though she knew he'd not touched a gun since he'd injured his sister, she remembered how steady he'd held the weapon. She didn't doubt he would have shot the man. But it would have affected him—brought back memories that would be hard to quash.

"I guess I should go upstairs as well." She stood and strode toward the door. She didn't want to be alone. She wanted the man she loved to hold her. When she'd been standing in the loft with that madman, she'd feared she might die without telling Elliot that even though he'd set out to deceive her, she knew he loved her. She knew it by the way he touched her. The way he looked at her. *I'll trade my life for hers.* His words repeated in her head.

She turned around. "Are you coming?"

As if startled, he stared at her for a long moment. "If

you wish me to. I would like that more than anything else in the world."

She held out her hand, and they climbed the steps together.

In bed, she set her head on Elliot's chest and listened to the strong beat of his heart. His large hand swayed up and down her back as if he wished to comfort her. And his touch did. She had a feeling it always would. That in times of trouble, she would seek solace in his arms, and Elliot would seek it in hers because that is what those who loved each other did.

And they did love each other. She'd never been surer of anything in her life.

Epilogue

The contentment within Nina made her smile as she and Elliot stepped into their bedchamber. She'd hoped the first family gathering at Ralston House would be a success, and so far, it was going splendidly. Grandmother was behaving. Elliot and her brother James were getting on marvelously. Well, perhaps *marvelously* was an overstatement, but they'd not snarled at each other once, and a few times she'd noticed them smiling while engaged in conversation.

James was still playing the role of the overprotective brother, but he'd told her only yesterday how he admired Elliot's hard work and commitment to running Langford Teas.

Sometimes, she wasn't as pleased, since Elliot worked long hours, but she knew her husband was right—this business would not only be their future but their children's future as well. And in a few months' time, he believed the profit would be substantial enough to hire a sales manager who would take over the task of garnering new accounts. He still refused to use the money from her dowry, stating it was hers and their future children's.

Her job as illustrator for the *London Reformer* kept her busy as well, but she would not trade it for the world. It gave her immense pleasure to see both her illustrations and caricatures published. She and Elliot were part a new breed of nobility who didn't hide the fact they took pleasure from working in trade. Whether Grandmother liked it or not, the status quo was changing.

"I think this gathering is going quite well," Elliot said, pulling her from her thoughts and repeating her own sentiment. He stepped behind her, wrapped his arms about her waist, and nuzzled her neck. "So far, James and I haven't come to blows once."

"Don't be shocked, but I believe James is coming to like you."

"Really? Well, that would be a nice change." He released her, strode to the bedroom door, and poked his head out.

"What are you doing?"

"Checking to make sure the coast is clear, and your family and my sister are all snuggled into their beds."

She tipped her head to the side. "Why?"

"Come with me." He took her hand in his and led her out of the room and down the corridor.

"Where are we going?"

He pressed a finger to his lips. "Shhh. We don't want to wake anyone up. They aren't invited to this party."

She grinned, knowing exactly where they were headed, and a bubble of excitement burst in her stomach as Elliot opened the door to the roof. As soon as they stepped onto the flat structure, Nina spotted a pallet loaded with blankets and pillows at the center of the roof, far away from the edges, but tonight there was no telescope set up.

"Where is the telescope?"

"I thought tonight, instead of stargazing, we could make love under the stars."

Anticipation curled in her stomach. She set her hand on Elliot's chest. "Have I told you I like the way your mind works?"

Chuckling, Elliot embraced her and brushed his lips against hers. The kiss turned hungry. His tongue stroked hers.

She wrapped her arms about his neck and, wanting more contact, arched against him. She almost purred as one of Elliot's hands slid up to mold itself to the soft flesh of her breast.

With a growl-like noise, he scooped her up in his arms and laid her on the blankets and gave Nina her first lesson on making love under the stars, but she was sure it wouldn't be her last.

Books by Bestselling Author
Fern Michaels

___The Jury	0-8217-7878-1	$6.99US/$9.99CAN
___Sweet Revenge	0-8217-7879-X	$6.99US/$9.99CAN
___Lethal Justice	0-8217-7880-3	$6.99US/$9.99CAN
___Free Fall	0-8217-7881-1	$6.99US/$9.99CAN
___Fool Me Once	0-8217-8071-9	$7.99US/$10.99CAN
___Vegas Rich	0-8217-8112-X	$7.99US/$10.99CAN
___Hide and Seek	1-4201-0184-6	$6.99US/$9.99CAN
___Hokus Pokus	1-4201-0185-4	$6.99US/$9.99CAN
___Fast Track	1-4201-0186-2	$6.99US/$9.99CAN
___Collateral Damage	1-4201-0187-0	$6.99US/$9.99CAN
___Final Justice	1-4201-0188-9	$6.99US/$9.99CAN
___Up Close and Personal	0-8217-7956-7	$7.99US/$9.99CAN
___Under the Radar	1-4201-0683-X	$6.99US/$9.99CAN
___Razor Sharp	1-4201-0684-8	$7.99US/$10.99CAN
___Yesterday	1-4201-1494-8	$5.99US/$6.99CAN
___Vanishing Act	1-4201-0685-6	$7.99US/$10.99CAN
___Sara's Song	1-4201-1493-X	$5.99US/$6.99CAN
___Deadly Deals	1-4201-0686-4	$7.99US/$10.99CAN
___Game Over	1-4201-0687-2	$7.99US/$10.99CAN
___Sins of Omission	1-4201-1153-1	$7.99US/$10.99CAN
___Sins of the Flesh	1-4201-1154-X	$7.99US/$10.99CAN
___Cross Roads	1-4201-1192-2	$7.99US/$10.99CAN